THE BAD BOOK AFFAIR

Also by Ian Sansom

IAN SANSOM

The Bad Book Affair

FOURTH ESTATE · *London*

First published in Great Britain in 2010 by
Fourth Estate
An imprint of HarperCollins*Publishers*
77–85 Fulham Palace Road
London W6 8JB
www.4thestate.co.uk

Visit our authors' blog: www.fifthestate.co.uk

A catalogue record for this book is available from the British Library

ISBN 978-0-00-725593-1

Typeset in Meridien by Palimpsest Book Production Limited,
Grangemouth, Stirlingshire
Printed in Great Britain by
Clays Ltd, St Ives plc

For my correspondents,
with all due respect

1

'Here we are, then,' said George, opening the creaking, paint-flaking, hinge-rusted, wood-rotting brace-and-ledge door to the former chicken coop that was now home to Israel Armstrong (B.A., (Hons.)), certainly Tumdrum's and possibly Ireland's only English Jewish vegetarian mobile librarian.

'The King of Siam,' said Ted, striding in. 'Let's have a look at him, then.'

Israel lay on his metal-framed bed in the middle of the room, dirty quilt pulled up around him, broken-backed books everywhere, empty bottles of wine and Jumping Jack cider stacked around like giddy sentinels. A row of broad-shouldered peanut butter jars stood lined up on top of the rickety shelves next to the bed, staring down disapprovingly at the squalor below.

Israel raised his head wearily and dismissively from his book as George and Ted entered.

'Quite a sight, eh?' said George.

'Ach, for goodness' sake,' said Ted.

'Morning, Israel!' said George.

Israel placed his index finger on the page of *Infinite Jest* that he was currently reading, and rereading, and rereading again, looked up at his visitors, returned to the book.

'This what he's been like the whole time, is it?'

'Well, I only came across him last week,' said George. 'I was wondering why I hadn't seen him for a while. He'd not been in the house and I hadn't seen him leaving for work.'

'Hmm,' said Ted, going up to the end of the bed, like a doctor on his ward rounds. 'What's with the auld face-lace, then?'

'I think he's growing a beard,' said George, quietly.

'That's always a bad sign,' said Ted.

'He might look all right with a goatee,' said George.

'I wouldn't have thought it,' said Ted. 'They look all right on goats, but . . . Maybe a moustache.'

'Ach, no,' said George. 'No one has a moustache these days. They went out with the Troubles.'

'More's the pity,' said Ted. 'I had a nice moustache once. Back in the day.'

'Sorry. Excuse me? Can I possibly help you two?' said Israel, rubbing his forehead as if in great pain. 'You do seem to have just barged into my home here.'

'I've brought Ted to see you,' said George.

'I can see that,' said Israel. 'And do neither of you normally knock before you enter someone's home?'

'Don't ye dare get sharp with me,' said Ted.

'The door was open,' said George.

Israel tutted.

'Bit of fresh air is what ye need in here,' said Ted.

'Yes,' agreed George quietly. 'It is a bit . . . rich, isn't it. It's damp, I think. And the chickens, maybe.'

'That's not chickens,' said Ted.

'Well, his personal hygiene,' said George, whispering. 'He has let himself go a bit, recently.'

'Lost the run of himself entirely,' said Ted, picking up a discarded tank-top thrown on the bed and rubbing it disdainfully between forefinger and thumb.

'I think it's because of the split with his girlfriend,' said George.

'Ach,' said Ted. 'He needs to pull his finger out.' He glanced over at Israel. 'Mind ye, difficult to pull your finger out if it's never been in.'

'Hello?' said Israel. 'I don't want to appear rude, but could you leave, please? Is that too much to ask? A little privacy here, in the comfort of my own home?'

Ted tensed and stared at Israel fiercely. It looked for a moment as though he might actually reach out and grab Israel and throw him off the bed, but he seemed to think better of it and instead he turned his back on him, and wandered slowly round the coop, which didn't take long – it was only one room – sniffing and poking around at the books and clothes piled on every surface. T-shirts. Toby Litt. Alice Sebold. Pants.

Israel's ambitious programme of refurbishment for the coop had stalled some time ago – his most recent acquisition, an old sofa that he'd found in someone's yard, was wedged tightly between the wardrobe and the Baby Belling cooker balanced precariously on a stool. The place clearly hadn't been cleaned or tidied for quite a while.

'He'd always the breath of a garlic-eater,' said Ted, fanning his hand in front of his face, in a vain attempt to dispel the room's fumes.

'I don't think he's been eating much,' said George.

'No,' said Ted, removing a spoon from an open jar of peanut butter.

'Hey!' said Israel. 'Leave that alone! That's mine!'

'Shall I leave you boys to it, then?' said George.

'Yes,' said Ted. 'I think that'd be best.'

'No problem,' said George. 'I thought it wise to get you in, Ted. I hope you don't mind. We were all getting a wee bit worried about him. I wasn't sure if I should have called the doctor.'

'Don't ye be worrying about him any more, my dear. No need for the doctor. I'll soon have him sorted,' said Ted.

George shut the chicken coop door behind her.

'Right, ye brallion,' said Ted, stepping briskly towards the side of Israel's bed. 'What are ye on, the auld loonie soup?'

'What?'

'What in God's name d'ye think ye're doing?'

'I'm not feeling well,' said Israel.

'Aye, right, me elbow. Lying in yer bed when there's work to be done – yer head's a marlie.'

'What?' said Israel. 'What are you talking about? Bob Marley?'

'God give me strength,' said Ted. 'Right. Up. Come on. It's no good you lying there.'

'I can't get up, Ted. I'm . . . cultivating my mind,' said Israel, dreamily, stroking his beard. 'Like Saint Jerome.'

'Who?'

'He's the patron saint of libraries.'

'Patron saint of my arse. You can cultivate your mind out in the van with me. Come on.' He went to grab Israel's arm. Israel shrank back.

'Get off! I'm on holiday,' said Israel.

'Aye,' said Ted. 'Ye were. But ye've had your two weeks off and another week off sick.'

'I've not been feeling well.'

'I'm not surprised,' said Ted. 'Ye been in this stinking pit the whole time?'

'More or less.'

'Right. Good. Time to get out, then.'

Ted threw the bedcovers from Israel, scattering books and toppling wine bottles in the process – Merlot and Roberto Bolaño everywhere.

'Hey!'

'Up! Come on, let's go.'

'Leave me alone!' said Israel.

'That I shall not,' said Ted. 'Ye might be able to run rings round the others, but you can't fool me.'

'I'm not trying to fool anybody.'

'"We were all a bit worried about him",' Ted said, mimicking George.

'There's no need to be worried about me, thank you,' said Israel.

'Good. Up and out yer stinking pit, then. Lyin' in bed like a cripple—'

'We don't say "cripple" these days, Ted.'

'Aye. Lying in like a woman—'

'You can't say—'

'No wonder ye don't know what end of you's uppermost.'

'What?'

'Come on. Up and out, ye bedfast.'

'Ted. Sorry. No. I'm staying here.'

'Ye're due in work, boy. Come on.'

'Ted. Look. I really can't be bothered.'

'Can't be bothered?'

'No.'

'Can't be *bothered* to *work*?' said Ted, incredulous.

'That's right.'

'If a man work not, then how shall he eat?'

'Yeah, all right, spare me the lecture,' said Israel.

'That's not a lecture, ye fool, that's the Bible. Now come on. Get yerself up and let's go.'

'Don't talk to me like I'm a child, Ted.'

'If you act like a child, then I'll talk to ye like a child.'

'Well, I would appreciate it if you could just moderate your language and talk to me in a calm and rational fashion.'

'Calm and rational?' said Ted. 'Calm and rational? What do you want me to say? "Please come back, Israel. We all miss you on the mobile library"?'

'Well, that might—' began Israel.

'Of course we don't miss ye on the mobile library. Ye blinkin' eejit. Ye've got a job to do. And you're expected to do it, like anyone else. And don't expect me to be covering for ye, because I'm not. Linda Wei'll

6

hear about this before ye know it, and ye'll be out on yer ear.'

'So?' said Israel.

'So? I'll tell ye what's so. I'm stepping outside here for a smoke and ye've got five minutes to get out of yer stinking bed before I lose my temper.'

Ted walked outside.

And Israel readjusted himself on the bed, pulling the quilt back up around him, plucking David Lean's *Great Expectations* out from under the covers – he'd wondered where that had got to. He'd joined an online DVD postal delivery service, which was very good – unlimited DVDs, no late fee, £12 per month, delivered to the door of the farm – and he'd been steadily working his way through the British Film Institute's Top 100 films. *The Third Man*, *Brief Encounter*, *The Thirty-Nine Steps*, *Kes*, *The Red Shoes*. Often he'd fall asleep in the coop to black-and-white images and then wake up in the morning to the sound of the shipping forecast on the World Service. Alfred Hitchcock, Dirk Bogarde, 'And now the shipping forecast, issued by the Met Office on behalf of the Maritime and Coastguard Agency at 0520 today. There are warnings of gales in Rockall, Malin, Hebrides. The General Synopsis: low, Rockall, 987, deepening rapidly, expected Fair Isle 964 by 0700 tomorrow.'

Sometimes he didn't know where he was. Or what year it was. It was like he'd come adrift in his life.

He thought maybe he'd try ringing Gloria on his mobile again. He'd only rung a couple of times so far today. She hadn't answered the phone to him since he'd arrived back in Tumdrum.

Straight to voicemail.

He'd try again later.

He picked up *Infinite Jest* again. Laid it back down. Started flicking through a month-old *Guardian*.

He scanned the job ads. He was seriously thinking about retraining. Administration. There were always jobs in administration. Israel knew he would make a great administrator. He just needed the right thing to administrate. How difficult could it be, being an administrator? 'Israel Armstrong is *The Administrator*.' He could see it, in his mind's eye. 'When the going gets tough there are men who know how to take charge. Men who know how to make things happen. Men who know how to *administrate*.' He had many times cast the film adaptation of the book of his life – he imagined John Cusack playing him, or someone younger, maybe Owen Wilson, he would be fine, he had an intelligent face, and Harvey Keitel as Ted, maybe, and a nice little cameo for Steve Buscemi, although obviously he'd have to beef up a bit, and Salma Hayek would be perfect as Gloria.

The trouble was, though, he wasn't in the film of the book of his life. He was *in* his life, in which he had split with his long-time girlfriend Gloria, was living in a converted chicken coop, and was paid exactly £15,000 a year as a mobile librarian on the northernmost coast of the north of the north of Northern Ireland. And he was nearly thirty. He had somehow become a shadow of himself, as though he were somewhere else and this thing – this body – was having experiences on his behalf. It was as if his own life had become a series of ancient lantern-slides, or an old video, or a shaky cine-show, or a snippet on YouTube, or a cinema trailer for a block-busting main feature called *Failure*. He had no idea what he was doing here, or what the point was, or how he was feeling. All he knew was that sometimes, in the chicken coop, he'd wake in the night sobbing and sobbing, his chest heaving, and there were these black beetles all over the floor, and when he switched on the light the beetles froze, as if they were holding their breath, waiting for something, their own destruction, or salvation, possibly, or the dark again, and that's *exactly* what he felt like . . .

'Time up!' said Ted, bashing back through the door. 'Not ready?'

'Look, Ted, I'm really not feeling the best this morning. Can we maybe reschedule?'

'Reschedule?'

'Yeah, look—'

'*Reschedule?*'

'Yeah. Just, if you could give me a couple of days maybe and I'll get back to you.'

'Ye'll get back to me?'

'Yeah. I just need a little time to take stock and—'

'*Take stock!?*'

'Yes.'

'Ach, Jesus. Fine.'

At which Ted walked over to the bed, bent down, locked his knees and grabbed hold of the bed frame.

'I'll tell ye what,' he huffed. 'Take stock.' Huff. 'Of.' Huff. 'This!'

And he stood, flinging the metal frame up as he stood.

Israel fell on to the floor, only the quilt protecting him from serious injury and a thousand cuts from the smashed wine bottles.

'What the hell are you doing, you madman!' screamed Israel, leaping up, winceyette-pyjama-clad, from the floor. 'I could have broken my back!'

'Your back!' said Ted, straightening up. 'Your back! I could have broken *my* blinkin' back, ye eejit!'

'Yes, but—'

'Ahh!' said Ted, painfully.

'Are you all right?'

'Of course I'm not blinkin' all right, ye eejit! Aahh!'

'Shall I get George, or—'

'No, ye shall not,' said Ted, drawing himself up stiffly to his not inconsiderable shaven-headed height. 'What ye'll do is get dressed in the van is what ye'll do, or I'll—'

'What?' said Israel.

'Ahh!' said Ted.

'Are you sure you're all right?'

'Yes. Just, some of these joints haven't been moved in a while, that's all. Now. Where were we?'

'You were just—'

'Ach, aye. Yes. In the van, come on. Now.'

'Or?' said Israel.

'Or,' said Ted, 'I'll ring your mother.'

'No—' said Israel. 'You wouldn't.'

'Yes,' said Ted, hobbling towards the door. 'I would.'

Israel's mother had recently made a brief and disastrous visit to Tumdrum, where, as a loud, extravagant, wildly hand-gesturing, menopausal, scarf-wearing, middle-aged north London Jew, she had made quite an impact on the local dour, largely Presbyterian, muttering community. She and Ted had formed an unnaturally close bond, and Ted had spent much time with her, taking her to visit Northern Ireland's supposed tourist attractions – the place where the *Titanic* was built, for example, and the colourful sectarian murals of Belfast – leaving Israel to single-handedly man the mobile during the day and having to sit up waiting for their return late in the evenings, flushed and smelling suspiciously of cigarettes and drink. Israel's mother had successfully managed to embarrass Israel the entire length and breadth of Tumdrum, including at an agonising dinner at the Devines', the farm where Israel stayed as a lodger, during which she had flirted outrageously with old Mr Devine, and had spent all evening urging George to adopt a rigorous daily beauty routine.

'And I'll tell ye what,' said Ted, gesturing towards the debris in the coop. 'When she hears about all this auld nonsense she'll be over on the next flight.'

'No!' said Israel. 'You wouldn't—'

Ted had his mobile phone in his hand.

'Five minutes,' he said. 'In the van. And don't ye dare waste another moment of my precious time.'

Five minutes later, Israel was in the van.

'There we are, then,' said Ted.

'Humpff,' said Israel, miserably.

'I tell ye what, son, ye want to learn to count your blessings,' said Ted, as he slammed the van into first and pulled out of the Devines' yard.

'What?'

'Ouch!' said Ted.

'You OK?'

'My back. Never mind it. Yer blessings. Ye want to count them.'

'Right. All right, Ted, thank you. I'm here, all right? I don't want to hear any more—'

'Go on, then.'

'What?'

'Count 'em.'

Israel sighed.

'Go on,' repeated Ted. 'Count 'em.'

'Ted. I'm really not in the mood. I have a headache and I'm really not well.'

There was a pause of a few seconds.

'Ye counted 'em?'

'I am not counting my blessings, Ted. Thank you.'

'How many d'ye get?'

'I'm not counting blessings!'

'Aye. Because ye're scared.'

'What? Scared of what?'

'That yer miserable life is not as blinkin' miserable as ye like to think, ye streak of misery. I tell ye what, as long as ye're dodging the undertaker ye're doing OK.'

'Right. Sure.'

'Good. Are ye ready?'

'Do I look like I'm ready?'

'Count them.'

'All right. All right,' said Israel, who had learnt from long experience that the only way to conclude an argument with Ted was to lose it.

Israel attempted to tot up his blessings in his mind, while Ted pulled on to the main coast road back into central Tumdrum.

'So, how many d'ye get?' said Ted.

'Two,' said Israel. He was alive, after all. And he wasn't starving.

'Two?'

'Yes,' said Israel.

'That it?' said Ted. 'Two?'

'Yes,' said Israel. 'Alas.'

'Well, that's better than one,' said Ted, 'isn't it? Sure, some people have no hands.'

'What?' said Israel, watching the grim outer-lying estates flashing by.

'No hands,' repeated Ted, sticking his own arm out of the window as they approached the first of Tumdrum's many mini-roundabouts. 'Must get that indicator fixed.'

'Some people have no hands?' said Israel.

'That's right. I saw a programme on the television the other week, about a fella with no legs.'

'No legs?'

'Aye. Makes ye think, doesn't it? Come back to me when you're in that sort of a position and start complainin' and I might start listening to ye.'

'Right, OK. When I've lost my legs in some horrific—'

'Or yer arms.'

'Or my arms.'

'Aye. Get back to me then with yer troubles.'

'I will, Ted, most certainly get back to you when I have lost either my arms or my legs—'

'Or both.'

'Both.'

'And ye might get some sympathy then. In the meantime,' continued Ted, 'turn the peat.'

'What?'

'It's a saying.'

'Right.'

'And get a haircut and a shave as well while ye're at it, that'll cheer you up.'

'I don't need cheering up, Ted.'

'You need a haircut and a shave, but.'

'All right, thank you. Let's drop this whole conversation now, can we?'

'Well, I promised yer mother I'd look out for ye and I don't intend lettin' her down.'

'I don't need you keeping an eye on me, Ted, thank you.'

'Well, believe me, it's the last thing I want to do either, but I told your mother I would, and I will. She's a good woman, yer mother.'

'She doesn't need to worry about me.'

'Of course she needs to worry about ye,' said Ted. 'That's what mothers are supposed to do.'

'Right.'

'You know what they say.'

'No. What?'

'You always meet your mother when you're young.'

'Right,' said Israel. 'Well, thank you, Martin Buber. Illuminating as ever.'

They were approaching the square, the downtown of Tumdrum.

'Ye probably just need a new challenge,' continued Ted.

'Probably,' agreed Israel.

'A hobby,' said Ted, 'is what you need.'

'A hobby?'

'Aye. A choir, or something.'

'A choir?'

'Or line dancing.'

'Line dancing?'

'Aye, or a jigsaw even.'

'A jigsaw?'

'Or walk a good brisk mile every morning. That'd cure you.'

'A jigsaw?' repeated Israel.

'Yes.'

'And a good brisk walk.'

'Aye.'

'I'm sure that'd do the trick, Ted. But can we talk about something else now, please?'

'It wasn't me got us started on the subject of yer hartship,' said Ted.

'Anyway,' said Israel.

They pulled off the main road.

'Ye all ready for the morning, then?' said Ted.

'Oh yes,' said Israel, who wasn't ready at all. He'd spent the best part of two weeks in bed reading David Foster Wallace, and he'd lost all track of time, place, sense, meaning, or himself. 'What day is it? Where are we going?'

'It's Friday. All day. Morning in the lay-by. And then we're off to the school.'

'Oh God. No.'

'No language, thank ye.'

'Oh Jesus,' said Israel.

'Shut up,' said Ted, leaning over and slapping Israel across the back of his head. 'I'll not tell ye again.'

Israel and Ted were back in business.

2

Tumdrum. Tumdrum. Tumdrum was not the back of beyond. No.

It was much, much farther.

No. Farther.

A little bit farther.

There. That's about right.

Tumdrum, the armpit of Antrim, on the north of the north coast of the north of Northern Ireland, a place where the sky was always the colour of a pair of very old stone-washed jeans, beaten and rinsed, and where the only pub, the First and Last, was a harbinger of Armageddon, and where the Bible Shop was the bookshop, where the replacement of what little remained of Edwardian and Victorian historic architecture with stunning, high-spec turnkey apartments was almost complete, and where a trip to Billy Kelly's edge-of-town Car and Van Superstore ('Please Pull In To View Our Massive Stock With No Obligation') represented a day out, and where scones – delicious, admittedly, served warm, buttered and spread with jam – were the height of culinary sophistication at Zelda's Café, the town's 'Internet Hot Spot: The First And Still The Best'.

And here, of all places, was Israel Armstrong, back at his post in this godforsaken Nowheresville, sitting on the mobile library, parked up in a lay-by, doing nothing but issuing true crime books about local thugs, and thinly fictionalised books about local thugs, and books *by* local thugs, and memoirs by the wives of local thugs, while enjoying all of the usual banter and craic with his regular readers. Such as Mr McCully.

'I'm looking for the De Saurus.'

'Sorry?'

'The DE SAURUS.'

'Right. And it's a foreign author?'

'A foreign author?'

'De Saurus. Like the Marquis de Sade?'

'The what?'

'Or De Maupassant?'

'Are ye having me on?'

'No. No.'

'Are ye having a wee laugh?'

'No. Not at all. I'm trying to help.'

'Good. So, it's the book with the words in it.'

'Well, sir, I think you'll find that . . . most books have words in—'

'Don't ye be patronising me now, ye wee skite, I know exactly what your game is.'

'I can assure you, Mr McCully, that the last thing I would do would be to patronise *you*.'

It was as if he'd never been away.

'Come on, then. The De Saurus. The book with all the words in it.'

'The book with all the words in it,' repeated Israel. 'The . . . Book . . . With . . . All . . . The . . . Words . . . In . . . It.'

'Aye! THE DE SAURUS!'

'Ah, right! Yes! Roget's *Thesaurus*?'

'No. That's not it.'

'I think it might be, actually. If you want to have a look here . . .'

'No.'

'The classic book of synonyms and antonyms?'

'No! Cymbals and Antimals?'

'I think it's the *Thesaurus*.'

'It is not. The *De Saurus*.'

'OK, well, sorry. We can't help you with the De Saurus.'

'D'ye have any books on the Foreign Legion, then?'

'Certainly.'

'And a guidebook to Prague for the wife?'

'Of course.'

He was harmless, really, Mr McCully. They were all harmless: the only real harm they did was to Israel's fragile mental and emotional health.

Like Mrs Hammond, for example.

'I'm looking for a book.'

'Yes, Mrs Hammond. Good. You've come to the—'

'It's a true story.'

'OK.'

'About a man.'

'Good. What kind of a man?'

'It was on the telly yesterday, sure. A fella was talking about it.'

'I see. And the man was . . .?'

'It was the fella on the telly. The English man. With the lovely hair.'

'Right. The man who wrote the book was an English man with lovely hair? Or the man who the book is about is an English man with lovely hair?'

'Ach, no, the man with the programme on the telly with the lovely hair.'

'Ah. The man with the programme on the telly . . . who interviewed the man . . .? about his book . . . about the man . . . is an English man . . . with lovely hair?'

'That's right.'

'Well, let's see what we can find here.'

And Hughie Boyd.

'I was in last year, sure, and there was a book on a shelf down there, but it's not there now.'

'Right.'

'D'ye not have it, then?'

'Erm. Whereabouts on the shelf was it exactly?'

'Just there, look. There.'

'Here?'

'No! There!'

'Ah. Oh. Right. There. Well. I'm afraid we've moved that book.'

'Typical.'

'Thank you, Mr Boyd! Lovely to see you! Have a nice day!'

And George Kemp.

'D'ye have Bibles?'

'Yes, indeed, we do, Mr Kemp. Bibles. Bibles. Let me see. *A* Bible, anyway. Here we are. Yes.'

'I'll take it.'

'Erm. Well. It's reference only, I'm afraid.'

'What do ye mean?'

'I can't issue it to you.'

'But it's the Bible.'

'Yes, I know.'

'You can't stop me getting out the Bible.'

'Well, yes, I can, actually, if it's a reference book.'

'It's not a reference book!'

'Yes it is. It's—'

'It's the Word of God.'

'Yes. But I'm afraid it's our reference copy of the Word of God. I'm afraid you can't take it with you right now. I can get you a copy on interlibrary loan for next week.'

'That's no good to me, is it? I want to read it now.'

'Well, you can read it here, if you want to.'

'In here? Are ye mad? I want to read it in the privacy of my own home. It's for the purposes of private devotion.'

'Well, I'm sorry, I can't—'

'Yer not a Christian, are ye?'

'Erm . . .'

'Ye're not washed in the blood of the Lamb?'

'Erm . . .'

'You know you're going to hell, unless you turn to Jesus.'

'Right. Good. Thank you, Mr Kemp. Have a nice day!'

And of course Mrs Onions' friend, Noreen.

'Now, young man, will ye choose me a book?'

'Yes, of course, Noreen. I . . . Just remind me, what sort of books do you like to . . .'

'I've read them all now.'

'OK. What, *all* the books in the library?'

'Every last one of them.'

'All the books?'

'Aye.'

'Everything?'

'Aye. I'm eighty-four, you know.'

'Yes. Well done.'

'I waited fourteen years for a knee replacement.'

'Uh-huh.'

'It was crumbling away.'

'Right.'

'I've read all these books, you know.'

'Yes, you said.'

'All the Mill and Boons.'

'There are other books you could try, Noreen . . .'

'Ach, no. I don't have time for them. I had a friend, she died while she was reading one of them other books.'

'I'm sorry to hear that.'

'You're all right – it wasnae a library book. She bought her own books.'

'Right.'

'Her son looked after her rightly. Not like mine. I've not a phone call from them from week to week.

I wonder, would ye be able to do me a few bits of shopping in?'

Misplaced, that was the word for it. That's what he was, Israel. That was his problem. He was misplaced. He rightly belonged in delightful places, Israel, filled with delightful people: Ravello, for example, in the 1920s, or somewhere around Lake Como, perhaps, with people who enjoyed painting watercolours of old buildings, and who drank prosecco, and grappa, from small tumblers, while enjoying intellectually stimulating and ever-so-slightly-erotically-charged conversations. His natural habitat was formal terraced gardens, swagged with wisteria, with ancient fig trees and vine-covered trellises, and shaded patios leading into light-filled villas with shutters and faded parquet flooring. Even back home in leafy north London, with access to good coffee and a reliable broadband service, that'd do. Instead, he'd somehow ended up as the mobile librarian in a town where Pat's Manicure and Footcare ('Manicure, Polish, Acrylics, Corns, Callouses, And Verucas') in the town square was a popular meeting place for young and old alike, and where local fishmonger Tommy Turner's recent winning of the local Chamber of Commerce's Small-To-Medium Business Personality of the Year Award was a cause for celebration ('Small-To-Medium Personality of the Year Awarded to Local Man', ran the headline in the *Impartial Recorder*).

Israel had always liked to think of himself as a warm, outgoing, friendly sort of an individual who could rub along with anyone. Until he came to Tumdrum, where warm, outgoing, friendly sorts of individuals who thought they could rub along with anyone but who weren't from round here were generally considered to be pushy, uppity good-for-nothings. He was a square peg in a round hole, a fish out of water, out of step, out of time, and out of place. He was a misfit, though admittedly a slightly lighter, bearded misfit, after his two weeks in bed, contemplating the meaning of life, the universe and everything, and weeping over Gloria, and the plight of the Hebrew people, and the thought of his forthcoming thirtieth birthday, which he would be celebrating, unbelievably, in Tumdrum. Alone.

He grimaced at his reflection in the windscreen. He'd lost quite a bit of weight, what with pretty much surviving on wine, cider and spoonfuls of peanut butter for the past few weeks, with only the occasional variation.

Not that he was on a diet. Not as such. Since he'd split up with Gloria he'd been losing weight at a rate of several ounces a day – the equivalent of about a bag of lean beef-mince a week – and had gone down from a size 36 waist to a 32 in just a couple of months, achieving a weight and a size that he'd last seen when he was a schoolboy. He was using safety pins on his trousers, and had had to trim some of the vast expanses of his shirt-tails and use them for rags. His duffel coat flapped around him like a dirty brown toggle-tie blanket left out on the line to dry.

It wasn't that he'd decided not to eat. He just found that he couldn't eat; he wasn't able to eat. It wasn't a diet; it was more like an unofficial hunger strike: his body was refusing him. Tayto cheese-and-onion crisps – certainly the best and possibly the only good reason for living in Northern Ireland – tasted like ashes in his mouth. And champ – often he couldn't manage more than a mouthful of old Mr Devine's creamy champ at dinner, all that potato and spring onion and good salted butter going to waste, scraped away for the pigs. Potato bread likewise. Sodas. Even the tray bakes – he'd not been able to finish a tray bake for weeks. At lunchtime he'd go to the Trusty Crusty and buy himself a couple of caramel squares, and a church window, a fifteen, maybe a Florentine – just the normal day's Tumdrum home-baked snacks – but it was no go. He'd be about to tuck in, and suddenly his body seemed to just give up, seemed to say, 'What's the point?' Since splitting up with Gloria he'd changed from a coffee-guzzling, comfort-eating, vaguely troubled fat person into a graze 'n' nibbling, wine-bibbing, deeply troubled thin person. He was hardly eating anything, but felt bloated the whole time. His hunger, which had always been his friend, had seemingly deserted him. His headaches were worse than ever, and at night he was having these dreams, vivid dreams all the time – bobbing around on a life raft, scanning the horizon, no land in sight; tripping down mountainsides; wandering lost through vast deserts . . . abandonment.

He was not only a misfit. He was an eating-disordered misfit.

* * *

As he was musing on his profound, increasing, ageing misfittedness, a young woman had come up the steps into the library. Israel glanced up. She looked to be in her mid-teens, although it was difficult to tell, because she had long, blonde hair hanging down over her face, big mascaraed eyelashes, and a black beanie hat pulled down tight over her head. Israel gave her a second glance: if she was indeed in her mid-teens, she should probably have been at school. They had this problem all the time, children bunking off school and skulking around the library. They called it 'mitching off', the children. 'Aye, I'm mitching off, what are ye going to do about it?' they would retort to Israel's polite suggestion that they return to school. He always felt vaguely responsible for truants, in the same way he felt vaguely responsible for the future of the rainforests, and global warming, and the war on terror. He felt bad, ineffectively bad, *ruminatively* bad. He felt bad, but could do absolutely nothing about it. He wasn't a politician, or a policeman, or a teacher, he was just a librarian, and alas librarians aren't able to save the world, or even to act *in loco parentis*. He was powerless. In the end Israel's only real responsibility was towards the books, rather than the readers. There wasn't really much he could do for readers. The books he could cope with. The great thing about books is that they don't talk back – unlike the teenagers, and the Mrs Hammonds and Hughie Boyds and Mrs Onions of this world. Israel absolutely dreaded teenagers coming on board the mobile library, more even than he dreaded reading to the children of Tumdrum Primary, or even dealing with Mrs Onions. Children are bad enough – children are rude, selfish, greedy and unthinking individuals who are unable to distinguish between their own selfish wants and needs and the wants and needs of others. And adults are children with money, alcohol and power. But that in-between stage, the teenage, is even worse, the interim between childhood and adulthood. In the interim between raging, selfish, impotent childhood and raging, impotent, insignificant adulthood you have adolescence, which is childhood with hormones. He hated Tumdrum's teens.

The girl was wearing a short, black skirt, and thick black tights, and heavy black boots, and a long black jumper, and she carried over her shoulder a black bag covered all over in black plastic spikes. It was a bag that looked as though it might have been useful as a cat-scratcher, or as a kind of orthopaedic aid for people with lower back problems caused by bad posture from sitting staring at a computer all day playing multi-user-dimension games.

She looked like trouble. She looked like a Goth. He hated Goths.

'I don't like the Goths,' he'd mentioned to Ted one day.

'Why not?' said Ted.

'I don't know. They look like they're in the Addams Family.'

'That's the idea, isn't it?' said Ted.

'Yes, but it's . . . weird.'

'Weird!' said Ted. 'Weird?'

'Yes, weird.'

'Aye, and ye'd know weird, right enough.'

'Yes. I would.'

'Aye, ye see, that's just like ye – you're a terrible hypocrite, so you are.'

'I am not.'

"Course you are. You're all for this political correctness, and then ye're after saying ye don't like the Goths.'

'Well, I don't.'

'Ach, ye're a sickener, so you are.'

'They come in wearing trench coats and . . .'

'What's wrong with trench coats?' said Ted. 'You don't like people wearing trench coats?'

'No. It's just . . . People wearing long black coats and . . .'

'Who are those people in Israel?' said Ted.

'Jews?'

'Yes, them. The ones in the long black coats and the hats.'

'That's different. That's religion.'

'Well, it's the same thing for the young ones here.'

'It's not a religion.'

'It is to them.'

'Anyway, Ted. I do not like the Goths coming on the library and smoking. And we're not meant to be issuing them with X-rated DVDs and . . .'

'It'll do them no harm, sure. And at least if they're on the van they're not out cloddin' stones.'

'Clodding?'

'Throwing stones, ye eejit.'

28

'Right.'

'Not a jot of harm in 'em.'

'How do you know there's not a jot of harm in them?'

'I just know,' said Ted. 'When you've known people as long as I have, you just know.'

'Well, when the Goths go on the rampage and . . .'

'Ach, Israel, will ye lighten up for just one minute, will ye? It's like listening to an auld man, so it is.'

Israel peered at the girl Goth over his book – *Infinite Jest*. She did look familiar, the Goth, but then all Goths looked the same to him: pale faces, dark clothes, like priests, or Pierrots, or members of Parisian mime troupes. The only discernible difference between all of Tumdrum's Goths seemed to be in size: there were fat ones, and thin ones, but nothing in between. There didn't seem to be any such thing as a medium-sized Goth: Gothicism seemed to be a minimal and a maximal kind of a teenage subculture.

'There are no medium Goths,' he remarked idly to Ted one day.

'A medium Goth is called an emo,' said Ted. 'Keep up, ye eejit.'

Ted, of course, had no problem with Tumdrum's Goths. Or the emos. Because, of course, Ted had no problem with anyone: Goths, emos, drunks, loonies, children, Mrs Onions, OAPs. As part-time driver of the mobile library, and proprietor-driver of Ted's Cabs ('If You Want To Get There, Call The Bear'), Ted knew everyone in town by name, and mostly from birth. He certainly knew all of Tumdrum's Goths from when they were mewling and puking in the children's book trough, and so was able to handle them with his usual aplomb, which mostly meant slagging, mocking and teasing them, but also allowing them to smoke on board the library when it was raining. Ted called the Goths the Whigmaleeries, or the Wee Yins.

'And what are Whigmaleeries when they're at home?' asked Israel.

'They're Wee Yins,' said Ted.

So that had cleared that up.

The young female Goth hovered nervously around the fiction shelves for a few moments, glancing over her black-jumpered shoulder.

'Good morning, madam,' said Israel, breaking the Gothic silence. 'How can I possibly help you?' He found sometimes that if he *pretended* to be positive and helpful it made him *feel* positive and helpful, for a brief moment at least. Were all positive and helpful people just pretending? 'Edgar Allan Poe, perhaps?'

'What?'

'Edgar Allan Poe?' he said. 'Master of the macabre.'

The girl looked blankly at him.

'Sorry,' he said. 'I was just . . . You know. I like to guess sometimes which books people are going to borrow, just from the way they . . . You know . . . big . . . fat person, probably going to borrow a . . . diet book. Child, probably going to borrow . . . a children's book . . . And a weird-looking person is probably going to . . . Anyway.'

Israel looked at the young woman's unsmiling face. Either that was very heavy make-up and eyeliner she was wearing, or she had a very pale complexion and hadn't slept for weeks.

'I'm looking for something . . .' said the young woman. She looked around again, over her shoulder and lowered her voice. 'From the *Unshelved.*'

'Ah,' said Israel, lowering his voice conspiratorially also. 'Of course. *The Unshelved.*'

'Yes.'

Israel winked at her and reached down under the issue desk.

The Unshelved was an unofficial category of books that the library service – under considerable pressure from representatives from churches, and so-called 'community' groups and local political parties – had agreed not to display on open shelves in the mobile library. The arrangement had been made long before Israel's time in Tumdrum, but apparently, *unbelievably*, it had been agreed that because of the unique status of the mobile library – its stock being so small, and its serving such diverse communities – certain books would be kept under the issue desk, duly catalogued and available for loan but unseen by the young, the impressionable and the mentally infirm who thronged the van's potentially virulent, morally infecting eight-foot-by-three-foot browsing area. Books in the Unshelved category included perennial favourites such as *Lady Chatterley's Lover*, *A Clockwork Orange*, *Nineteen Eighty-Four*, and *American Psycho*, and one or two racier titles such as Nancy Friday's *My Secret Garden* and *The Hite Report*. During quieter moments in isolated lay-bys Israel had been known to have an occasional glance at the latter titles. There was, it seemed, no limit to human ingenuity and imagination. He'd also spent one entire uneventful afternoon on the van counting the various offensive words in *Lady Chatterley*. Thirty fucks or fuckings; 14 cunts; 13 balls; 6 each of shit and arse; 4 cocks; and 3 pisses. Which was quite a lot, really, when you thought about it.

Not that he agreed with censorship. Not at all. On the contrary. He did not agree with the Unshelved, on principle. As a north London Jewish vegetarian liberal freethinker – someone who would most certainly be reading the *Guardian* on a daily basis, if the *Guardian* were available on a daily basis in Tumdrum – Israel saw no problem with open access to all available books and to all of the rich and peculiar outpourings of the human mind. Once you were about eleven, frankly, in Israel's opinion, you could and should be reading whatever was out there. You might not be able to drink alcohol, or marry, or drive a car, but surely you should be allowed to read *Under the Volcano*, and *Madame Bovary*, and *Crash*? How else were you going to learn? Personally, Israel had gone through all of William Burroughs, and D. H. Lawrence, and Norman Mailer, and *Lolita* in his local library back home in north London in his early teens, looking for the dirty bits, which usually someone else had already found and had marked on your behalf, and it hadn't done him any harm at all. Or not much.

The only books in the library that Israel had any real doubts about were in fact the young adult readers, which were proudly and openly displayed on the mobile on the 'Teen Fiction' shelves, in their garish jackets with their sub-literate jacket blurbs. Israel avoided uplifting, joyous, life-affirming reads as much as the next man – who cares about the *Five People You Meet in Heaven* with Morrie? – but even he found some of the young adult material depressing and creepy. In Israel's experience as a librarian most young teenagers these days seemed to be reading deeply disturbing, adult-sanctioned psycho-sexual fantasies about zombies and vampires. This probably tells you something very profound about where we are as a society, but Israel would have needed the *Guardian*, or perhaps the *Daily Telegraph*, to remind him exactly what.

The Goth waited patiently while Israel scooped up the dozen or so books from the shelf under the desk, and placed them on the table. It was always a slightly awkward moment, the displaying of the great Unshelved – you never knew if the borrower really was looking for George Orwell, or was really angling for Madonna's *Sex*. Israel suspected that *Nineteen Eighty-Four* was borrowed more times out of embarrassment than out of choice. He always preferred to absent himself while the borrower . . . browsed.

'I'll, er . . . just tidy a few books here,' he said.

When the young woman's nervous shuffling made it clear that she had made her decision, Israel swiftly and discreetly issued the books with half-closed eyes.

'Thank you, then. Enjoy your reading!'

Philip Roth. *American Pastoral*: the young woman would not be disappointed.

Israel glanced at his watch.

Eleven o'clock.

Which in a town like Tumdrum, wherever you were, meant only one thing.

Zelda's.

He called Gloria, again, quickly.

No reply.

3

Pearce Pyper was wearing an oatmeal jumper – or, at least, a woollen jumper of an oatmeal colour – and a pair of bright red, corduroy, paint-splattered plus-fours, and worn brown leather sandals, and knee-length papal yellow socks, and a black beret. Two of his dogs, the mongrels, Picasso and Matisse, in their matching blue paisley neckerchiefs, sat by him, eyes closed, tongues lolling, like a couple of huskies exhausted from some long artistic hike. Pearce had a greasy-looking cap down at his feet, a viola in one hand, and a straggly bow in the other. He had recently grown a thin, grizzled beard, and he wasn't looking at all well. He was standing like a wind-cracked Lear on the stormy heath, except he was in Tumdrum, standing outside Zelda's Café, staring into the distance, a rheumy, faraway look in his eyes, as if he'd suddenly caught sight of his own destiny and it wasn't looking good.

'Pearce! How are you?' said Israel, as he and Ted approached the door.

'Israel, Israel!' said Pearce, his voice thin but still forceful, the gingery voice of George Bernard Shaw on an old wax cylinder. 'How lovely are the . . .' He started coughing. 'Feet of thee . . .'

'Er . . .?'

'Israel . . .?' asked Pearce.

'Armstrong,' said Israel, generously. 'Israel Armstrong.'

'Ah!' Pearce pantomime-smacked his forehead. 'Of course!'

'The librarian?' offered Israel.

'Yes. Yes. Have you lost weight?'

'Maybe a little bit.'

'And the beard?'

'Yes.'

'*El Barbaro,*' said Pearce. 'Had dinner once with Castro. With my second wife. Pork. Relentless talker.'

'Aye, that's the two of yous, then,' said Ted.

'Sshh,' said Israel.

'Is he dead?' asked Pearce.

'Fidel Castro?' said Israel. 'No, Pearce, I think he's still going strong.'

'I heard he'd died,' said Pearce.

'No, that was maybe Che Guevara.'

'Oh. Really. But how are you . . .?' asked Pearce.

'Israel.'

'Israel, yes.'

'Good, thanks, yes . . . Erm, Pearce?'

'Yes, my dear?'

'You're playing the violin?'

'Viola, Israel. Viola. You can tell the difference, surely? Oxford-educated man like yourself.'

'Oxford Brookes,' said Ted, taking a last, deep, desperate draw on his cigarette before going into the café. 'Wasn't it? The polytechnic.'

'*Ex*-polytechnic,' said Israel. 'Thank you, Ted. *Ex*.'

'Aye,' said Ted, coughing.

'Oxford,' said Pearce, reverently, as though describing a lover. 'Much darker tone.'

'Sorry?' said Israel. 'You've lost me. Oxford has a much darker tone than . . .?'

'The viola,' said Pearce. 'Compared to the violin. Much darker. Voice of the soul. C. G. D. A.' Pearce plucked at the strings of the instrument in his hand. 'Prelude to the Bach cello suites, arrangement by an old friend of mine. My first wife – beautiful soprano voice. Igor wrote something for her mother . . .'

'Erm.' Israel hesitated. Pearce had recently been showing signs of memory loss and confusion. He'd been found as far away as Belfast, on his bicycle, claiming that he was riding in the peloton in the Tour de France. 'You know you're outside Zelda's, playing your violin?' said Israel.

'Viola,' said Pearce. 'I'm collecting money for the Green Party. Forthcoming elections. Need every penny.'

'You're busking,' said Israel.

'That's illegal,' said Ted, spitting on the pavement.

'Fund-raising,' said Pearce. 'Spare a few coppers, guv'nor?'

'Not likely,' said Ted.

'I didn't know you were a Green Party supporter,' said Israel.

'Isn't everybody these days?' said Pearce, breaking into another racking coughing fit, which doubled him over, his slight frame shaking as he stood himself up straight again.

'No,' said Ted.

'Sssh,' said Israel, staring hard at Ted. 'Are you all right, Pearce?'

'Yes,' coughed Pearce. 'Fine.'

'Good,' Israel said. 'Good for you.'

'It's not good for me,' said Pearce. 'Not at all. That's not the point of it, my dear. It's good for the planet.'

'Yes,' said Israel, soothingly. 'I meant—'

'I've been planting trees up at the house, you know, carbon offsetting. About a thousand now, I think.'

'A thousand trees?'

'Indeed.'

'That's a lot of trees,' said Israel.

'Hardly,' said Pearce. 'You can never have enough trees.'

'No,' agreed Israel. 'They don't grow on . . . trees.'

'Sorry?'

'They don't—' began Israel.

'Just ignore him,' said Ted. 'And he shuts up in the end.'

'Handbook of the soul,' said Pearce. 'A tree.'

'Is it?' said Israel.

'Of course.'

'Right. Yes. Probably it is.'

'Irish oak. Native species. *Sorbus aucuparia. Sorbus*

38

hibernica . . . I had a friend who grew hurley ash for profit, you know. Nice little business.'

'Aye, all right,' said Ted. 'Let's get in here for our coffee, Israel, shall we?'

'Yeah, sure. Pearce, do you want a cup of tea or anything to keep you warm? We're just going into Zelda's here—'

'No, thanks,' said Pearce. 'No time for tea. Work to be done. Planet and what have you . . . Raging against the . . .' He hawked up some phlegm and spat it into a polka-dot handkerchief. 'Dying of the light.'

'OK. Good to see you,' said Israel. 'Look after yourself, OK?'

'Aye, you enjoy yourself there,' said Ted.

'I've been measuring my pond at home,' said Pearce.

'Right ye are, auld fella,' said Ted to Pearce. And 'Let's get in here, my back's killing me,' he said to Israel.

'One hundred and two feet,' said Pearce.

'Very good,' said Israel. 'Excellent.'

Pearce raised the viola and the neckerchiefed dogs stirred at his feet, preparing themselves. 'I'll see you on Sunday, of course?' said Pearce.

'Yes,' said Israel. 'Of course.'

'Sunday?' said Ted.

'I visit him sometimes on Sundays.'

'Very cosy,' said Ted.

'Sshh,' said Israel.

'Good,' said Pearce, waving them away with his bow. 'Now, no time to chat. Must get on. Bach.'

'Ing,' said Ted.

'Sshh!' said Israel.

'Bloody header,' said Ted, as they walked into Zelda's.

'I like him,' said Israel. 'He's my favourite person in the whole of Tumdrum.'

'Aye,' said Ted. ''Cause he's not all there, an' a big lump trailin'.'

'What? What does that mean?'

'He's as bloody crazy as you are.'

4

They waved goodbye to Pearce playing his viola outside and pushed into the crowds. Even by the usual packed standards of Zelda's on a Friday morning, Zelda's was packed: you couldn't move for the thick fug of car coats, steamed milk and potpourri.

'Oh God. What the hell's happening in here?' said Israel.

'Busy,' agreed Ted.

Zelda's Café was a kind of holding area for the nearly departed, a place where the retired of Tumdrum assembled for coffee and scones before ascending towards the Judgement Seat and the Gate of Heaven; it was a place neither in nor entirely of this world, or certainly not of the world that Israel wished to inhabit; not a world he could ever feel a part of. It wasn't that they were bad people, the ever fragrant coffee-and-scone crowd in Zelda's. In fact, they were very decent people – sweet, sweet milky coffee ran in their veins, and they were as good hearted as the glacé cherry in a cherry scone. They just weren't Israel's kind of people. And here they all were, gathered together, just about every last one of them: it was as though Zelda's were staging the worldwide scone-and-coffee fest. Scoffest.

'We'll never get a seat,' said Israel, staring at the heaving throng. 'Shall we go somewhere else?'

'There is nowhere else,' said Ted.

'Ah,' said Israel. 'Yes. You see. There's the rub.'

'Give over,' said Ted.

'Come on, ye, on on in,' said Minnie, bustling over, frilly pinny on, brown cardigan sleeves rolled up. 'Plenty of room, gents, plenty of room!'

'God. Really?' said Israel. 'Isn't it a little—'

'And none of yer auld language here today, please. We've a visitor. Come on on.' She waved them forward and started to lead them through the crowded café, like a guide taking tourists through a souk in Marrakesh.

'Who's the visitor?' said Israel, squeezing between car coats.

'A Very Important Person,' said Minnie.

'Who?' said Ted.

'Nelson Mandela?' said Israel.

'Och!' said Minnie.

'The Berlin State Philharmonic?'

'What?' said Minnie.

'You know you've got Pearce outside busking?'

'Ach, he's harmless, bless him,' said Minnie.

'He's away in the head,' said Ted, demonstrating what

he considered to be a state of away-in-the-headness by rolling his eyes and lolling his tongue.

'He's not well,' said Minnie.

'It's the Haltzeimers,' said Ted.

'The what?' said Israel.

'Have you lost weight, pet?' said Minnie, glancing behind her.

'Just a bit,' said Israel.

'He's depressed,' said Ted.

'I am not depressed,' said Israel.

'Split up with his girlfriend back in London,' said Ted.

'Oh dear,' said Minnie. 'And you've grown a beard as well,' she added.

'Adding insult to injury,' said Ted.

'Top-up of coffee when you've a minute,' said a man in the traditional Zelda's get-up of car coat, plus a suit and a tie, and a zip-up pullover, with a *Racing Post* propped before him, as Minnie bustled by.

'Make that two,' said his similarly attired companion.

'And I'll take another date-and-wheaten scone,' piped up another identically clad man at another table.

'And me!'

'Cinnamon scone, and a large cappuccino?' called someone else.

'Och, all right,' said Minnie, squeezing past women whose calorie intake had clearly exceeded recommended daily amounts for some years, and men whose red, flushed faces suggested that an occasional tipple had become a rather more regular routine, 'give me a wee minute here, will ye?'

Zelda's was not the Kit Kat Club.

'So who's the VIP?' said Ted. 'Not the fat boy off the radio? He gets everywhere.'

'Stephen Nolan?' said Israel. 'Oh God, no. Not him.'

'Stop it,' said Ted, pointing a finger at Israel. Ted insisted on the highest standards of non-blaspheming. 'I like him.'

'No,' said Minnie. 'Maurice Morris.'

'Oh God, not him, the f—' began Israel.

'I said no language!' said Minnie. 'He's getting worse,' she said to Ted.

'I've warned you,' said Ted to Israel. 'Ye bad-mannered bastard.'

'Come on now,' said Minnie. 'Let me squeeze you in the wee huxter here, and I'll see if I can't bring Maurice over for a wee chat. I'm sure he'd love to meet you.'

'No!' said Israel.

'I'll be back in a minute for your orders,' said Minnie, bustling away.

'Maurice Morris,' said Ted. 'Well, well, well. The Man With The Plan.'

Maurice Morris, The Man With The Plan: Independent Unionist candidate for Tumdrum and District, out on the stump, one of Northern Ireland's most popular politicians, admired by all and loved by many, until he'd fallen from favour and had been defeated – crushed, humiliated – by the Democratic Unionists at the last election, not because of any policy or political crisis, but because of the small complicating matter of his affair with one of his constituency workers, and the accompanying slight whiff of financial impropriety, which never came to more than a whiff, but which was more than enough for the good people of Tumdrum, the scone-and-coffee crowd, who could smell a rat when they saw one and who had turned their car-coated backs to him and set their po-faces against him. It had taken Maurice years to patch things up and make himself anew and only now was he seeking to regain his seat, which is why he was here in Zelda's, the very heartland of Tumdrum, busy working the crowd, jacket off, sleeves rolled up, receding hair swept boldly back from his vast, lined but deeply untroubled forehead, looking every thickset square inch the comeback politician. In his campaign literature Maurice liked to draw attention to his confidence-inspiring six-foot-five-inch frame and his well-cut suits – suits for which he was, according to his campaign literature, renowned Province-wide. His Savile Row pinstripes and his Jermyn Street shirts and ties, he believed, spoke for themselves, and they most certainly did; they told you everything you needed to know about Maurice Morris, or M 'n' M, as he preferred to be called. His sparkling white teeth and his perma-tan spoke eloquently also – they sang out on his behalf – as did his reputation as North Antrim's most successful independent financial adviser. What M 'n' M did not know about mortgages, repossessions and trusts in kind simply was not worth knowing: Maurice was the man, the big man in the big picture, financially, politically and socially; this was a man who had been photographed consistently, for over a decade, in the *Ulster Tatler*, and the *Belfast Telegraph*, and the *Impartial Recorder*, with every Irish and Northern Irish celebrity, major and minor, excepting Bono, who was still on his wish list. Maurice was not just a politician, or a businessman: he was a brand and a celebrity, and he was not a man to be underestimated, overlooked, doubted, mocked, questioned, queried, or in any other way challenged. Maurice Morris had been blessed at birth – by whimsical, apparently homonymic- and possibly crossword-puzzle-minded parents – with his own surname for a first name, and he had known from an early age that this somehow made him impregnable and unassailable, like God with Jesus and the Holy Spirit. Maurice was like New York, New York. He was entirely in and of himself; he was, according to his campaign literature, The Man With The Plan. His ostensible plan was accountable government, investment in jobs, reform of the planning process; all of the usual. His actual plan was to win back power by any means necessary. He'd done his penance; he'd made his apologies; and now he wanted back in. Israel had followed Maurice's charmless charm offensive on the many hoardings of County Antrim as he drove in the van every day, Maurice Morris's shining face staring down at him: dominant; necessary; and appalling.

'So what is it, gents?' said Minnie, returning to take orders. 'Two coffees and two scones of the day?'

'Aye,' said Ted.

'Right you are,' said Minnie. 'And I'll make sure Maurice comes and has a quick word with you.'

'I heard he'd had a cafetière fitted,' said Ted.

'A cafetière?' said Israel.

'Aye.'

'A cafetière is what you make the coffee in,' said Minnie.

'Not a cafetière, then,' said Ted. 'Something like that.'

'A catheter?' said Israel.

'Well, I don't want you asking him about *that*,' said Minnie.

'I don't want to meet him anyway,' said Israel. 'Thanks.'

'The man running to be your own elected representative?' said Minnie.

'Sure, you probably vote for the Shinners,' said Ted.

'The whatters?' said Israel.

'Now!' said Minnie. 'We're one big happy rainbow nation these days, Ted.'

'Does he have any actual policies, Maurice Morris?' asked Israel.

'Aye,' said Ted. 'The same as the rest of them. Snouts in the trough and selling the rest of us down the river. I tell ye, I've some questions for Mister Morris if he comes over.'

'That's fine,' said Minnie, beginning to walk away. 'Healthy democracy and all that – just you make sure you go easy on him, Ted. I don't want any trouble. Nothing personal. I'll be back in a minute.'

'Nothing personal!' said Ted. 'Adulterating so and so.'

'Ex-adulterer,' said Minnie, as a parting shot.

'Ex-adulterer?' said Israel.

'A leopard doesn't change its spots,' said Ted.

Israel watched, fascinated, as Maurice slowly worked his ex-adulterating way from wipe-down gingham tableclothed table to wipe-down gingham tableclothed table, firmly shaking hands with the men, and hugging the ladies, and kissing the babies – grandchildren, mostly – and grinning and winking with utter conviction, as though there were no other place on earth that he'd rather be right now, a-grinning and a-winking, than right here, in Zelda's Café. In his years out of office Maurice had read a lot of books about communication, and persuasion, and entrepreneurial self-realisation and reinvention, and during his time in the wilderness he'd learnt that in life generally and in politics in particular, no matter how you felt or what your circumstances, you needed to appear always as though *this* really mattered – *this* coffee morning, *this* photoshoot, *this* meeting, *this* community liaison event. Even if it didn't. Which it didn't. Maurice had become, even more than he was previously, an *of* the and *in* the moment kind of a guy. When Maurice Morris went out campaigning around Tumdrum and District he put all thoughts of himself, of his many personal successes and achievements, from his mind and focused instead on the little people and their problems and difficulties, and the amazing thing was, it worked. They flocked to him, the people, because he, Maurice Morris, was *in* the moment. He *was* the moment: he had presence, you couldn't deny it, and right now, at this moment, middle-aged and elderly women who should have known better were in the moment with him, giggling and photographing each other, posing cheek-to-cheek with him, using the cameras on their mobile phones, many of them for the first time, delighted that they'd upgraded, as their daughters and the suited salespeople in the Carphone Warehouse in the Fountain Centre at Rathkeltair had wisely suggested. There were mega-pixel flashes, and much automatic red-eye reduction, and laughter, and good-natured banter and repartee, and even though it was Zelda's, and even though it was a Friday morning in September, and even though it was softly raining outside, it felt like a glittering gala event. Maurice Morris was about as glamorous as it got on the North Antrim coast. Short of George Clooney himself turning up in Zelda's, as part of some promotional tour for a new film about the Giant's Causeway – *Atlantic Ocean's Eleven*? – Maurice Morris was *it*.

'Come on now, fellas, sit up straight,' said Minnie, returning with coffee and scones.

'What?' said Israel, mesmerised by this manifestation of pure, adulterated charisma in their midst.

'Sit up straight for goodness' sake,' said Minnie. 'You make the place look untidy. He'll be over in a minute.'

Minnie leaned across and pulled Israel's T-shirt collar straight.

'There,' she said, 'that's better.'

'I'm not a child,' said Israel.

'Well . . .' said Ted. 'I wouldn't say that exactly. The mental age of a—'

'It's my birthday next week, actually,' said Israel.

'Ah. Really?' said Minnie. 'How old are ye going to be, pet?'

'About a hundred and twenty?' said Ted.

'Sssh,' said Minnie. 'I asked *him*, not you. Do you know how old he is?'

'Not a clue,' said Ted. 'But I could guess. What do you reckon?'

'Well . . .' Minnie looked Israel up and down: the mess of hair, the scrap of beard, the sullen cheeks, the gold-rimmed spectacles pushed up on to his forehead, the broken-down brogues, the baggy corduroy trousers, the 'Triple H' World Wrestling Entertainment T-shirt, featuring a grimacing, sweaty-looking man with long hair in black underpants, one of Brownie's. 'Difficult to say,' she concluded, diplomatically. 'What do you think?'

'Hello?' said Israel, trying to break into the conversation, unsuccessfully.

'He carries on like a wee cappy and he blethers on like a grumphie old man,' said Ted. 'I'd place him around fifty.'

'Fifty! I'm not fifty!' said Israel. 'Fifty! Do I look fifty?!'

'Early fifties?' said Ted.

'It's the beard, maybe,' said Minnie.

'Fifty! I'm nowhere near fifty! I'm going to be thirty!'

'Thirty?'

'Yes.'

'Oh,' said Minnie.

'Middle age,' said Ted. 'Make anybody depressed.'

'It's not middle age,' said Israel. 'And I am not depressed.'

'Might be older than middle age,' said Ted.

'Depends when ye're going to die,' said Minnie.

'Right,' said Israel.

'No man knoweth the hour,' said Minnie.

'Right,' said Israel.

'Never mind,' said Ted.

'Never mind what?' said Israel.

'Thirty. Bad age.'

'It's not a bad age. I have no problem with reaching thirty. That's the least of my problems.'

'Good,' said Ted.

'I'll leave you boys to it, then,' said Minnie. 'Enjoy your coffee. And happy birthday for next week.'

'Thanks,' said Israel.

'Thirty,' said Ted, shaking his head.

Israel had no problem with thirty, actually. Thirty is not that old. When you think about it. At thirty, really, you're still on the cusp of your twenties. At thirty you're an honorary twentysomething – that's a good way of looking at it. It's like you're the top of your year at school. You're a September baby. At thirty you might still conceivably be a late developer. You have a whole lifetime still ahead of you. At thirty the world remains your proverbial oyster . . .

'Buddy Holly,' said Ted, slathering his scone with butter.

'What about Buddy Holly?' said Israel.

'He died young,' said Ted.

'Right. And your point is?'

'I'm just saying, like. He was, what, twenty-one, twenty-two?'

'Right.'

'And the other fella.'

'Which other fella?'

'The actor fella. The leather jacket and the T-shirt.'

'Marlon Brando?'

'Ach, no, the other one.'

'James Dean?'

'Aye, that's yer man. How old was he when he died?'

'I have no idea, Ted,' said Israel.

'Twenty-five? Twenty-six?'

'And?' said Israel.

'You're a young man no more at thirty,' said Ted, taking a huge bite of scone, as if the scone itself might bite him back if he didn't get at it quick enough.

'Yes you are,' said Israel. 'Of course you are.'

'You're not in your twenties in your thirties,' said Ted, chewing, his mouth wide open.

'Yes, right, that's very true, Ted. Brilliant. Thank you for pointing that out. You're not in your twenties in your thirties. You did maths in school, then?'

'Big difference, twenties and thirties,' said Ted, ignoring Israel, swallowing. 'Big, big difference.'

'No it's not.'

'I'm telling ye. Yer movers and shakers, they've all done their moving and shaking by thirty, haven't they?'

'Well, some of them have, but—'

'Maurice Morris here.' Ted nodded towards the pinstriped figure of Maurice moving among them. 'Look what he'd achieved by the time he was thirty.'

'I have no idea what he'd achieved, actually. But I'm sure—'

'Well, what about yer Romantical poets, then? What about them?'

'Who?'

'All done in, weren't they, by thirty?'

'Who?'

'Kates, and—' Ted attacked the scone again.

'Keats?'

'Aye. All hanged themselves, didn't they, by the time they were—'

'No, they did not all hang themselves,' said Israel, factually. 'And I think Wordsworth lived till—'

'Exception that proves the rule,' said Ted. 'Like Johnny Cash.'

'What?'

'Oldest swinger in town.'

'You're losing me, Ted.'

'That's why you're depressed. The birthday, and breaking up with the girl—'

'I am not—' said Israel.

'The beard. The diet.'

'I'm not on a diet!'

'Have it your way.'

'I will. Thank you. I think thirty is a fine age.'

Ted finished his scone. Israel looked around Zelda's. Thirty was an absolute disaster.

At thirty you could no longer pretend that you might have lived a different, more extraordinary life, because you'd already lived a large part of your life – thirty useless years, for goodness' sake! – and it was utterly ordinary and straightforward and dull, dull, dull. Ted was right. At thirty you have lost touch for ever with the great and the good and the rich and the famous – the simple fact is, you do not move and you do not shake. At thirty there's no way you're going to start behaving like . . . whoever the hell you are, it doesn't matter, because in fact you're just a half-decent butcher, or a baker, or a candlestick-maker, or even a librarian, let's say, for the sake of argument, a mobile librarian named Israel Armstrong, on the northernmost coast of the north of the north of Ireland, and your whole life – let's just pretend, for who could possibly imagine a life of such inanity and nullity? – is preoccupied with cataloguing, and shelving, and making sure you remember to switch off the lights before you go home to the pathetic little converted chicken coop – imagine! – where you live on a farm – oh God – in the middle of the middle of nowhere around the back of beyond, and your idea of a good time is coming here to Zelda's to drink ersatz coffee with elderly men and women in car coats . . .

Basically, his life was over.

'Israel?' said Ted.

Israel did not answer.

'Hey?' Ted clicked his fingers in front of Israel's face. 'Wakey wakey.'

'What?' said Israel.

'Ye eatin' yer scone?' said Ted.

'I suppose,' said Israel, as though a scone were all he deserved in life. 'What is it today?'

'Bacon and cheese,' said Ted.

'Oh God. Not again. Why do they do that? That's not a scone!'

'That's a scone and a half,' said Ted.

'Exactly: that's lunch,' said Israel.

'Ye not having it, then?'

'I'm a vegetarian! How many times do I have to tell you!'

'Can vegetenarians not eat scones?'

'*Vege*-tarians,' said Israel.

'I didn't know they couldn't eat scones.'

'Not with bacon in they can't.'

'Aye, well,' said Ted, reaching across. 'There we are now.'

Minnie bustled over with the coffee pot.

'Refill?'

Israel took a hasty sip of coffee.

'It tastes off,' he said, grumpily.

'What does?' said Minnie.

'The coffee,' said Israel.

'It doesn't.'

'Coffee can't go off,' said Ted.

'The milk can.'

'Our milk is not off,' said Minnie.

Israel sniffed the milk in the jug.

'It's fine,' said Ted.

'It must be the coffee, then,' said Israel. 'It has a sort of fishy smell. Is this an Americano? Are you using that chicory stuff again?'

'Ach,' said Minnie, 'the machine's not working.'

'That machine has never been working,' said Israel.

'It has, so it has,' said Minnie.

'When?'

'It's usually working.'

'Not since I've been living here.'

'How long have you been living here?' said Ted, in an accusatory fashion.

'Long enough,' said Israel.

'Aye,' said Ted.

'Life sentence,' said Israel.

'Ooh, did you see *Prison Break*, Ted?' said Minnie.

'That the one with the tattooed fella?'

'Aye.'

'Was it on last night?'

'Aye.'

'I think I Sky-plussed it. I was watching this programme last night about the American security services on the History Channel.'

'Ooh. Really? Was it any good?'

'In America,' said Ted, raising his fingers, as though about to conduct. 'In America, they have sixteen security agencies.'

'Sixteen?' said Minnie, impressed.

'I bet you didn't know that now, did you?' Ted said to Israel.

'No, I must admit, I didn't—'

'There's the CIA,' said Ted.

'Oh God,' said Israel. 'Are you going to—'

'The FBI. The NSA.'

'Never heard of it,' said Israel.

'National Security Agency,' said Minnie.

'How do you know that?' said Israel.

'The Defence Intelligence Agency,' said Ted, counting on his fingers. 'And . . . some others.'

'Drugs Enforcement Administration?' said Minnie.

'Aye, that's one,' said Ted.

'How the hell did you know that?' said Israel.

'Sure, wasn't Denzel Washington in one of those films?'

'Was he?' said Ted.

'Aye.' Minnie turned to Israel. 'Now what's up with ye? You've a face'd turn milk sour.'

'The coffee,' said Israel, grimacing. 'It really is—'

'I was telling ye, we can't get the parts,' said Minnie.

'How long have you had the machine?'

'The Gaggia?' said Minnie. 'I don't know. Forty years?'

'Right. Well, there you are,' said Israel. 'It's obsolete.'

'It's a very good make,' said Minnie.

'It's an antique,' said Israel. 'Like everything else in this godfor—'

Ted reached forward and clipped Israel round the ear.

'He smells lovely,' the women at the next table were agreeing among themselves at that very moment, as Maurice Morris wafted over to them, and he did, they were right, Israel could smell it, as he ducked down with the force of Ted's blow; he smelt absolutely lovely, Maurice; it was the sharp, sweet, lemony smell of a Turkish cologne, which Maurice had discovered while on holiday with friends at a luxury golf resort hotel in southern Turkey some years previously, a cologne to which he had become famously – according to his campaign literature – addicted, and which he had sent over specially from London, and whose smell of exotic sweetness had until recently cut famously and decisively through the manly whiff of his cigar smoke, though alas, since the beginning of his campaign, Maurice had – also famously – given up smoking. You had to make certain sacrifices in politics, Maurice believed, and politicians were expected to set an example. Also, smoking was no longer a vote winner, so the cigars had had to go. A politician caught smoking cigars in public these days might as well have been caught patting a secretary on her pert little behind, or having an affair – for the sake of argument – with one of their constituency workers; those days, the good old cigar-chomping, camel-coat-wearing, secretary's-pert-little-behind-patting and constituency-worker-bedding days were long gone, and they sure as hell weren't ever coming back. You had to keep moving with the times and keep on moving forward in politics, according to Maurice, which could be easier said than done, frankly: since giving up smoking he'd put on a few pounds around the waist and if he was absolutely honest the last place he wanted to be was in a café surrounded by grey-haired men and women in car coats discussing coffee and cakes, but if these good people – his people, his constituents – wanted to talk tray bakes, Maurice talked tray bakes. He was like Jesus, Maurice Morris: his life was a living sacrifice.

'Tasty, ladies?'

'Yes,' said one of them.

'That was a statement rather than a question,' said Maurice, winking.

'Here you are,' offered one woman, 'would you like a wee nibble of mine?'

'Well, thank you,' said Maurice, leaning down, teasingly. 'It's not often I get an offer like that.'

'Go on, then,' said the woman, blushing, and reaching forward with her fork, the dark brown confection poised perilously on the end. Maurice closed his mouth around the cake, winked at the assembled crowd, smacked his lips around the cake, and exaggeratedly chewed and swallowed.

'Mmmm!' he exclaimed, sub-orgasmically. 'That is delicious. So rich!'

'I think it's made with buttermilk,' said the woman.

'Really?' said Maurice, entirely as if the use of buttermilk in cakes were a point of great interest to him.

'You have to use buttermilk,' piped up someone from the crowd.

'I can't get buttermilk these days,' said someone else.

'Buttermilk,' repeated Maurice, confirmingly.

'Me neither,' said another woman.

'You ladies can't get buttermilk?' said Maurice.

'No,' they all chorused.

'That sounds to me like a problem,' said Maurice. 'Is that a problem?'

'Yes,' chorused the ladies.

'Well, let's make a note of that,' said Maurice. This was where he really came into his own, M 'n' M; this was where his years of independent financial advising and his reading of *Neuro-Linguistic Programming for Dummies* really came into play: he profoundly understood that people liked to think that they were being consulted, even when they weren't, that you had to give people at least the illusion that they were in charge of their lives and their destinies. Hence one of his favourite phrases, 'Let's make a note of that'. Maurice didn't make actual notes of anything himself, of course; that would have been ridiculous; he always had a secretary with him – whose pert behind went noticeably unpatted – whose job it was to make notes of things.

'Buttermilk,' he said as he got up from the table. 'Let's see what we can do about that. Ladies, I hope I can rely on your vote.'

Of course he could rely on their votes: Maurice was the tallest, and the best-dressed, and the most pointlessly and aggressively articulate Unionist politician in Northern Ireland, where there was plenty of competition in the pointlessly aggressive articulation stakes and no competition whatsoever between parties outside of their secure geographical and sectarian areas, which made Maurice's re-election a real possibility. All he needed to do was to win back the popular vote, and to get people on his side again – including his wife, Pamela, who'd stood by him through thick and thin, even though she had every reason not to, given the . . . unique . . . stresses and strains that Maurice's career had placed upon their marriage.

'Here he comes!' said Minnie. 'Quick! Sit up!'

'*Macher*,' said Israel.

'What!' said Ted.

'It's Yiddish,' said Israel.

'I don't like the sound of it,' said Ted.

'It's just a word,' said Israel. 'It means—'

'I don't care what it means,' said Ted. 'Shut up. Here comes his Lordship. I'm going to give him a—'

And then there he was, in the flesh, Maurice Morris, looming over them, teeth a-sparkling, tan a-glowing, body a-facing them – whenever Maurice spoke he consciously moved his body to face the person he was talking to, so that they could feel the full force of his personality.

'Gentlemen, I'm Maurice Morris. I wonder if I can rely on your vote next Wednesday?'

'Aye,' said Ted, resolve failing, and blushing like a schoolgirl.

'Marvellous. And how about you, young man?'

Israel looked up at Maurice Morris, up at the blue suit, at the shiny tie, the rosy cheeks, the hair with some sort of shiny product in it, and he smiled.

'Nope,' he said. 'Thanks.'

'Oh,' said Maurice Morris.

'He's Jewish,' said Ted, apologetically.

'Ah,' said Maurice Morris.

'What?' said Israel.

'Also, he's not from round here,' added Ted. 'So he's probably not illegible.'

'Eligible,' corrected Israel.

'It depends if he filled in the census,' said Maurice Morris, speaking to Israel as though he were wheel-chair bound. 'Did you?'

'I have no idea,' said Israel. 'But I'll not be voting for you anyway.'

'So, anyway,' said Minnie, glaring at Israel, begin-ning to usher Maurice Morris away.

'Well, good to meet you, gents. Enjoy your coffees,' said Maurice, ready to move on.

'Hold on,' said Israel. 'I've got a question for you.'

'Ssshh,' said Minnie.

'No, no, fire away,' said Maurice. 'Always open to questions.'

'It's a policy question,' said Israel.

'Good,' said Maurice.

'What are you going to do about global warming?'

Global warming was one of the many things that Israel felt bad about.

Minnie frowned but Maurice smiled his weird politi-cian's smile. This was not the usual tray-bake kind of a question. This was one of those questions that he'd said something about in his brochure. One of the things that had always distinguished Maurice from his rivals, according to his campaign literature, was the sheer quality and quantity of his campaign literature; his election brochure had been printed at an expense and in a style that might more properly have been used to advertise the first release of a complex of luxury apartments in Majorca, or a major development opportunity on the north coast, and Maurice also blogged (at mnmblogspot.com), and did email circulars and had a MySpace site; he was, according to his brochure, Northern Ireland's first and most successful cyberpolitician. And he couldn't remember for the life of him what it was he'd said in the brochure about global warming.

'That's still one for the scientists,' he told Israel.

'Not according to the scientists it's not,' said Israel, one of whose only companions these days was the BBC World Service late at night and early in the mornings.

'Ha!' said Maurice, changing the subject rapidly. 'Well, it's been good talking to you.'

'I would still like an answer,' said Israel.

'Sorry, I don't think we've met,' said Maurice to Israel. 'You are?'

'I'm a librarian,' said Israel.

'Really?' said Maurice.

The phrase 'I'm a librarian' usually excited a number of depressingly predictable responses, in Israel's experience, responses that usually began with an 'Oh' and were soon followed by a vague and slightly uncomfortable look in the eye. Maurice's response was unusual.

'The *mobile* librarian?' said Maurice.

'Yes,' said Israel.

'Isaac Angstrom?'

'*Israel Armstrong*,' said Israel. Had Maurice been reading John Updike? *Couples*?

'Israel Armstrong,' said Maurice, savouring the words in his mouth. 'The mobile librarian.'

'Yep,' said Israel. 'That's me.'

'Well, I hope you're ashamed of yourself, you sick bastard,' said Maurice, striding away.

5

'Ach, brilliant!' said Ted, again and again, after they'd left Zelda's and they were driving to their next port of call, Tumdrum Primary School, where Israel was expected to help the children with their reading. 'Brilliant! Brilliant. Priceless.'

'All right, thank you, Ted,' said Israel.

'The look on his face, but. Brilliant. Brilliant. You must have done something bad to upset him! Oh, brilliant!'

'He's just a miserable bas—' began Israel.

'Language!' said Ted. 'Mebbe he just doesn't like the look of you.'

'Horrible,' said Israel. 'A creepy, slimy, rude, horrible man.'

'Ach, he was maybe in a bad mood, just, eh? "I hope you're pleased with yourself, you sick bastard!" Oh dear, oh dear.'

'He's got some sort of problem,' said Israel. 'Personality disorder probably.'

'It's the election, isn't it?' said Ted. 'Pressure getting to him.'

'I know the feeling,' said Israel.

'What? Pressure?'

'Yes,' said Israel. 'Do you have any Nurofen?'

'Ach, wise up,' said Ted, as though Nurofen were a heroin substitute. They pulled into the school playground. 'Who'd ye think ye are, Barack O'Bana?'

'Obama,' said Israel. 'O.Ba.Ma.'

'Aye,' said Ted. 'His family were from Kerry, weren't they?'

'What? He's a black man from Hawaii,' said Israel.

'I'm not arguing with you about it,' said Ted. 'Just get on with it. Come on. We're late.'

They visited the school once every two weeks and the routine was always the same: the children would choose their books from the library under Ted's menacing gaze and without major incident – no tears, no fights, no tantrums – and then Israel would trudge with them into the classroom for the compulsory story time, and all hell would break loose.

Israel was just not a story-time kind of a librarian: he absolutely hated children's books, for starters. Most of them were mind-bogglingly bad, illustrated by the artistically challenged – can no one draw hands any more? – and with words by people who clearly hated words. He was always trying to read *Where the Wild Things Are*, or *Green Eggs and Ham*, again, but the children, being children, wanted novelty, and the teachers wanted something more appropriate to the national curriculum's reading strategy. So Israel would read something dull and appropriate in a dull and appropriate monotone, and the children would inevitably fidget, and then this would lead inevitably to shoving and poking, and then usually to a fight, and hence to chaos. It didn't help that Israel also didn't much like children, per se. He could never remember their names, or if he could remember them, he couldn't pronounce them.

'How do you say the name of the boy with the big ears?' he asked Ted, as he always did.

'Who?' said Ted.

'The one who always asks the difficult questions.'

'*Pod-rig*,' said Ted.

'I thought last time you said it was more like . . .' He puckered up his lips. '*Pahd-rag*.'

'Ach, I don't know,' said Ted. 'I'm not good with these Irish names.'

'You're Irish,' said Israel.

'I'm an Ulsterman,' said Ted.

'Right.'

'Big difference,' said Ted.

'Sure,' said Israel.

'It might be *Paw-rick*.'

'Right,' said Israel.

'It just depends,' said Ted.

'On what?'

'I've no idea,' said Ted.

'So, is it *Pod-rig*? Or *Paw-rick*?'

'*Paaah-ric*?' said Ted, rolling the vowels around in his mouth. 'I don't know. *Paw-drig*.'

'Oh, come on,' said Israel.

'Just call him Paddy,' said Ted. 'That's what I do.'

'Marvellous,' said Israel.

'I'll just have a wee smoke here, then,' said Ted.

'But—'

'Me back's a bit sore, still. You hurry on there, sure.'

While Ted waited cosily in the van Israel trudged towards the classroom and the moon-faced children of Tumdrum, who stared up at him, as they always did, loudly fidgeting, while Tony Thompson, headmaster of the school, sat at the back, in his shiny black suit, and his grey shirt, and black tie, smirking, and poor Israel droned.

The reading was bad enough. He read from a super-sized book about someone called Red Ted, who sat on a shelf and did very little else, except clearly demonstrate some pointless rule of phonics. There were the usual skirmishes. It was awful. But there was worse to come. Question time. He absolutely hated question time.

'Yes, Laura,' said Tony Thompson, when Israel had finished reading about Red Ted, on his shelf. 'You have a question for Mr Armstrong – the *librarian*.'

Tony somehow always managed to make the word 'librarian' sound dirty and sinister, as though a librarian were a sort of a book pimp.

'Why have you grown a beard?' asked Laura, a girl with pure pale blue eyes, and a full head of fizzing ginger hair, like a changeling out of a horror film.

'Erm.' Israel was thrown. 'Just to make my face look . . . smaller. Any other questions?'

'Are you on a diet?' asked Laura.

'No. I am *not* on a diet. Any *book* questions?'

'Do you *make* books?' asked Laura, without pausing for a beat.

'No,' said Israel, trying to muster what might pass for a tone of infectious enthusiasm. 'No, personally, I don't actually make the books myself, I just . . .'

Laura's eyes bored into him, withering his confidence.

'I just . . . look after the books,' he continued. 'Like a . . . zookeeper looks after the animals.'

'Thank you,' said Mr Thompson. 'Any other questions for Mr Armstrong, the bearded book *zookeeper*?'

A hand shot up. It was Padraig.

'Any other questions?' said Israel, eyeing up Padraig. 'Anyone else?'

No hands were raised.

'Sure?' said Israel. 'No one else? Any questions?'

Silence.

'Good. So . . . Yes . . . Paddy,' said Israel.

'My name's Padraig,' said Padraig.

'Ah, yes, sorry. Of course. *Porr-idge*?'

'What do you do?' said Padraig.

'What do I do?' said Israel. 'I'm a librarian.'

'But do you have another job?' interrupted Padraig. He had intricate whorl-like ears, Padraig, and a head like a pug.

'No,' said Israel, 'I don't have another job. This is my actual job.'

'D'ye not have another job?'

'No. I don't. It's actually quite a busy job, being a librarian. You have to . . . sort the books out, and put them on the shelves, and . . .'

'Thank you, Padraig,' said Tony Thompson. 'Any final questions for Mr *Arm*strong this week before he rushes off to rearrange his books on the shelf?'

Hands again.

'Yes, Billy?'

'What are books?' asked Billy, whose face was as wide as it was tall.

'What are books?' said Israel. 'Erm. Books? Good . . . question. Excellent . . . question.'

'I'm sure we'd all like to hear your answer to that question, Mr Armstrong,' said Tony Thompson. 'What is a book? Listen, children, to what Mr Armstrong has to say.'

'A book is . . .' Israel was struggling here slightly. 'Well, a book can be about . . .'

'Sorry,' said Tony Thompson. 'Sorry to interrupt you, Mr Armstrong. But I think what Billy was asking was not what is a book *about*, but a wider and more general question – wasn't it, Billy?' Billy nodded obediently, his pure white lardy child-jowls shaking. 'About what exactly a book *is*.'

'Ah, yes, what is it? A book?'

'Indeed,' said Tony Thompson.

'A book?' repeated Israel. 'What is a book?'

'Yes,' said Tony Thompson. 'That's the question, Mr Armstrong. And the children would love to hear your answer.'

'Well, a book is a kind of . . .' Israel looked around desperately for inspiration. 'It's a dead tree, basically.'

'A dead tree,' repeated Tony Thompson, grinning and showing his teeth. 'Really?'

'Yes,' said Israel, 'basically.' He got the sense he was maybe losing his audience here, but he'd started so he'd have to finish. 'Not a tree that's been killed, exactly, by a . . . gun or anything. It's more . . . I mean, more like a piece of a dead tree.'

'A piece of dead tree,' said Tony Thompson.

'Yes. That's one way of looking at it,' said Israel. 'Or, I know . . . a tree flake.' Oh God. 'Yes! That's it, that's what books are. Tree flakes. Little parts of the body of a tree, you see, that have been . . . Like pork scratchings . . . It's not something alive, anyway. If you turn it over in your hand.' He turned over the supersized *Red Ted on the Shelf* in his hand. 'Here we are, then,' he said. 'Listen! Can you hear it saying anything?' He held the book up to his ear. 'Hello, Mr Book? Red Ted? Anybody there? No? No. That's because a book is not a disembodied voice. Can you hear it, children?'

Tony Thompson was shaking his head.

The children were leaning forward in their seats.

A hand shot up.

'Yes?'

'I can hear it, Mr Armstrong.'

'No. No. You can't. That must be a . . . voice in your . . . head. You can't hear the book,' continued Israel, changing tack. 'Because a book can't speak. Because a book is not . . . a person.'

'Is it imagination?' asked Laura.

'Yes. Well, not exactly. A book is not itself imagination, or an idea, or anything like that. It's just . . . A book is basically . . . I mean, literally of course a book is just . . . paper covered in ink, like lots of . . . little black . . . maggots crawling around on a big . . . white sheet, or snow, or . . .'

'Thank you, Mr Armstrong,' interjected Tony Thompson. 'I think that's enough this morning. Thank you very much for your little talk. As enlightening as ever.'

'No, thank . . . you,' said Israel.

'Good to be back in the saddle, eh?' said Ted, when Israel – mentally and emotionally drained, and dizzied by his ordeal – arrived back at the van.

'You're not meant to smoke in the van,' said Israel.

'Ach, wise up,' said Ted. 'Glad to be back in the swing of things, though, eh?'

'No,' said Israel.

'Good,' said Ted. 'Go all right?'

'It was horrific,' said Israel.

'No,' said Ted. 'Having no arms and legs would be horrific.'

'Right,' said Israel. 'Yes. Of course. I forgot. I am lucky to have the use of my arms and legs.'

'Exactly,' said Ted. 'Count your blessings.'

Israel counted his blessings all the way to the visitors' car park at the Myowne mobile home park, their last stop of the week, 1 p.m.–5 p.m., the traditional rush as Tumdrum's many mobile home dwellers changed their books for the weekend.

'So,' said Israel, staring out at the grey expanse of the strand.

'So,' said Ted, producing his ancient orange-coloured Tupperware lunchbox. 'Back to normal, then.'

'Yes,' agreed Israel.

'Do you no good, lying in yer bed,' said Ted.

'No,' agreed Israel, for the sake of peace and quiet.

'Weather's not looking the best,' said Ted, tucking into the first of his customary two-ham-sandwich lunch. 'It's autumn, mind. So what do you expect?' In the absence of anyone else to actually argue with, Ted enjoyed arguing with himself. He was pretty much self-sufficient, conversationally.

'What are books, do you think, Ted?'

'What are books?'

'Yes.'

'Are you losing your mind?' said Ted, with sandwich poised.

'No. I'm just . . . interested.'

'Ye're not eating right,' said Ted. 'Your mother'd be on to me if she knew.'

'Right.'

'What are ye eatin'? Weetabix and lettuce? D'ye want a bite?' He held out his sandwich between his fingers.

'No, thank you.'

Ted then proceeded to peel open the two slices of white bread and peer carefully inside, as though he were Howard Carter uncovering the entrance to the tomb of Tutankhamen.

'They're ham.'

'I know they're ham. You have ham every day, Ted. You have eaten a ham sandwich every lunchtime ever since I've known you. You *only* eat ham sandwiches at lunch.'

'Aye, well, and I'm offering you a bite, seeing as the

condition ye're in, but it's an offer I'll not make again in all pobability, given your attitude.'

'Probability,' said Israel.

'Exactly,' said Ted.

'You're offering me a bite of your ham sandwich?'

'Aye.'

'Well, I would accept, under normal circumstances,' said Israel, wearily, 'but as you well know, Ted, I'M A VEGETARIAN.'

The vegetarian conversation was another one of the conversations that Ted and Israel had had at least once a day every day since Israel had arrived in Tumdrum – along with the conversation about Israel resigning, and why there were no longer any great Irish boxers – yet the memory of it seemed to leave no trace with Ted, like the taste of tofu, or Quorn. Ted took a long and very noisy slurp of tea from the plastic cup of his old tartan Thermos flask.

'Aye, well, the vegetenarianism'd be yer problem. Ye've the skitters, have ye?'

'What?'

'Aye, all them there fruit and vegetables, skittering the guts out of ye. It's a wonder ye're not on the po the whole time.'

'I have been vegetarian for many years, Ted. And my digestive system remains in good working order, thank you.'

Ted finished one sandwich and then slid another from under the firmly elastic-banded lid of his lunchbox.

'So ye're just off yer food, are ye?'

'I suppose so.'

'Ye frettin' about yer birthday, eh? And the girl?' Ted spoke with his mouth full, pointing at Israel with the sharp end of the sandwich.

'No. I am not fretting about my birthday. And no, I am not fretting about Gloria.'

'Well, it's strange but, isn't it, seeing as ye were a wee ball of lard when you were with her.'

'I was not a "wee ball of lard" when I was with Gloria, thank you, Ted.'

'Wee bunty, so you were. Ye want to get back on the stew and the Guinness, boy. Get a good rozner in ye, ye'd be right as rain.'

'A rozner?'

'A good feed, boy, and ye'll be out gropin' the hens again.'

'Well. Thank you for your dietary and relationship advice, Ted. To the point, as ever.'

'I tell ye, ye'll be playing the vibraphone on your ribs soon enough ye keep this up.'

'Right.'

'It's not healthy, so it's not, losing all that weight like that. Ye'll see. Ye'll put it all back on again. Ye're depressed, just.'

'I am not depressed, Ted.'

'Good.'

'I've just got things on my mind,' said Israel.

'Very dangerous,' said Ted, mid-mouthful.

Ted finished his sandwich in silence, screwed the cup back on the top of his Thermos, and looked at his watch.

'Books,' said Israel.

'Books?' said Ted.

'What are they?'

'Ach, knock it off,' said Ted.

'I mean a book is not a person, is it? Or an idea. Not just an idea.'

'No,' said Ted, uninterested.

'It's not an issue or a theme.'

'No,' said Ted. 'I'll tell you what it is: a book is a blinkin' book, for goodness' sake. End of conversation.'

'But—' began Israel.

At which point a man entered the van.

'Hi!' he said.

'Hello,' said Israel.

'Saved by the bell,' said Ted. 'I'm away for a smoke here. Think you can cope?'

'Yes, I think so,' said Israel.

'Not going to go crazy in my absence?'

'No, Ted. I am not going to go crazy.'

'Good,' said Ted. 'Watch him,' he instructed the man. 'He's a bit . . .' – he tapped a finger to the side of his head – 'ye know.'

The man was wearing a navy crombie jacket, faded jeans, and cowboy boots, a look that was one part bohemian to one part gentleman farmer, to one part middle manager in corporate marketing. He also sported a goatee beard, which added to the overall effect, and which gave him a rather sincere appearance, as if he'd just made a decision and was mulling over the consequences, and he also had close-cropped hair, which made him look as if the decision he'd just made was a serious one, possibly related to the military, or

the sale of some new kind of social-networking software. Israel wondered whether it might be an idea for
him to have his hair cut short, to look as though he
were making important decisions relating to weapons
technology, or new media. Unfortunately, when Israel
had had his hair cut short in the past, it made him
look as if he meant to commit a serious crime.

'Neil Gaiman,' said the man.

'Pleased to meet you,' said Israel. 'I'm Israel
Armstrong.'

'No, sorry,' said the man, laughing. 'I mean do you
have any books by Neil Gaiman.'

'Ah,' said Israel. 'Right. Yes! Of course. I think we're
all out actually. Sorry. We could always do an interlibrary loan request.'

'No, that's OK, I'm not really in for borrowing,' said
the man.

'Right,' said Israel. 'You're not one of our regulars?'
And as he spoke these words Israel almost choked: he
knew the regulars; he had become a local; he was mired,
inured and immersed in Tumdrum.

'No,' said the stranger. 'My parents are originally
from here. But I live in Belfast.'

'Well, nice to see a new face,' said Israel. Oh God.

'My name's Seamus,' said the man. 'Seamus
Fitzgibbons. I'm the Green Party candidate for the forthcoming election.'

Seamus stuck out a friendly hand.

'Oh. Hello. I'm Israel. Israel Armstrong.'

'Look, thanks for coming,' said Seamus.

'That's OK,' said Israel. 'I work here.'

'Oh, yes!' Seamus laughed. 'I'm so busy at the moment with meetings and meet-and-greets it's difficult to remember where I am.'

God. Israel would give anything to not know where he was. He knew exactly where he was: stuck. Seamus looked to be about Israel's age, but while Israel had drifted and gone from job to job, aimlessly, Seamus had obviously set out with a goal and achieved a position of responsibility – prospective parliamentary candidate! A position where he wasn't sure where he was, and conducted meetings and meet-and-greets! And he was a man who looked as though he enjoyed shouldering the responsibility; it was something in his eyes. If you looked closely in his eyes you could see Atlas with the world upon his shoulders.

'Let me come straight to the point, Israel,' said Seamus. Israel could never get to the point. That was how people who shouldered responsibility spoke! They got straight to the point. 'We in the Green Party don't have a campaign bus.'

'Uh-huh,' said Israel.

'And so . . .'

'Yes?' said Israel, like a rabbit caught in the headlights.

'Well, we were wondering if we could perhaps use the mobile library?'

'Ha!' said Israel.

'Is that a yes?'

'No!' said Israel, instinctively. 'I mean yes . . . No. I mean no.'

'Oh.'

78

'No. No. I don't think so. No, Linda would go mad.'

'Who's Linda?'

'Linda Wei, she's responsible for library provision in Tumdrum and—'

'Well, maybe I should speak to Linda directly, if you're unable to make those sorts of decisions.'

'Well. I . . . It's not that I . . . I mean, I am responsible for the mobile library.'

'But that sort of bigger decision would be out of your hands?'

'Not entirely,' said Israel, smarting rather from the implication that he was a powerless functionary. 'I do have some . . . sway with these things.' He had no sway with anything: he didn't even have sway with himself.

'Well.'

'I could probably take it to the mobile library subcommittee,' offered Israel.

'Well, the election's in less than a week now, so we would really need to know very soon,' said Seamus.

'Ah,' said Israel.

'I don't suppose it could be justified on the basis of educational benefit?'

'I don't think so,' said Israel.

'Look,' said Seamus. 'I really didn't want to put you in a difficult position. It was worth asking, but.'

'Yeah, sure.'

'If you don't ask you don't get,' said Seamus.

'That's true,' said Israel. Israel didn't ask. He didn't get.

'Look, that's fine. Let's forget about using the van. Maybe I could just leave you some of these.' He produced from a battered old leather satchel a thick bundle of election leaflets.

'Sure,' said Israel. 'Just leave them there.'

Seamus carefully fanned out the leaflets on the issue desk.

'There,' he said, proudly.

'Recycled paper?' said Israel, pointlessly.

'Of course,' said Seamus. 'Look, thanks a million for your help.'

'My pleasure,' said Israel.

'Look,' said Seamus – he liked to say 'look', a lot. 'Look, I'm afraid I need to get on here. The campaign's hotting up in the final few days.'

'Of course,' said Israel. 'Yes.'

'We've got to keep out Maurice Morris.'

'Quite,' said Israel.

'I think the tide's turning towards the Greens,' said Seamus.

'Good. Good,' said Israel. He thought he might vote Green, actually.

'Well, lovely to meet you, and thanks again,' said Seamus.

As Seamus left, Ted re-entered, smelling of cigarettes. He homed in immediately on the leaflets.

'What are these?' he said, disdainfully.

'What?' said Israel, who was still trying to decide whether or not to vote Green.

'These.'

'They're leaflets.'

'I can see they're leaflets.'

'The man just left them.' They featured a picture of

Seamus, with his goatee and cropped hair, in what looked like an orchard, eating an apple. 'They're for the Green Party. For the election. I'm thinking I might vote Green, actually.'

'Ach,' said Ted.

'No, I might,' said Israel.

'Aye, you would,' said Ted. 'But we're going to have to get rid of these.' And he scooped up the leaflets from the counter.

'We're allowed to carry public information leaflets,' said Israel.

'Public information,' said Ted. 'Aye. But this isn't public information, is it? This is propaganda.'

'It's not propaganda,' said Israel.

'It is, so it is.'

'What about all the hoardings Maurice Morris has up everywhere?' said Israel. There was one, in fact, looming above the van even now, high up on a telegraph pole, with Maurice's face grinning out into the cold wind.

'Aye, well, he's entitled, isn't he. He's paid for that. The Greens want to get organised themselves, get some hoardings up, nothing to stop them.'

'They probably can't afford it.'

'Well, whose fault is that?' said Ted.

'Anyway,' said Israel, grabbing the leaflets back out of Ted's hands. 'I told him I was going to display his leaflets.'

'We're not supposed to,' said Ted.

'Well, I told him, and I will.'

'Ach,' said Ted.

'It's censorship if we don't,' said Israel.

'Censorship!' said Ted. 'I don't know anything about censorship. But I do know that Linda wouldn't like it.'

'Well, Linda doesn't need to know, does she?' said Israel, fanning the leaflets back out on the counter. 'How would she find out?'

6

'He did what?' said Linda Wei, who was not only Israel's boss, but also Tumdrum's only and most prominent lesbian Chinese single mother, and who was currently sipping a large glass of restorative Friday night Chardonnay at the bar of the back room of the First and Last. Linda was wearing her habitual heavy make-up and her trademark sunglasses, perched film-star-ishly high up on her forehead, and she'd pushed the sartorial boat out even farther than usual this evening, with a red beret, a voluminous bright purple silk blouse, and a pair of green-and-brown camouflage combat trousers, teamed with blazing pink, customised plastic clogs: she looked like she was ready for anything, from the catwalk to the playgroup, to her own show on a shopping channel, to tackling insurgents in the jungles of Belize.

'Hmm,' said Ron, chairman of the Mobile Library Steering Committee, who was wearing his grey suit and nursing a glass of tap water. 'Leaflets.'

'Is he a total idiot?' said Linda.

'And what with lending out the Unshelved—' said Ron.

'But Maurice Morris's daughter!' exclaimed Linda. 'Is he out of his tiny mind! The Unshelved! To Maurice's daughter!'

'Aye,' said Ron, who was a man of few, and usually rather depressing, words. 'Alas.'

'How old is she?'

'Fourteen.'

'Fourteen!' said Linda. 'God love her. What do they know at fourteen? My eldest's sixteen, for goodness' sake, and he's a wee babby still. Fourteen!'

'Just turned fourteen,' said Ron. 'Closer to thirteen, actually.'

'Oh! What's she been borrowing?'

'I don't know. I would think the usual suspects,' said Ron, meditatively.

'*Lolita*,' said Linda, with disgust. 'I bet. *Slaughterhouse-Five*.'

'*Wuthering Heights*,' said Ron. 'Very strange.'

'*Wuthering Heights*! That's not Unshelved,' said Linda.

'We read it at school,' said Ron. 'I found it very strange.'

'*American Psycho*,' said Linda. 'That's what we're talking about here, Ron. Filth.'

'*Sex and the City*,' said Ron.

'That's a TV programme,' said Linda.

'But, I suppose, girls mature more quickly . . .'

'Have you ever read *American Psycho*?' said Linda.

'I'm more of a Patrick O'Brian man myself,' said Ron.

'You could live till a hundred and twenty and still not be old enough to read that sort of filth!' said Linda. And then, 'Filth!' she repeated, for good measure.

'Patrick O'Brian?' said Ron. 'Aubrey and Maturin? There's nothing wrong with them, so there's not.'

'No! *American Psycho*,' said Linda. 'That sort of stuff. Denigrating to women.'

'Bad books,' said Ron.

'Exactly!' said Linda, adjusting the angle of her beret. '*Bad books*. Have you any idea how damaging this is to our reputation as a responsible library service? When I get a hold of that idiot I am going to . . .'

Israel, who had no idea that Linda was on the bad-books warpath, waved to her from his table across the other side of the room, and was about to call out in greeting when the Reverend England Roberts announced, 'Let's Get Busy with the Quizzy!' and the one-hundred-plus people crammed into the back room of the First and Last suddenly quietened, put down their – mostly non-alcoholic – drinks and took up their pencils.

Because if it was the last Friday night of the month – and it was – then it was Fish and Chip Biblical Quiz Night in Tumdrum. The idea for Fish and Chip Biblical Quiz Nights had come originally from a friend of the Reverend Roberts, a man named Francie McGinn, a millionaire minister who ran his own rapidly growing house church movement and Christian franchise business a little way down the coast from Tumdrum. Francie McGinn's inspiration was an American pastor called Rick Warren, founder of the phenomenally successful

Saddleback Church in South Orange County, California, and the author of *The New York Times* No. 1 bestselling *The Purpose Driven ® Life*, *The Purpose Driven ® Church*, *The Purpose Driven ® Life Journal*, and *The Purpose Driven ® Life Scripture Keeper Plus*. Pastor Warren's was a kick-ass-go-getting-positive-mental-attitude-plus-sacrificial-prayerfulness kind of a philosophy, which Francie McGinn, after facing a number of personal and financial difficulties and setbacks, had taken seriously and taken on board and had applied diligently to his own life and work, managing to build up both his congregation and a range of businesses, which now included the very popular chain of Family Viewing DVD rental shops, the nationwide Christian Eventides Homes, and the Jacob's Well Christian day spas and nail and beauty bars. Francie had also acquired the UK and Irish distribution rights for a range of Christian snack bars and health drinks, which meant that throughout the length and breadth of the land, from the supermarkets of County Down to the corner shops of County Cork, you could now purchase the Seeds of Samson ('A Holy Good Mixture of Sunflower Seeds, Pumpkin Seeds, Cashews and Peanuts'), and a range of – mostly honey-based – Sweet Shalom Smoothies, the Lion Bar of Judah, Land of Beulah Yoghurt-Coated Raisins, and Jacob's Ladder energy drinks ('We Are Climbing Jacob's Ladder, With Added Ginseng'), all of which came with inspirational scripture verses prominently displayed on their packaging.

Fish and Chip Biblical Quiz Nights were one of Francie McGinn's rather more niche ideas. Churches subscribed online to a complete Biblical Quiz Night package and were then able to use the material either as an evangelism tool, or as an alternative to traditional Bible Study groups, or as a means of congregation team-building, like white-water rafting, or paintballing. The Reverend England Roberts, Tumdrum's incongruously black South African Presbyterian minister, preferred to use the quiz nights as a simple excuse for a good night out, and he stood proudly now, microphone in one hand, Diet Coke in the other, at the back bar of the First and Last, wearing his Lord of the Rings-style 'One King to Rule Them All, One Son to Find Them, One Love to Bring Them All, One Spirit to Bind Them' T-shirt.

'Pencils at the ready!' he boomed.

Israel had been dragged along by his landlady, George Devine, and her grandfather, old Mr Devine. Mr Devine had come in his usual garb of flat cap, ancient stained suit and sturdy shoes, but George had dressed up: she was out of her usual dungarees and wearing a green velvety dress, with a little cardigan, and these pointy little shoes, and her raven hair was swept back from her face, and she was wearing earrings, and it looked as if she was maybe wearing make-up. She looked like a 1940s film star: Israel was thinking maybe Dorothy Lamour, in *Road to Zanzibar*, with Bob Hope and Bing Crosby, one of the DVDs he'd been watching when he'd been lying in bed, thinking . . .

About Gloria. He shifted uncomfortably in his seat. He'd texted her earlier. No reply. Gloria was more Lana Turner than Dorothy Lamour. And Lana Turner in *The*

Postman Always Rings Twice. She had so many clothes and shoes, Gloria, he wondered sometimes whether she was maybe a shopaholic. When they'd first been together, and they were students, she'd been fine, but then she'd got the big legal job with the firm and she'd had to upgrade. And as she'd been promoted she'd upgraded again, and again, until the only thing she hadn't upgraded was Israel. And so eventually she'd upgraded him. In the good old days they'd go shopping together to second-hand shops, and Camden Market, but then she'd moved on to Next, and Monsoon, and then it was Ghost, and finally little places that she knew in Kensington and Chelsea that friends had recommended, with Israel sloping along after her while she bought clothes and shoes, although somehow she would never have the right shoes to go with the clothes, or the right clothes to go with the shoes, and if Israel liked it, it was wrong, and if he didn't, it was wrong, so he felt like he couldn't win, and of course in the end, he hadn't. He'd lost.

'Question One,' said the Reverend. 'How many books are there in the Bible? And for our Jewish brothers and sisters in tonight,' he added –

'Hooray!' said Israel, pathetically, alone. He felt one hundred pairs of Christian eyes bore into him.

'– I am referring to the Christian Bible. That's Question One, brothers and sisters: how many books are there in the Bible?'

'God, I have no idea,' said Israel, turning to his companions.

'Do not use the Lord's name in vain,' said old Mr Devine.

'Shit, sorry!' said Israel.

'Sssh,' said George, nudging him, but not unpleasantly, thought Israel, not in the way she might usually nudge him. She'd been very kind to him since he'd been holed up in bed for three weeks. Maybe it was the beard.

'Sixty-six,' whispered old Mr Devine.

'Really?' said Israel. 'Are you sure?'

'As sure as there's an eye in a goat,' said Mr Devine, narrowing his already narrow eyes under his cap.

'Right. And of course there is an eye in a goat,' said Israel.

'Aye,' said Mr Devine.

'Unless it's a blind goat!' said Israel, who had already finished his second pint of Guinness and started, unwisely, on his third. 'Boom boom!'

'Sixty-six,' repeated Mr Devine.

'Isn't that like the number of the beast?' said Israel.

'That's six-six-six,' said George, who was drinking sparkling mineral water.

'Oh. Right. I don't know if I'm going to get many of these.'

'No,' agreed old Mr Devine, who wasn't drinking anything at all. He'd had a lemonade on his arrival and was saving himself for the fish and chips. The Fish and Chip Biblical Quiz Nights cost £5: fish and chip supper, plus one free drink, all profits going to an orphanage in Romania.

'I'll tell you what, shall I write?' said Israel, reaching out for George's pencil.

'I'll write,' said George, patting away his hand. 'Thank you.'

It was the first time anyone had touched Israel in a long time – except for Ted, which didn't count, because Ted was usually walloping him round the back of the head. Israel suddenly remembered being on the Underground with Gloria one night, travelling back home in an empty carriage, and his pulling Gloria on to his lap, and—

'Question Two,' said the Reverend Roberts. 'What is the longest book in the Bible?'

'I know what the longest book *outside* of the Bible is,' said Israel.

'Tssh,' said old Mr Devine.

'*A la Recherche du temps perdu*,' said Israel, in his best French.

'You mean *A la Recherche du temps perdu*,' said George, in her better French.

'Thank you,' said Israel.

'Pleasure,' said George. 'But what about *War and Peace*?'

'No,' said Israel. 'That's nowhere near.'

'I always preferred Dostoevsky,' said George, pushing hair back behind her ear.

'Me too!' said Israel, overenthusiastically, although it was a long time since he'd read either Tolstoy or Dostoevsky. Working on the mobile library, he'd found himself drifting inexorably towards chick lit and misery memoirs. He found he quite liked chick lit – it was like reading Anne Tyler, without trying – and he'd even started wondering about writing his own misery memoir, title: *The Books in My Life*. Subtitle: *And How They Have Disappointed Me*. A book about the mocking of his expectations of what life should be, based on his reading of great literature. Every student of literature would buy a copy of that, surely? A book about slight emotional deprivation and bourgeois career disappointment? Dostoevsky, Kafka, Knut Hamsun, Robert Musil, Philip Roth, Fernando Pessoa: eat your bitter little hearts out.

'The Psalms,' said Mr Devine.

'What?' said Israel.

'The Psalms: longest book in the Bible.'

Israel remembered the way he and Gloria would sit around when they were first together, discussing books, reading to each other, thrilling over food, drinking wine, lolling around in bed, making love, drinking more wine, and then reading together, exchanging meaningful kisses while reading out bits of Milan bloody Kundera! Oh God.

'Question Three,' said the Reverend Roberts. 'What council – I repeat, what *council* – adopted Sunday as the Sabbath day?'

'Tumdrum District Council?' said Israel.

'Sssh!' said George, throwing her head back slightly and laughing.

'But you have to put your bins out on the Monday,' said Israel.

'The Council of Laodicea?' said Mr Devine.

'Are you sure, Granda?'

'Let's try it,' said Mr Devine.

'Let's live dangerously,' said Israel.

'Yes,' said George. 'Let's.'

Gloria had been a thrill-seeker: she was that kind

of a person. She had to push herself to the limit and beyond. She'd done sponsored parachute jumps, and marathons. Husky sledging. Team-building weekend city-breaks in Europe, arriving back on Monday mornings and going straight into work. And there were other things also . . . Israel stirred again uncomfortably on his seat.

'Question Four,' said the Reverend Roberts. 'What is the shortest chapter in the Bible?'

'I don't know,' said Israel. He turned to George. She was definitely wearing make-up. 'The shortest chapter in the Bible? What do you think?'

'I have absolutely no idea,' said George. With a slight pout, he thought. Was that a pout? She was definitely doing something with her lips. Like Dorothy Lamour.

'It's a psalm,' said old Mr Devine.

'Are you sure?' said Israel.

'Ach, ye're an aggryvatin' boy,' muttered Mr Devine. 'Of course I'm sure!'

'Yes,' said Israel, placatingly. 'I'm sure you're right. A psalm,' said Israel. 'I was just going to say that myself.'

'Aye,' said Mr Devine. 'Which psalm?'

'There are a lot of psalms,' said Israel.

'Psalm 117,' said old Mr Devine.

'That's so funny! That's just what I was going to say!' said Israel.

George looked at him and smiled.

She definitely smiled. At something he said. He couldn't recall another occasion when she'd smiled at something he said. Maybe it *was* the beard.

'Next question,' said the Reverend Roberts. 'What

is the *longest* – I repeat, the *longest* – chapter in the Bible?'

'It's a psalm,' said old Mr Devine.

'We've moved on, actually,' said Israel.

'It's a psalm,' said old Mr Devine.

'No,' said Israel. 'We're on the *longest* chapter in the Bible. *Long-est*.'

'It's a psalm,' said old Mr Devine.

'Everything is a psalm!' said Israel. 'Psalm, psalm, psalm. It can't possibly be a psalm.'

'Why not?' said Mr Devine.

'Because we just put that for the shortest chapter.'

'Things vary in length,' said George.

'So I've been told,' said Israel, unthinkingly.

'Are you being suggestive, Armstrong?' she said.

'No, no. No,' said Israel.

'Good,' said George.

Israel had never quite mastered the art of double entendre.

'Now. Maths,' said the Reverend Roberts.

'Oh no!' said Israel.

'Porches at the pool of Bethesda multiplied by the shekels of silver plundered by Achan, divided by the number of sons of Haman.'

'What?' said Israel.

'Let me repeat that, for the hard of hearing, and those of you who didn't go to Sunday school,' said the Reverend Roberts, who kindly repeated the sum.

'A billion?' said Israel.

'Ach,' said Mr Devine, scribbling down figures.

'Zero?'

After more questions of a scriptural and mathematical nature – the number of daughters of the priest of Midian, the height of Nebuchadnezzar's image, the weight of a talent, the length of a cubit – the Reverend Roberts announced a short break, when fish and chips were to be served, and there was to be a collection for a Romanian orphanage, and a rickety-wheel raffle for packets of Seeds of Samson and Sweet Shalom Smoothies, and Jacob's Ladder energy drinks, and Linda Wei came boldly striding across to Israel's table. Israel was on pint five. He was on great form. He was really enjoying himself.

'Linda!' said Israel. 'Good evening! Or should I say perhaps *Bonsoir*!'

Linda's hand instinctively flew up and protectively patted her beret. Her face was set.

'*Ça va?*' said Israel.

'Mr Armstrong,' said Linda.

'What is the weight of a talent?' said Israel.

'The weight of some our talents will be greater than others,' said Linda.

'Ah, very good,' said Israel. 'I see what you're doing there! Very funny. Seriously, you don't know the length of a cubit, though, do you? Even Mr Devine here was struggling with that one.'

'No.'

'Oh well, not to worry. Who's on your team tonight?' said Israel.

'You haven't forgotten your appraisal meeting on Monday morning?' said Linda.

'Sorry?'

'Your six-monthly appraisal is scheduled for Monday morning. You haven't forgotten about it?'

'Yes, I had actually.' He laughed, and then, realising that Linda was not laughing with him, he added, 'No. No. Of course I hadn't forgotten. Only joking.'

Linda continued not to smile.

'No. Sorry. I mean, yes.'

'You have or you haven't forgotten?'

'I definitely haven't forgotten it, Linda.'

'Good. We have a lot to discuss.'

'As always!' said Israel.

'Probably more than always,' said Linda. 'Given recent events.'

'Recent events?'

Linda leant over to Israel. 'Your unexplained absence. Leaflets promoting political parties. Maurice Morris.'

'Maurice Morris?'

'His daughter?'

'Sorry, Linda, I have—'

'Lending the Unshelved to the under-sixteens?'

'Sorry, I have—'

'I'll see you Monday morning,' said Linda.

'Right,' said Israel. 'Yeah, yeah.'

'First thing.'

'*Oui. Oui. D'accord,*' said Israel.

'Please do not speak French to me,' said Linda.

'That's not what the girls usually say to me!' said Israel.

'Mr Armstrong!'

'Sorry,' said Israel. 'Just the . . . beret. I . . .'

'We are ready to resume, brothers and sisters,'

announced the Reverend Roberts. 'If you could take up your pencils, please.'

A hundred Tumdrum Presbyterians laid down their chips and took up their pencils.

'And we'll start with a difficult one,' said the Reverend Roberts. 'Just to get you in the mood. There are seven things that the Lord hates, brothers and sisters, seven that are detestable to him. Can you list them?'

'George W. Bush!' yelled Israel.

'Sssh!' said George, old Mr Devine, and a dozen others.

'Sorry,' said Israel. 'U2?' he said more quietly.

George punched him. But not in the usual punching-him way she had. This was more of an affectionate, rabbit-punch kind of a punch.

'Haughty eyes,' said old Mr Devine.

'What?' said Israel.

'A lying tongue.'

'Are you making this up?' said Israel. 'How do you know all this sort of stuff?'

'Hands that shed innocent blood.'

'Quite right.'

'A heart that devises wicked schemes.'

'George W. Bush. See, I said.'

'Feet that are quick to rush into evil.'

'There. There!' said Israel. 'I'm right.'

'How many have we got?' said old Mr Devine.

'Hold on.' George counted them up. 'Five.'

'We need two more,' said Israel.

'Oh, well done. That's the only question you've answered correctly all evening,' said George.

'A false witness who pours out lies,' said Mr Devine.
'And a man who stirs up dissension among brothers.'

'Bingo!' shouted Israel. 'Housey housey!'

'Thank you,' said the Reverend Roberts.

The evening wore on.

'What seed did manna look like? Was it: a) coriander;
b) mustard; c) cumin; or d) peppercorn?'

'What part of King Asa's body was diseased? Was it a)
his hands; b) his bowels; c) his stomach; or d) his feet?'

'What about his di—'

George punched him a little harder that time, and
Israel's chair tipped back, and the last thing he remembered of the evening was lying on his back, George
standing over him.

'The ferret is mentioned in which book of the Bible?'

7

At precisely seven o'clock in the morning, as every morning, except on Sundays, and Christmas Day, and when he was away golfing in Turkey, or in Spain, Maurice Morris sat down to breakfast, freshly shaved and eau de cologned, hair neatly combed, and wearing a red pullover and blue blazer, a reflection of his profound broad-mindedness. He had all of the papers laid out on the vast granite breakfast bar before him, and coffee in his bone-china cup, and just a lick of unsalted butter on his granary toast; he was going to stay trim if it killed him; he wasn't going to go down the tray-bake route. He had the big wall-mounted HD plasma screen television on, with the sound muted – he liked the lady who did the news in the mornings, even though she was a little chubby, and maybe even a little old to be doing the whole breakfast-news-on-the-sofa thing, but there was just something about her that gave him a kick, he was addicted to her, the slight sense of unpredictability in the way she moved, which reminded him of someone – and he was also listening to BBC Radio Ulster. He never missed the local news headlines. Knowledge was Power. That was another one of his mantras. He'd thought about having them all painted up on the wall, to remind himself: a kind of inspirational Wall of Positive Thinking. He could maybe get them mounted on boards: YOU ARE 100% RESPONSIBLE. FAILURE IS NOT AN OPTION. FEEL THE FEAR AND DO IT ANYWAY. But his wife wouldn't have allowed it.

Maurice's house was out in the country, but not so far out in the country as to be actually *in* the country; Maurice did not appreciate or enjoy the actual rural. He was uncomfortable with the country: he didn't enjoy the solitude, or the silence. He didn't like mud and mess. He just couldn't identify with trees and hedges and tillable land: you got nothing back from them; they just *were*. To Maurice, the countryside represented opportunity and potential, rather than being an entity in and of itself. To Maurice, the countryside was a suburb in waiting. Where his wife saw bosky woods and thickets, and the seasons, and little creatures, and leaves changing colour, Maurice saw cul-de-sacs-to-be, and opening-soon light industrial units thronging with people happily at their work. Maurice needed people as much as people needed him: his every landscape, internal and external, imaginary and real, was a landscape with figures.

The house itself – 'The Grange', as Maurice had styled it – was an old farmhouse that had been ambitiously extended and expanded over the years until it resembled now more a luxury gated community or a compound than a family home: it was a house that implied other people. What had once been outbuildings now housed rooms for guests, and entertaining, and playing games in, though the family rarely played games, or entertained, or had guests. The barn was an office which Maurice Morris rarely used, preferring always to be out meeting people. And the stables housed a horse that their daughter no longer rode. Only the old grain store, which had been turned into a light-filled artist's studio for Maurice's wife, Pamela, saw much use, though Pamela hardly ever made any actual art in it: she would sit, rather, and smoke and drink coffee and stare out at the surroundings, as though perhaps they might inspire her to rediscover whatever it was she seemed to have lost during the past twenty years of her marriage to Maurice Morris.

The house was surrounded on three sides by green fields and faced out on the other to the chill Irish Sea. The only approach was a long, sweeping drive, whose uniform, loosely crunching gravel gave Maurice perhaps more pleasure than any of his other achievements: to have your own long, sweeping, crunchy-gravel driveway! He had even gone so far as to plant lime trees to line the drive, which, though only now semi-mature, gave the requisite impression of approaching a stately home in the south of England rather than a coastal farmhouse in Ireland. If this was not one of the finest homes in County Antrim then

Maurice Morris didn't know what was. There was an indoor swimming pool, a dedicated golf simulator room. Even the kitchen – which had once been the old coach house – was a work of art, specced-out to the highest standards imaginable, and perhaps a little more, for who in their right minds could possibly imagine a use for a gas-fired Aga, and an eight-burner (plus wok burner) range cooker, and a wine cooler, and a fridge-freezer the size of a closet? Not Maurice and Pamela. They ate mostly takeaways, and prick-the-plastic ready-meals.

Maurice looked away from the breakfast news lady and gazed out to sea. He'd considered having a helipad built out on the lawn, but his wife had felt it was vulgar, so that had been that. It was probably the right decision: the helicopter would have obscured the view. The sun was shining this morning – the sea looked like diamonds – and Maurice had been up since five, dealing with correspondence. This was one of the secrets of his success – by seven o'clock he had a two-hour lead on most of his rivals. Sitting on a stool at the breakfast bar, plasma screen to the left of him, diamond ocean to the right, two hours of good honest work behind him, Maurice Morris was the master of all he surveyed.

He was scanning the newspaper headlines when his wife appeared. She was still in her pyjamas and her hair was scraped back and she was thus far, at this hour, without make-up, but she still looked younger than her fifty-five years; she was lucky enough to have been blessed with a sharp chin and a firm jaw, and piercing eyes, precious gifts to the woman in middle age, almost as precious indeed as a husband ready and willing to help her keep body and soul together and topped up with Botox and unguents and herbalistic creams. She was also possessed, Mrs Morris, of a kind of natural, shocking vitality, the vitality of a tigress ready and willing to pounce at any moment but also, more importantly, to protect herself and her family from anything and anyone. If Mrs Morris had purred and patted you down with a big taloned paw, you wouldn't have been surprised. As it was, she sighed and poured herself a cup of coffee. Maurice didn't look up. She sat herself down at the opposite end of the breakfast bar and lit a cigarette.

'Would you mind?' said Maurice, without looking up.

'What?'

'Not.'

'What?'

'Smoking.'

'And good morning to you too,' said Mrs Morris.

'Outside at least?' said Morris.

'In my own house I'll smoke where I want.'

'The smell lingers,' said Maurice. 'People can smell it on my suits.'

Mrs Morris chose not to respond.

'Have you called her?' said Maurice.

'Yes.'

'I'm away from here in half an hour,' said Maurice. He batted away the smell of smoke. 'Sleeping late again.'

'It's a Saturday, Maurice.'

'She has hockey.'

'She'll be down in a minute. She's probably having a shower.'

'If she's expecting a lift—' said Maurice.

'I can take her in later,' said Mrs Morris, taking another long draw on her cigarette.

Maurice tutted.

'She shouldn't miss breakfast,' he said.

'Relax, Maurice. She won't miss breakfast.'

'Most important meal of the day,' said Maurice. 'You can't expect to perform at your best if you haven't—'

'She'll be fine,' said Mrs Morris. 'Stop fussing.'

'If you want to be on the top of your game you need to—'

'We've heard it all before, Maurice,' said Mrs Morris.

'Fine,' said Maurice, looking at his watch. 'Twenty-five minutes, or I'll be late.'

'For what?'

'It's a breakfast meeting.'

'At the golf club?'

'That's right.'

Mrs Morris snorted.

Maurice liked to get together every weekend with a few friends and fellow businessmen to play golf and to laugh loudly at one another's slightly off-colour jokes and to sit in the clubhouse and enjoy a few drinks. This was Maurice's downtime, among men who never spoke of their emotional lives, or of their families – companions rather than friends. People you could trust; people you could do business with.

They sat and sipped coffee in silence.

'I met the librarian yesterday,' said Maurice.

'The who?'

'The librarian who's been lending her those books.'

'What books?'

'Those books she's been reading.'

'What books are you talking about?'

'Adult sort of books.'

'Adult books?' Mrs Morris's eyes flashed, and she raised an already raised and plucked eyebrow. 'She's not mentioned any adult books to me.'

'I don't mean that sort of book. I mean . . . not children's books.'

'Maurice! She's not a little girl any more.'

'I know she's not a little girl any more.'

'So. She can read whatever she likes.'

'I don't think she should be able to read whatever she likes.'

'Why not?'

'She'll get ideas.'

'What sort of ideas?'

'About . . . things. You know.'

'Don't all books have ideas, Maurice?' Mrs Morris sighed.

'Yes, but I mean ideas about . . . sex.'

'Chip off the old block, then, eh?'

Maurice reddened: being reminded of his infidelities was the one thing that could cause him embarrassment.

Mrs Morris let Maurice's embarrassment fully ripen

before continuing. 'So, she's been reading *The Kama Sutra*, has she?'

'Good God, no!'

'*Lady Chatterley's Lover*?'

'No!'

'Well, she wouldn't need to get that from the library. She could borrow my copy. Along with *The Joy of Sex* and—'

'Sssh! She might hear you!'

'She's still in bed.'

'Good.'

'You wanted her up a minute ago.'

'Anyway, I told him what I thought.'

'Who?'

'The librarian.'

'Oh. Well, good for you, Maurice. Keeping the lower orders in their place. Librarians, lending people books? I don't know. What's the world coming to?'

Maurice ignored his wife and glanced up at the TV: his friend was still there on the sofa.

'Has she talked to you any more about her plans?' said Maurice.

'What plans?' said Mrs Morris.

'Her GCSEs. Is she making any other plans you know of?'

'No.'

'So?' said Maurice.

'She wants to stick with the Art and Media Studies,' said Mrs Morris.

'Mickey Mouse courses.'

'If she wants to go to the art college—'

Maurice huffed.

'There's nothing wrong with the art college,' said Mrs Morris.

'Art college!' said Maurice. 'She'd be better doing law.'

'She doesn't want to do law.'

'She'll come round,' said Maurice.

'Not if you're nagging at her she won't come round.'

'I didn't work all these years so my daughter could—'

'It's nothing to do with you, Maurice.'

'It's everything to do with me!' said Maurice.

'She'd be fine at art college.'

'Doing what? Hanging around a bunch of dope-smoking layabouts!'

'*Layabouts*? Nobody says layabouts any more, Maurice.'

'I say layabouts.'

'Anyway, she's got years to work it all out.'

'You have to plan ahead for these things, I keep telling you.'

'Maurice, you go on ahead and get yourself elected, and let me worry about her.'

'She's had a five-star education. Pony, clubs, the best of everything. When I was growing up on Corporation Street I'd have given anything to—'

'Maurice, please. You're on repeat. You're making a speech to me. I'm your wife. Remember?'

'How could I forget?'

'And I've not had my coffee yet. So let's not get into all this now.'

'Fine.'

Mrs Morris stubbed out her cigarette and took a final sip of her coffee.

'She'll be late,' said Maurice, 'if she doesn't get up soon.'

'She won't be late! Now just leave her be. God, you're such a control freak.'

Maurice was not a control freak. He had, for example, left much of the design and furnishing of the interior of the house to Mrs Morris, whose tastes in home furnishings ran rather to the exotic. Left to his own devices, Maurice would have tended towards basic dictator chic – chandeliers and gold plates, with brocaded curtains and brand spanking new mahogany. Pamela had more bohemian tastes: tapestries; antiques; curiosities. He'd even allowed her to paint a mural on the kitchen wall, bold and Bloomsbury style, when they first bought the house, depicting the mountains of Mourne, and the cottage they had there and which they used as their bolthole. But the kitchen had since been vigorously extended with steel and glass and a table that could accommodate a large, catered dinner party, and the Mournes mural with its little cottage had long since disappeared.

They sat in silence, the two of them, sipping their coffee, as distant as any long-married couple. Maurice looked at his watch.

'All right,' said Mrs Morris. 'I'll go and get her up.'

'Thank you,' said Maurice.

The right order had re-established itself.

*   *   *

As he explained to the police and to the press later that day, the first thing Maurice Morris knew about his daughter's disappearance was the sound of his wife screaming.

8

Sundays were always the real challenge for Israel in Tumdrum. On Sunday, Tumdrum's sheer Tumdrumness somehow intensified: the place seemed to hum not only with its average, everyday senselessness and pointlessness, but with an extra tone, a deep overtone or undertone – a void – of doom, as if a dark-cloaked chorus had arrived and was lamenting the steady encroachment of catastrophe in the last scenes of some long, depressing opera about the terrible fate of Everyman: Sibelius; Benjamin Britten; *Don Giovanni*; *Simon Boccanegra. O Tumdrum! Weh mir! Weh mir!* And on Sundays, as a consequence, with the thrum of doom in his ears, Israel always suffered from a combination of queasiness, headaches and a nausea of a kind both physiological and philosophical, which would doubtless be familiar to anyone who'd been out on a Saturday night drinking, or at an amateur production of a play by Harold Pinter, or at home listening to the Saturday night play on Radio 4: *He was a man of sorrows, despised, rejected and acquainted with grief.*

Sometimes, to dispel the Sunday doom and anxieties, Israel would go to the pub – the First and Last. But it only ever made things worse – the First and Last leaned more towards the Omega than the Alpha – and anyway, in the end he would always have to return home, to the converted chicken coop, his room like a prison cell, no more than twelve foot by twelve foot, with bare brick walls and a concrete floor, and an asbestos roof, a room that Israel had worked on and worked on over the past year and had managed to transform into a . . . room no more than twelve foot by twelve foot, with bare brick walls and a concrete floor, and an asbestos roof, with rugs, and a bed, and some books. A room of his own, to be sure, with his own enamel plates and cups. But no window. Fortunately, he wanted no window. For there was nothing out there to see.

Outside the coop was the yard, and the Devine farmhouse, and the garden sloping southwards, and the old glassless glasshouse, and the row of broken-down cold frames, and the couch grass and nettles where once had been blackcurrants and berries, and the walls of the walled garden, pitted with nails where apples and pears had once been carefully trained, and where there was now just mud, mud everywhere, and everywhere mud.

The Devine family farm wasn't just deteriorating, it was sinking: the heavy and seemingly continual rain during the summer had not been kind to the two-hundred-year-old building. Parts of it had begun quietly to slip away – irreparable damage to outbuildings with leaky roofs and big old wooden doors and hardboarded windows which had swollen up like weeping eyes. And even in the main house, old carpets had had to be removed – the place was unprotected, like a sponge, the damp infecting and soaking in through the render and seeping down the walls providing the perfect environment for mould and for mushrooms. A fair crop of little crumble-capped fungi had sprung up on the wallpaper, and old Mr Devine had simply brushed them off with the back of his hand, and scooped them up and tossed them on to the fire, and they'd filled the house with a sour, soapy smell which – mixed with the stench of damp cardboard and cabbage, and chickens – was overwhelming, organic, fundamental; the unmistakable stench of decay. Israel gagged every time he went into the kitchen, which was decay, plus dogs, plus fat, plus Irish stew. Black mould, dry rot, condensation. Sum total: miasma. George did everything she could to maintain the property but she was fighting a losing battle: it was simply impossible to fix everything that needed fixing, and paint everything that needed painting, and clean everything that needed cleaning. She often crawled into bed at midnight and then was up again at five to begin the day's chores. The animals were cared for, but the windows were rotten, and the floorboards were rotten, and the walls were rotten; even the septic tank was rotten. There was continual surface run-off from the fields, and groundwater levels were rising; the farmhouse was like a rusting ship in an unforgiving ocean, and George was

like Sisyphus, Tantalus and Captain Smith of the *Titanic*.
She could not cease in her lonely task; couldn't leave
her post; could not desert her command. Her duty was
to the farm – and 'the farm' they all called it, not 'our'
farm, or 'our house', or 'our home'. It was 'the farm',
as the church was the church, and the government
was the government, and the law the law. It was an
entity, a being, an institution. It was not a way of life,
it *was* life.

The farm was where George had grown up. It was
where she remembered her parents living, and where
she'd played down by the stream, and had run around
in the fields. The farm was her entire world: she could
imagine no world without it, although outside, the
world was passing it by, superseding it, speeding up
and crashing, colliding, collapsing and rapidly remaking
itself. Outside was progress, for better or for worse;
inside, the Devine household was stasis. The furniture
was heavy and inherited; the carpets were orange and
thin. Mr Devine would sit in the good front room by
the fire, with crumbling, swirling turquoise wallpaper
coming slowly down upon him, with a large pair of
foot-operated bellows made of wood and leather at his
feet. There was still a butter churner in the kitchen,
and earthen bowls, and old brass candlesticks, and a
big old mahogany wall clock, with a TV in teak to
match. At night George used a brass bedpan with a
long wooden handle to warm her in her loneliness,
and next to her bed sat a Teasmade, her only
companion.

George's bedroom was her sanctuary, or the closest

thing to it, and she'd arranged it exactly as she liked: old Roberts radio next to the bed, and her library books in their thick plastic protective covers, and her one concession to luxury, a Cath Kidston floral bedspread that she'd had sent over from London, a concession not merely to luxury, indeed, but to herself; an allowance. Weighing heavily against it was the old woodworm-racked pine clothes cupboard, made by her father, and not made to last, and her parents' old double bed – a rickety iron-frame affair that had been in the farmhouse for generations. Inheritance. She'd been born in the bed, and would probably die there too, just like her grandmother before her. The only picture in the room was a poor watercolour, painted by George's mother when she was young and first married and had come to live there, a painting of the farm, all pure white against green fields and blue skies, expressive of all her hopes of the life she was going to live. Big dreams. Dark red Donegal tweed curtains hung at the windows and down over the deep window ledges, which had been painted over so many times that where the paint was chipped it was possible to see years of colours going back, from whites through creams and down to deep dark browns, like geological strata. Sometimes George would sit picking at the paint, staring out at the fields spread before her, wondering about her own deepening layers, and she would listen to the trills and calls of the birds, and if she closed her eyes she could see her father still, in rolled-up shirt-sleeves, tall and spare, always on the go, out in the garden, or in the distance on the tractor. She'd kept all the old accounts books, their covers smudged with white mould, and sometimes she would read through them in bed, reading her father's, her grandfather's and her great-grandfather's careful detailing of income and expenses. She did all of the accounts on a laptop now – Brownie helped her when he was home from university. But she knew that ultimately it was pointless, that the forces of decay and modernity were about to overwhelm her and the farm, and sweep them all away, and there was nothing she could do about it, that what had once been a farm employing half a dozen men, and which was now little more than a smallholding, would soon become nothing.

And of course she spoke of this knowledge, these fears, to no one. And certainly not to Israel Armstrong, whose lodgings in the chicken coop brought the Devines almost half of their monthly income.

Israel had got up late, as usual, this Sunday morning, neurasthenically, and had washed, and dressed, and not shaved, and had eaten his customary spoonful of peanut butter and drunk his customary pot of coffee and had now wandered, aimlessly, but much refreshed, outside to the yard, where George was busy working, paintbrush in hand.

'What are you doing?'

'What does it look like I'm doing?'

'Erm. I'm guessing here . . . Painting?'

'Whitewashing,' corrected George.

'Is that the same as painting?'

George just looked at him, eyes wincing.

'Well, anyway,' continued Israel. 'Sorry about Friday night, by the way.'

'It's fine.'

'I . . .'

'It's really fine.'

'I just had one or two too many.'

'It's fine.'

'Are you sure?'

'Yes.'

'OK, then. We're fine, then?'

'Yes.'

'Well. That looks like fun.'

'Really?'

'Yeah.'

'Fun?'

'Absolutely. Nice way to spend a morning—'

'Afternoon.'

'Whatever. Painting, though. Brightening the place up a bit. Looks very satisfying.'

'Does it?' said George. 'Well, here, you satisfy yourself, then.' She handed Israel the brush and stood with her hands on her hips.

'Well, that's not an invitation I receive very often from a—'

'Just paint, Armstrong.'

'Well, I'd love to help, obviously, but I . . . erm. I have a few things I need to do.'

'Really?'

'Yes. It's Sunday. I need to . . . go and see Pearce.'

'I see.'

'Yes. What's the time?'

George looked up at the sky.

'About half past two.'

'How do you do that?' said Israel. 'I've always—'

'Do what?'

'Tell the time by looking at the—'

'Armstrong, I need to get on, if you're not helping.'

'Sure. Yes. Sorry.' He handed back the paintbrush. Their hands touched briefly. Israel coughed. George looked away. It was nothing: nothing had passed between them.

'Why are you painting the shed?' asked Israel. 'Spring clean?'

'It's September, Armstrong.'

'Yes. Well. A late spring clean.'

'We're selling the goats,' said George.

'Oh, really? Why? I quite like the goats.'

'Why do you think we're selling them?'

'I don't know.'

Israel's grasp of real-world economics was not great: 'sketchy', in fact, might be the word. Or 'feeble'. Or 'poor'. Risible. Rum. Quaint. Or pathetic. He was a salaryman, when it came down to it, a public employee, so the gulf between him and someone who had to earn their living by the literal sweat of their literal brow was as big as the gap between, say, a primitive tribesperson and the Christian missionary come to save them.

'Goats must be sold,' continued George.

'It does seem a shame, though,' said Israel.

'Shame doesn't come into it,' said George. 'It's a shame when you can't eat.'

'True. True. Good point,' said Israel. 'So why are you painting the shed, if you're selling the goats?'

George took a deep breath: it was a family trait. Old Mr Devine did the same when he was roused: an attention to and awareness of one's own anger, which Israel always found impressive; he was always utterly shocked and surprised by his own emotions.

'To set them off when people come to see them,' explained George, patiently.

'Ah,' said Israel. 'Right. Presentation. A sort of framing device, for the goats?'

George looked at him, unimpressed.

'Anyway,' continued Israel, sticking his head round the shed door and sniffing. 'What's that smell? Is that the—'

'I've bleached the floors,' said George.

'Ergh!'

'And it'll be the alkalis in the whitewash. You don't want to breathe too much in.'

'Ugh!'

'And don't touch the walls!' she said, as Israel touched the walls. 'It'll have the hand off ye,' said George. 'You have to wear gloves.'

'Ahh,' said Israel, staring at his hands. 'I touched it!'

'Well, go and rinse your hands, then,' said George.

Israel jogged quickly across the yard to the outside tap, George laughing.

'Here, do me some more whitewash while ye're there, would you?' she called over to him.

'What?'

'Hydrated lime. Salt. In the cans in the barrow there. Plus water.'

'All right, all right,' said Israel.

'But watch your hands,' said George.

'OK!' said Israel.

'And don't rub your eyes,' shouted George.

'Ahh!' said Israel, who'd rubbed his eyes.

Having washed his hands and rinsed his eyes, Israel started adding water and lime and salt into the old cut-down oil drum on the barrow.

'How much water?' he called across the yard to George.

'About two gallons,' called George back.

Israel didn't want to ask how much two gallons was, so he hosed what he thought looked like two gallons into the oil drum and wheeled the barrow unsteadily back over, oil drum filled to the brim. He was trying to remember from school how many pints were in a gallon. Was it twelve? Or three? Or thirty-six? Or was that inches in a yard? He'd grown up metric in north London: gallons were as foreign to him as was bitter Sumatran coffee to the coffee crowd in Zelda's Café.

And as he wobbled back over towards George, for a moment it felt good to both of them, to be working together, to have a purpose. It reminded George of her parents: in harmony, and in tandem. Each knowing what the other needed, and taking care to provide it. Helpmeets. Partners. Farmers. And Israel enjoyed doing something for George, because it felt as though he was not alone, as though his life was in parallel with another's. For a moment.

George paused from slopping on the whitewash, turned, looked into the oil drum.

'What's that?' she said.

'It's the whitewash,' said Israel.

'That's not whitewash,' said George. 'I said two gallons of water.'

'That's about . . . two gallons, isn't it?'

'How many gallons in an oil drum?' demanded George.

'I don't know. I've never—'

'Fifty-five!' said George. 'And this is a half-drum, so—'

'About twenty-seven gallons?' said Israel.

'You're an idiot, Armstrong,' said George.

'Sorry,' said Israel.

'Don't say sorry for being an idiot!' said George. 'Say sorry for wasting all that lime and—'

'Sorry,' said Israel.

'Stop saying sorry!'

'But you just said—'

'I don't care what I just said!'

'Well, I—'

'Leave it. I'll do it myself,' said George, grabbing one of the handles of the wheelbarrow.

'No. No, I'll do it,' said Israel, grabbing the other. 'It's fine, I just didn't know how—'

'Leave it!' said George, pulling at the handle. 'I'm doing it.'

'Let me help,' said Israel, yanking back. 'I want to—'

And it tipped, of course, the oil drum with its gallons of whitewash, tipped slowly and inexorably towards Israel, first splashing and then toppling, the murky white water coming over him like a torrent, and the drum rolling and shrieking across the yard like a wounded animal, the whitewash flooding in its wake. Israel staggered back, soaked, George's eyes riveted on him.

'Sorry!' he said, not sure how she'd take it.

'Sorry,' she said.

'Yes. Sorry,' said Israel.

'All that waste,' she said, staring as the whitewash soaked into the concrete.

'Sorry,' repeated Israel.

'Just go,' she said, quietly.

'I'll help—'

'Just go away, Armstrong.'

'No, it's fine,' said Israel. 'I'll—'

'Leave me alone!' screamed George, suddenly.

'But—'

'Go!' she yelled. 'Go! Away!'

So Israel went. He went back into the chicken coop and shut the door. And George set about putting things right in the yard.

And once again absolutely nothing had passed between them.

9

The lane from the Devines' to Pearce Pyper's was one of the most beautiful places Israel knew around Tumdrum, a place so beautiful in fact that it was almost enough to restore his proverbial and habitual and today very particular low Sunday spirits. But not quite. An overgrown, winding, one-way gravel track suitable for single traffic only, and hemmed with high hedges and tall trees, the lane made him think of Gloria, and England, and of long, lacy and weepy Victorian and Edwardian narrative poems. It was a route he walked every Sunday on his way to read with Pearce, and it usually had an effect of uplift. The fields to either side of the lane sprang alive with rabbits and hares and the sound of blackbirds, and then suddenly, with a parting of the trees, there was the arrival at Pearce's, which was always like stumbling upon a previously undiscovered ancient Aztec ruin, what with Pearce's eccentric sculptures flanking the driveway and scattered throughout the grounds – the chunky painted concrete, and the driftwood things, and the totem poles made of old railway sleepers – and the avenue of trees extravagantly pleached, espaliered and cordoned, and then finally the house itself, Pearce's mad, grand baronial-cum-Corbusier home.

Israel had spent the afternoon tidying his coop, avoiding George, who had also been avoiding him, and he stood now – confused and chastened, but also at least a little cheered and chivvied by nature – and yanked at Pearce's big chain doorbell, which rang, as big chain doorbells always ring, ominously.

Pearce's housekeeper, Joan, answered the door. She was not a woman who wasted her words: she was a woman who looked as if she permed her own hair. Unwillingly.

'Yes?' she said. Up until recently Israel had come every Sunday to see Pearce, and Joan had always greeted him with the same thin, suspicious 'Yes?', as though anything more would be an invitation to unwonted intimacy.

'I'm here to see Pearce,' he said.

'He's not well.'

'Oh dear,' said Israel. 'Shall I call back at a more convenient time?'

'There'll be no more convenient time,' said Joan, and she turned her back on Israel and made off through the house.

Israel closed the big oak door behind him, and hurried to catch up with her. The house, always huge, always echoing, but usually somehow full and present with energy, somehow felt today as though it had been

drained of life, like an abandoned theatre, as though
the theatrical impresario had already left, packing up
in a hurry and moving on to his new home. It felt like
Kane's Xanadu; a vast, complex, empty puzzle.

Usually on his Sunday visits Israel would sit in the
drawing room with Pearce, who would insist on plying
Israel with wine – 'Into the old sluicery,' he would say,
and into the old sluicery it would be, and 'Don't be such
a silly prawn,' he would say, when Israel refused another
glass, or 'Tosh!' he would say, to anything he disagreed
with, which was most things – and he taught Israel how
to open bottles of champagne with nutcrackers, and
how to decant, and the difference between a good Lafite,
and a fine Latour, and an acceptable Margaux. Pearce's
hand did not stint, nor in old age had his appetites
wearied: just a couple of months ago, during one of
their Sunday afternoon sessions, they'd polished off
between them a nice half-bottle of Sancerre, and a
Pinot Noir from the Salgesch, and a Pinot Noir from
Yvorne, all the while discussing the meaning of life,
and art, and the pros and cons of the Futurist Manifesto,
and the war in Iraq.

Over time, the arrangement had become more
formalised and Israel would arrive and read from one of
Pearce's favourite books – *Madame Bovary* ('Incomparable!'
Pearce would exclaim. '*Sans pareil*!'), or some George Eliot
('The best-looking English novelist'), or Dickens ('The
great farceur!') – and then they would drink, and eat
Madeira cake. They had become their own miniature
literary salon, a twenty-nine-year-old-soon-to-be-thirty-
year-old mobile librarian, and an eighty-two-year-old

Anglo-Irish aesthete. Israel had found it a most curious and refreshing experience, reading out loud to Pearce, the complete opposite of reading out loud to the children at Tumdrum Primary, where the real challenge was keeping order and hanging on to his dignity. Reading to the elderly Pearce was for Israel like becoming a child again, being able to become absorbed and enfolded in a book. Israel found that as he read his mind would often wander, in a kind of dreaming concentration, and he'd find himself somehow *with* Madame Bovary romanticising, or *with* Magwitch swimming with his heavy chains, or Maggie Tulliver cerebrating. It had something to do with the rhythm of the language: he would find himself breathing with the books.

'The sound of an English voice,' Pearce would say, when Israel read, and 'Con*t*roversy,' he would say, when Israel said *con*troversy. 'You're not American, are you?' And '*Ca*nine,' he would say. 'People do insist on calling it cay-nine.' It reminded Israel of being a child, when his father had told him stories – fairy tales, and Irish legends, the story of Finn McCool, which was why he'd arrived in Ireland in the first place, he was sure, because of the fantasy of Irishness, and now he was living its reality. Pearce Pyper's was an oasis.

Sometimes when Israel was reading Pearce would fall into a deep sleep and Israel would let the housekeeper know, and he'd creep out of the house and walk down the lane back to the Devines' with a curious sense of peace and terrible sadness, the very feeling he'd associated with reading as a child, a sense of great possibilities and endless disappointments. Pearce had tried to insist on paying Israel for his time and trouble, but Israel had steadfastly refused. Reading out loud to Pearce was not a job; it was a joy. And then Pearce had hit upon the idea of paying him in kind.

'What sort of a palate do you have?' he'd asked Israel one Sunday afternoon, after they'd drunk their sherry and eaten their slice of cake.

'Erm.'

'I've a Spanish palate myself, I'm afraid.'

'Right,' said Israel.

'I find the Italian reds and French very high in tannins.'

'Ah. Yes. Uh-huh.'

'So I have my supplier in London – Moreno, do you know them?'

'Erm. No.'

'Excellent. Been with them for years. I find you have to spend so much to get a good drinking claret these days.'

'Right.'

'Anyway. I have them send me mostly New World, and Spanish. Which I hope you'll be able to enjoy.'

'Sorry?'

'I doubt you'll need more than a case a month, will you?'

'A case of wine?'

'I've taken the liberty of arranging it to be delivered to you at the Devines'. I do hope it's convenient.'

'A case of wine?'

'Riojas, mostly. But some New World. As a small token of my—'

'Oh, no, Pearce, I couldn't possibly . . .'

'You could, definitely,' said Pearce. 'And you shall. No arguments, thank you!'

'No. I couldn't, really.'

'Next chapter, please,' said Pearce, with a flourish of his arm from the chaise longue. 'Where were we?'

'Charles is about to perform the operation on the club-footed man.'

'Ah!' said Pearce. '*Quel dommage!* Read on! Read on!'

They were special times together.

But things had changed.

Pearce wasn't in the drawing room today, and there was no wine, and no craic. He was in the library, which was decorated in the Edwardian style, by Edwardians, with a stencilled frieze running around the tops of the shelves, and large, thread-bare Persian rugs on the dark stained floorboards, heavy furniture highly polished, and windows draped with thick red velvet curtains. He lay stretched out on an old leather chaise longue by his writing desk, eyes closed, his hands folded on his lap, a black shawl draped around his shoulders. Even from a distance you could see that he wasn't well, that something had gone wrong: his skin looked tight, and luminous, and pale, like a veil drawn across his face. He looked like a very sick and very weak Whistler's mother; he had that peculiar, childlike, otherworldly grace about him that only the very old acquire, as though life were just one long, wasting, harrowing journey back towards home. His eyes had sunk far into his face, but his hair had been cut short and neat, as though ready for an important occasion: a birthday, perhaps, or an anniversary.

'He's wandering,' whispered Joan, as she ushered Israel into the library. 'You have to be patient. And don't let him give you anything,' she warned. 'He's giving people things at the moment.'

'I see.'

'If he gives you anything, just leave it behind when you go.'

'Has he seen a doctor?'

'Doctor's been.'

'And?'

'Exhaustion. Flu. On top of everything else,' she said, disapprovingly, adding, 'He's going to go into a home.'

'No?' said Israel. 'You're not serious? You can't make him leave here and—'

'Yes,' said Joan. 'We can.'

'But . . . What about his family?'

'There is no family.'

'But to take Pearce from here, would be . . . He'll . . . And what if he gets better?'

'He's not going to be getting any better now.'

'Why? What do you mean? Isn't he just—'

'This is it now,' said Joan, forcefully.

'No. He's fine,' protested Israel. 'He's just—'

'He has vascular dementia,' said Joan.

'Oh. Well.' Israel didn't know what to say. 'I knew he wasn't . . . What is that?'

'It's like Alzheimer's.'

'Is it curable?'

'No.'

Israel and Joan stood facing each other at the door leading into the library.

'Anyway, you'll see for yourself,' said Joan.

'Well, what about . . .' Israel was struggling to take it all in. 'Is there no one else who could help look after him here?'

'Are you volunteering?'

'Erm.' Israel looked down at the floor. 'Well. I'd like to be able to—'

'He's going to need specialist care.'

'Have you told him?'

Joan nodded.

'And what did he say?'

'What do you think? Go on on in.' She nudged Israel forward.

Israel walked quietly across the squeaky floor into the library. The room was full with the smell of beeswax, old books, and sickness. He could see Pearce's chest steadily rising and falling. Before he'd reached him, and without opening his eyes, Pearce spoke.

'How nice . . .' he began. And then he began coughing – low, dry coughs. 'Nice of you to come,' he said. 'I do apologise . . . for my . . .'

Pearce's voice was still there, but it was thin, as though he were speaking from another room. It was the voice of man at the edge of somewhere. He drooled slightly as he spoke.

'Will you . . .' There were long, agonising pauses between his words. 'Have a drink?'

'No, thanks,' said Israel. 'Pearce, how are you?'

'Fine. The Russian novel?'

'Sorry?'

'*The Brothers Chestycough*?'

'Ah. Very good,' said Israel.

'Just a . . . cold,' said Pearce.

'That's because you were out in the damp on Friday, playing your fiddle.'

'Playing the fiddle?'

'On Friday? Don't you remember?'

'Heifetz I met once.'

'Yes, I know. But—'

'Where are we going?'

'We're not going anywhere, Pearce. I've come to visit you.'

Israel glanced enquiringly across at Joan, who had settled herself on a battered chesterfield by the door: she cast her eyes up to the ceiling.

'Would you like me to take your coat?' asked Pearce.

'No thanks, I'm fine, really, thank you.'

'If you are, so.' Pearce raised a withered hand and beckoned him closer. 'You need to . . . sit close.'

Israel pulled a high-backed chair close.

'Closer,' said Pearce. Israel glanced again at Joan, who nodded. He came and knelt by the chaise longue.

Pearce was wearing a linen shirt, buttoned all the way up to the neck, and a pair of black trousers, and canvas shoes with thick soles the colour of a North Antrim beach. Up close, the skin on his face looked thin and papery; his beard was barely there.

'I'm sorry . . .' he said. 'Hard of hearing.'

Israel tried to think of something to say.

'I saw a hare on the way here, Pearce. I thought you'd be interested.'

'A hare?'

'Like a rabbit?'

'Ah, yes,' said Pearce. '*Lepus* . . .' Israel could see Pearce's mind working, struggling, trying to remember. '*Timidus hibernicus*,' he announced, eventually. 'Michael Longley.'

'Sorry?'

'Poem.'

'I don't know it, I'm afraid.'

'Fine poem.'

'Right.'

'His father was in the same regiment as my uncle.'

'Right.'

'Ypres. The mud.'

'Uh-huh.'

'You never forget the mud.'

'Right.'

'Rats,' said Pearce, wearily. 'But how are you?'

Before Israel could answer, Pearce's dogs, Picasso and Matisse, came in, made for Israel, and started enthusiastically licking his face and hands.

'Are they being a nuisance?' asked Pearce.

'No, no, not at all,' said Israel.

'Good,' said Pearce, and then he whispered very quietly to Israel, his eyes suddenly filling with tears. 'They say I've dementia, you know. I've heard them.'

'I see,' said Israel.

'Stuff and nonsense!' said Pearce. 'They're trying to cart me off.'

'I'm sure that's not—' began Israel, gently pushing the dogs away.

'I'm staying right here!' Pearce said, suddenly much more loudly, so that Joan could hear. 'Tell that bloody woman! I'm not going anywhere. In the end . . . Nowhere. Staying. Leonard . . .'

'Leonard?' said Israel.

'Leonard Bast.'

'Right,' said Israel.

'You know what I'm talking about?' said Pearce.

'Yes,' lied Israel.

'Here!' shouted Pearce, with all his might. The dogs barked in response.

Israel looked over at Joan. She cast her eyes down, sadly.

'Right here! Do you . . . understand!'

'That's OK, Pearce,' said Israel, soothingly. 'I understand.'

'You're all alone, aren't you?' asked Pearce, suddenly quiet again.

Israel nodded.

'No sign of marrying?'

'No,' said Israel, 'there's . . .'

'You're young?'

'I'm nearly thirty,' said Israel.

Pearce gave a harsh, faint little laugh, as though in pain.

'Alone,' said Pearce.

'You still have plenty of friends,' said Israel.

'No,' said Pearce, gently. 'Eventually . . .' His voice trailed off. 'I wanted to ask you a question.'

'Ask away,' said Israel.

Pearce placed a hand on Israel's arm. 'The collection.'

'The collection?' said Israel.

'The books.'

'Yes,' said Israel.

'For the library,' said Pearce.

'I'm sorry, I don't understand,' said Israel.

'I want the library,' said Pearce, 'to have my books.'

There was a long pause. Israel could see Pearce struggling to stay on track with the conversation.

'Pearce?' prompted Israel.

'They say England's changed,' said Pearce.

'Yes, I suppose it has.'

'Ireland . . .'

'Yes?' said Israel.

'The Glens,' said Pearce, who seemed to be having conversations in his own mind. 'We're very lucky.'

'Yes,' said Israel.

'Glenn Patterson. The coast road,' said Pearce.

'Yes,' said Israel.

'Finer than the Grande Corniche. And Jim McKillop. Finest fiddle player in Ireland. Have you seen the Book of Kells?'

'No,' said Israel.

'You must see the Book of Kells! My brother is at Trinity, he'll take you to see the Book of Kells. All the magic people.'

Israel had no idea what he was talking about.

'Comedy of . . .' began Pearce.

'Errors?' said Israel.

'Manners,' said Pearce. 'Do you know how many words there are in a pencil?'

'Sorry?'

'Forty-five thousand.'

'I'm not following you, Pearce, sorry.'

'In a magazine. It said. Forty-five thousand words in a pencil.'

'Doesn't it depend on the size of the words?' said Israel.

'Very good!' said Pearce, laughing hoarsely. 'Very good! Oh, you'll go far, young man, mark my words.' And then 'The books!' he said suddenly – 'words' having apparently brought him back to the books. 'Keep them together.'

'Of course.'

'I trust you with the books.'

'I understand.'

'All of the paperwork has been done.'

'Good.'

'And there's a book I'd like you to have.'

'No. No. I don't need any books, Pearce.' Israel glanced nervously across at Joan.

'I . . . insist.' Pearce reached out a hand and closed it around Israel's wrist.

'Very important. You know Dewey?'

'No, I don't think so,' said Israel.

'Dewey. The . . .'

'Oh, the classification system . . .'

'Yes. Remind me. What are the . . .'

Israel recited the Dewey decimal system to Pearce.

'General works. Erm. Philosophy and psychology. Religion. Social sciences. Language. Science. Technology. Arts and recreation. Literature. History and geography.'

'Philosophy,' said Pearce. 'That's it.'

'Right.'

'Go on then. Fetch! Fetch!'

Israel got to his feet, followed by the dogs, who'd obviously taken the command to heart, and started making his way along the shelves, which were – loosely – arranged by the Dewey system. Halfway down the library he came to a halt and called back to Pearce, who had closed his eyes again.

'I've found Philosophy, Pearce.'

'J,' said Pearce, dreamily.

'J?'

'J.'

'What am I looking for?'

'Doctor Johnson. *Rasselas*. Do you know it?'

'No, I don't think I do.' Israel ran his finger along the shelf. 'Got it!'

Israel took the book down and brought it over to Pearce. It was bound in leather with fine embossed lettering. The pages were musty and the dust set Pearce to coughing – deep, deep coughing – and hawking, and then struggling for breath. His eyes welled up with tears again. His frail body was shaking with panic.

Joan hurried over. She held up his head and helped him hawk into a handkerchief.

'I think he needs a rest now,' she said.

'Yes, of course,' said Israel. 'Sorry. I . . .'

'Israel's going now, Pearce,' she said.

Pearce stared up at Israel, unable to find words. His eyes stared up at him – as if he were looking for something, searching for reassurance.

'Go on,' said Joan. 'He needs rest.' Israel hesitated. 'Please,' said Joan. 'He'd rather you went.'

'If you're sure.'

'Please,' said Joan, insistently.

Israel glanced back at Pearce as he left the room: the dogs were sitting quietly by him, Joan was fussing over him. Like he was a child, or a small broken bird.

It was dark as Israel walked down the lane back to the Devines' and there was a full moon, as though the scene had been carefully set for a theatrical performance. Normally, Israel didn't respond to nature – he responded mostly to books, and to his own narcissistic impulses and needs – but tonight, brushing past the cow parsley, and the whin bushes, and with the sound of his feet in the silence, it felt for a moment that he was outside himself, and outside time, and that the whole of nature was somehow audible and available to him, and he was overcome by a feeling of intense love, and of loss – as though he was completely connected to the world and, simultaneously, completely and irrevocably cut off.

He paused before reaching the Devines', in the little clearing by the big red barn, and stood in the bright moonlight and opened the book that Pearce had given him, turning to a page at random.

That the dead are seen no more, said Imlac, I will not undertake to maintain, against the concurrent and unvaried testimony of all ages and all nations. There is no people, rude or learned, among whom apparitions of the dead are not related and believed. This opinion, which perhaps prevails as far as human nature is diffused, could become universal only by its truth; those that never heard of one another would not have agreed in a tale which nothing but experience can make credible. That it is doubted by single cavillers can very little weaken the general evidence; and some who deny it with their tongues confess it by their fears.

And he burst into tears. And wiped his eyes. And walked on.

10

Monday morning, Linda's office. Israel's six-monthly appraisal.

He hadn't slept well. The usual sorts of dreams. And thinking about Pearce. About Gloria. About George. About his own deteriorating mental and physical health.

'Mr Armstrong, do you have a copy of your contract of employment with you?'

'No. Sorry,' said Israel. 'Was I supposed to—'

'That was in the email I sent you about our meeting.'

'Ah, well . . . I, erm . . . don't have very good . . . connectivity, you see, on the farm, in the chicken coop. It's wi-fi they've got. But I haven't quite hooked into it . . . somehow.'

'Well, Mr Armstrong, perhaps you can recall for me the Overall Purpose of your role here?' said Linda.

She had a tendency to speak like this, Linda, or at least certainly to Israel, and certainly for as long as Israel had known her – a tendency to stating the obvious as if it were both catastrophic and incomprehensible to mere mortals. She spoke as though she were reading the news for the deaf on regional TV.

Israel already had a headache.

'The Overall Purpose?' said Israel.

'Yes.'

'Of my role here?'

'Yes.'

'On earth, do you mean?'

Linda sighed a sigh of a kind that indicated not so much weariness as utter contempt.

'Clearly not, Mr Armstrong. I mean your overall purpose in your role here, as Learning Support Officer on the Learning Support Vehicle.'

'Mobile Librarian, you mean?' said Israel. It was a bone of contention.

'*Learning. Support. Officer,*' repeated Linda. 'Thank you. But go ahead.'

'Well . . .' Israel gazed out of the window.

'You might want to try and break it down into your primary responsibilities.'

'Yes. Of course,' said Israel.

'Go ahead,' said Linda. She had folded her arms across her chest in a way that suggested she was preparing for a wrestling bout.

'Erm,' said Israel.

'Would you like me to remind you?' said Linda.

'Well . . . sure,' said Israel. 'Yes. Go ahead.'

'To be responsible – and I quote,' said Linda, reading from a sheet of paper, 'responsible for the running and administration of Tumdrum's Mobile Learning Centre—'

'Mobile Library.'

'Mobile Learning Centre,' repeated Linda. 'And your principal accountabilities—'

'Sorry?'

'Your principal accountabilities.'

'Ah.'

'Are to develop and maintain a thorough under-standing and up-to-date knowledge of mobile learning centre resources.'

'Uh-huh.'

'To be responsible for taking forward specific campaigns in developing user participation; developing an appro-priate strategy for each campaign; monitoring and evaluating the effectiveness of the strategy; developing and building relationships with and between diverse groups; developing and supporting links with estab-lished groups at all levels; to promote a safe working environment by complying with Health and Safety regulations; and to undertake any other duties which may be required by your manager.'

'Right. That sounds like a pretty fair summary of what I'm doing, yes,' agreed Israel, jauntily.

'Does it?' said Linda.

'Yes.'

'Good. Well, perhaps, then, Mr Armstrong, you could tell me where in this list of responsibilities it mentions LENDING UNSHELVED BOOKS TO UNDERAGE READERS!'

Linda banged the desk so hard at this point that it shook all of her carefully placed soft cuddly toys.

'Sorry?' said Israel, rubbing his temples.

'You have been lending the Unshelved to underage readers,' said Linda, gathering herself.

'I don't think so,' said Israel.

'Maurice Morris's daughter!'

'Who?'

'Lyndsay Morris? She was—'

'The Goth?'

'Yes!'

'Ah,' said Israel.

'So?'

'Well, when people ask for the Unshelved, I . . . give them the Unshelved.'

'And she asked for the Unshelved and you gave her the Unshelved?'

'That's right.'

'Yet you know you shouldn't lend the Unshelved to the young and the impressionable and the—'

'She's sixteen,' said Israel.

'She's fourteen!' said Linda.

'Really?' said Israel. 'Gosh. They look older these days, don't they, the . . .'

'Fourteen!' repeated Linda.

'Well, even so,' said Israel. 'There's no proscribed list, as such, is there?'

'I know there's no proscribed list, Mr Armstrong! But it is our responsibility to protect our young people from—'

'What?'

'Things that they should not be exposed to as young people.'

'Like what?' said Israel. 'D. H. Lawrence?'

'Yes!'

'D. H. Lawrence? Oh, come on, you can't tell people what to read, Linda.'

'I am not suggesting for one moment, Mr Armstrong' – when Linda got really, really annoyed, she spoke more slowly, through clenched teeth, and dropped her voice – 'I am clearly not suggesting for one moment that you tell people what to read.'

'Well, what are you suggesting?'

'I am simply suggesting that you should steer young people away from what *not* to read.'

'Which amounts to the same thing, doesn't it?' said Israel.

'NO!' said Linda, banging her desk again.

Israel took some ibuprofen from his pocket.

'Sorry,' he said. 'Just a bit of a—'

'So. Can you please explain yourself?' said Linda.

'Sorry. Regarding?' mumbled Israel, as he swallowed the tablets.

'Regarding the Unshelved!' said Linda.

'Sorry,' said Israel. 'I don't really see the relevance of who's been borrowing what and when to my six-monthly—'

'Relevance?' said Linda. '*Relevance?* Relevance! You have seen today's *Telegraph*, I take it?'

'Er, no,' said Israel. 'I'm more a *Guardian* man, myself, although I've found some of their coverage of the—'

Linda flung that morning's *Belfast Telegraph* across her desk towards him.

'Maurice Morris's daughter has gone missing!'

'Sorry?'

'Maurice's daughter has gone missing.'

Israel read out the headline. '"Daughter of Local Politician Missing."'

'Read on.'

'"Police are this morning searching for the teenage daughter of local businessman and Independent Unionist candidate Maurice Morris. Lyndsay Morris (pictured), fourteen, went missing some time in the early hours of Saturday morning. Police are appealing for witnesses. Anyone with information is asked to ring Crimestoppers." Oh dear.'

'Oh dear?' said Linda.

'Yes, that's awful.'

'Is that the best you can do?'

'What? How do you mean?'

'This young girl has gone missing, and it turns out she's recently been borrowing adult books from the mobile library—'

'Well, they're not *adult* books, Linda, in the sense of their being "adult", they're—'

'They're not children's books are they?'

'No, but I still don't quite understand what you're suggesting.'

'I'm not suggesting anything, Mr Armstrong. My concern is what *other people* will be suggesting when they discover that we may have contributed to this poor young girl's disappearance!'

'What? You think there's a connection between what she's been reading and her disappearance?'

'Possibly,' said Linda.

'Well, that's ridiculous,' said Israel.

'When did she last come and borrow books from the library?'

'Erm. It was—'

'Friday,' said Linda.

'Right.'

'And she went missing on Saturday.'

'Well, that's just a coincidence,' said Israel.

'It might seem like a coincidence to you, Mr Armstrong, but I don't want to become the subject of a witch-hunt when it's discovered that this young lady had been borrowing unsuitable books which had influenced her to—'

'People don't just read books and then run off, Linda.'

'Oh, really? And you know that, do you?'

'Well. No. But . . . I mean, if I play *Grand Theft Auto* I don't suddenly go out and start stealing cars and shooting people, do I?'

'I have no idea what effect playing *Grand Theft Auto* might have on you, Mr Armstrong. I'm talking about this poor young lady, who has perhaps been influenced by your poor choice of recommended reading.'

'I didn't recommend her any books,' said Israel.

'Well, what books did she borrow?'

'Last week?'

'Yes, last week!'

'I think it was . . . *American Pastoral*.'

'*American Pastoral*?'

'Yes,' he repeated. 'It's a book, by Philip Roth.'

'Never heard of it,' said Linda, making a note. 'How do you spell Roth?'

'R. O. T. H.'

'And what sort of book is it?'

'It's a . . . a great work of literature,' said Israel.

'I'm not looking for a book review, Mr Armstrong.
I mean, is it a novel, or is it non-fiction?'

'It's a novel.'

'Right. And what sort of novel is it? Science fiction?
Crime?'

'No. It's . . . a great work of literature.'

'Yes, you said. "Literary fiction", then?'

Israel huffed. 'You know, I don't really agree with
the term "literary fiction", which seems to me—'

'Is there anything in this book,' said Linda, 'that
might have prompted this young lady to disappear?'

'Well, funnily enough—' began Israel.

'I don't think "funnily enough" is quite appropriate
in the circumstances, do you?' said Linda.

'No, sorry, I mean . . . Oddly enough, the book is
about a girl who . . . betrays her family, and runs away.'

'Oh, no,' said Linda. 'You are joking?'

'No. I mean it's a very complex book, really. I haven't
read it for a while, but it has all of Roth's, you know,
zest, and elaborations, and, erm . . . it's really a sort of
critique, I suppose, of the emotional bankruptcy, and
the . . . moral idiocy, and the intellectual dishonesty –
the pure badness – which—'

'All right, that's enough, Mr Armstrong. I'm going
to have to be contacting the police this morning with
information about this girl's borrowing record. They
may want to talk to you about it.'

'Right, well. Of course, I'd be happy to help, but I
don't think—'

144

'Good,' said Linda. 'We'll leave that to the police, shall we? In the meantime, I don't think I need to remind you, Mr Armstrong, that we do not lend bad books to impressionable young people.'

'Bad books?' said Israel. 'Bad books?'

Linda glanced up at the wall clock.

'Anyway, Mr Armstrong. This meeting was scheduled for your appraisal.'

'Yes. Of course.'

'And apart from your irresponsibility in this particular area there are a few other areas we need to look at.'

'Right.'

'So, it would probably be helpful if at the start of the appraisal I explain to you exactly what an appraisal is not.'

'Right. Yes. Fine. Go ahead.'

'An appraisal is the time we get together to look at some of the things you might want to do more of, or do differently, on the Mobile Learning Resource Centre.'

'The Mobile Library,' said Israel.

'Resource Centre,' corrected Linda.

'OK,' said Israel. 'Fine.'

An appraisal was not about telling Israel how to do his job. Absolutely not, said Linda. What she was interested in, she explained, was solutions, not problems. She was interested in staff development, not staff underdevelopment. And she saw her role, apparently, as helping Israel to begin to implement Quality Control in preparation for the forthcoming Quality Audit. And in order to do so we – and here she moved almost, but not quite, imperceptibly from the first person singular to the plural – we need to make sure that all of the appropriate methods of Quality Assessment are in place, which requires the setting of certain Benchmark Practices and the aligning of Assessment Conventions. She saw her role very much, she said, as assisting Israel in clarifying the threshold standards for Mobile Learning Resource Centre activities, which would allow us – by which she meant Israel – to apply the necessary Quantitative Performance Indicators in order to be able to rank the Mobile Learning Centre's effectiveness and long-term viability.

Israel was gazing out of the window, thinking about Philip Roth.

'Mr Armstrong?' said Linda. 'Mr Armstrong? MISTER ARMSTRONG!'

Israel brought his attention to the room.

'Yes, Linda?'

'I have been looking at your SAQs' – Israel had had to fill in a number of SAQs (Self-Assessment Question-naires) in preparation for the appraisal meeting over the past few weeks, including SAQ31, SAQ554, SAQ8A3, detailing the time he spent on various work activities, and scoring himself on a scale of Excellent/ Highly Satisfactory/Satisfactory/Unsatisfactory, and suggesting any 'Issues' he felt he needed to address. He had ranked himself, mostly, as 'Satisfactory'; to have ranked himself any higher would have seemed like hubris. 'I see you've not filled in the section asking you to describe,' continued Linda, 'in your own words, a typical period of UCT.'

'Erm . . .'

'User Contact Time—'

'Ah . . .'

'—And nor have you filled in the areas asking about the NIF.'

'Erm . . .'

'Nature of Information Flow—'

'Ah.'

'—Or what you think are new MAK—'

'Erm . . .'

'—Mechanisms for Acquiring Knowledge. Or the section asking you, through description and analysis, to provide suggestions for AICS.'

'Aches?'

'Actions for Improving Customer Service.'

'Erm. Yes. Well, some of those sections I found quite difficult to . . .'

'Well, let's do them now, shall we?' said Linda, handing Israel a pen.

'Sure.'

Israel quickly did his best to counterfeit some answers based on upper-case keywords such as FACILITATION and ENABLING and WIDER PARTICIPATION and Linda nodded and listened as Israel read them out and then she explained that she just needed to input this information into her computer, because the Education and Library Board, in cooperation with a number of leading software manufacturers, had developed some software that would enable her to instantly recommend some improvements in his librarian practice, based on his answers.

'Great,' said Israel.

'This'll take a few minutes,' said Linda.

'Fine.'

As Linda typed, Israel tried to remember every Philip Roth novel he'd ever read. *The Human Stain. Sabbath's Theater. Portnoy's Complaint. The Ghost Writer. Operation Shylock.*

'Oh,' said Linda. 'And while you're here, I almost forgot, we also need a doctor's note from you to cover your few days' sickness.'

'I see.'

'You need to go and see your GP and provide me with a note. For the records. Unauthorised days off would of course lead to an automatic salary reduction.'

'Right. Great.'

'Good,' said Linda. 'That should do it. We'll get a print-out in just a minute.'

'Right.'

'So, finally, training needs.'

'OK,' said Israel.

'Do you have any?' said Linda.

'Any what?'

'Needs,' said Linda, stressing the knee in 'needs'. 'Anything that would assist you in carrying out your duties?'

'Erm. No, I don't think so. Unless you count an apartment overlooking Central Park and a holiday home in the Caribbean,' said Israel.

'Don't be facetious, Mr Armstrong.'

'I'm not being facetious. '

'I can offer you a storytelling course,' said Linda.

'A storytelling course?'

'Yes, a lot of people have found it very helpful.' Linda began reading from a brochure. ' "Using narrative-based techniques to broaden children's horizons, participants will learn about—"'

'Storytelling,' said Israel.

'Exactly,' said Linda.

'I don't think so,' said Israel. 'Thanks anyway. That doesn't really appeal to me.'

'OK,' said Linda. 'Fine. Face painting.'

'Face painting?' said Israel.

'Face painting,' said Linda.

'You're joking,' said Israel.

'I'm not joking,' said Linda.

'You're proposing we do face painting in the library?'

'No, Mr Armstrong. It's a course available through the Education and Library Board, which can lead to an NVQ in Children's Entertainment. And which you may find useful in your work as Learning Support Facilitator—'

'Mobile Librarian.'

'—*Learning Support Facilitator.*'

'No,' said Israel.

'Fine,' said Linda. 'You do realise, Mr Armstrong, that you are required to complete a certain number of hours training as part of your continuing professional development?'

'Yes, but I don't think face painting is really the kind of professional development I'm interested in, Linda. Difficult to do the . . . lolling tongues and—'

'Lolling tongues?'

'You know, they always have sort of lolling tongues, with face painting, don't they?'

'What is the kind of professional development you're interested in, Mr Armstrong?'

'I'm not really sure,' said Israel.

'Self-defence?' said Linda.

'Self-defence?'

'"Designed especially for the council's public-facing staff,"' Linda began reading again, '"this course is designed to—"'

'Public-facing?

'Yes. That's you, Mr Armstrong. I'm sure you must sometimes encounter . . . difficulties with readers.'

'Ha!' said Israel.

'I'll take that as a yes, shall I?'

'Yeah!' said Israel. 'Right. The window lickers.'

'Sorry?'

'Window lickers. We call them window lickers.'

'Please do not refer to our customers as window lickers.'

'Fine,' said Israel. 'Nutters, then.'

'And do not refer to them as nutters.'

'Freaks?'

'Or freaks, clearly, Mr Armstrong. Anyway, the course is called Minimising Risk. I shall sign you up for—'

'The only way to minimise risk is not to let anyone on the library!' said Israel.

'Clearly,' said Linda. 'Computing?'

'I hate computing.'

'Health and safety?'

'No.'

'Fire safety?'

'No.'

'What about your PSV test?'

'No, I don't want to do the test.'

'It's run by the Road Transport Industry Training Board, down at Watt's Corner.'

'No, thank you.'

At which point the laser printer concealed under Linda's desk on a little shelf hummed awake like a tiny tiger and coughed up a sheet of paper, which Linda gratefully took, glanced at, signed, and pushed across her desk for Israel to countersign. The page was titled ISRAEL ARMSTRING, and contained two columns, one titled AKP (Addressing Known Problems) and AICS (Actions for Improving Customer Service), and listed problems and pointed out solutions, with dotted lines at the bottom asking for Israel's signature and the date.

Israel signed and dated. And then he signed and dated another. And another. One for Linda's records, one for Israel, and one for the Education and Library Board. This incriminating statement of failure and intent would be kept on file for future reference, Linda explained. Israel didn't even know he had a file.

'Good,' said Linda. 'Well, I think that was very helpful, wasn't it?'

'Very,' said Israel.

'I'll just be ringing the police and offering any assistance we can.'

'Super,' said Israel.

'And you'll be providing me with that doctor's note?'

'Absolutely.'

'Immediately.'
'If not sooner.'
'Good. Well, I think that's all.'
'Thank you, Linda.'

11

'Israel,' said George. 'I'm sorry.'

'You're sorry?'

'Yes.'

'You're saying sorry to me?'

'Yes. I . . . I'm afraid I have some bad news.'

They were in the Devines' kitchen. Israel had been on the library all day after his appraisal meeting with Linda. After a long day, returning to the Devines', for all its faults, felt like rejoining humanity. It was his little niche, his little place in among the Devines' familial smells, and the mess, and the debris and decay. There was a kettle whistling on the Rayburn. The dogs. The long, placid sound of the clock. The floor, washed and scrubbed clean, and the hot, over-rich smell of cleaning products and of deep, deep grime; the smell of dishes having been recently washed. It wasn't home, but it was the closest thing he had to home.

'Problems with the goats?' said Israel. He'd lived here

so long now he couldn't imagine worse news. And he couldn't understand why George was saying sorry. She never said sorry. And certainly not to him. Sorry for what?

'Sorry,' she was saying again, stony faced. She was wearing a white apron; the white apron she always wore in the kitchen.

'The chickens?' said Israel. 'Pigs?' George looked down at the floor. Israel looked to old Mr Devine, tucked up in his blanket on his seat by the Rayburn. 'OK,' he said, not getting a reply, and he stroked his beard. He'd taken to stroking his beard; it gave him something to do with his hands. 'What's up? You're not kicking me out of the chicken coop again?'

George looked him in the eye and held his gaze for a moment.

'I'm afraid it's Pearce.'

'What?'

George paused, just for a moment, and Israel realised: it was the pause. The pause that everyone dreads, and that everyone knows ultimately is coming, and whose meaning is as clear as any outpouring of however many words; the total eloquence of a moment's silence.

'No?' said Israel.

'I'm so sorry,' said George.

'No!' said Israel.

George averted her gaze.

'Oh, no.'

'I know you were fond of him.'

'But . . . I was . . . just. I just saw him, yesterday.'

'I know.'

George reached out and patted Israel's arm, and it was the touch that was like the pause, a touch entirely expressive and direct in meaning: the black spot; the bad news; the curse. And it suddenly brought everything back, the way she touched him: the day his father died. He was thirteen. His mother. They were in the front room. They had this new sofa – they hadn't had it long. You could still smell its newness – almost as if it'd been born into the room. And he was there, sitting on the sofa. He'd been watching TV. His father had been in hospital for some time. But Israel still somehow had no idea his father was going to die; it just hadn't occurred to him. He'd thought that it was like in a television drama – that it was a difficult story, but that everything sorted itself out in the end. As if life were like a drama. Like *Dawson's Creek*. And his mum was sitting on the sofa next to him, and she was saying his name, and there was a pause, and she ruffled his hair, and he somehow knew in that moment that everything didn't sort itself out. That things went wrong, and couldn't be put right, that beyond crisis there was . . . Nothing. Darkness. And everything after that moment, after his father's death, seemed to lose its colour, as if someone had literally put on a filter that had blocked out the light. As though a cloud had passed over. And the colours had never quite returned. As though the world were on mute. Which is why he read books. That was when he'd become a serious reader. To try to regain the colour. But he never could regain the colour. The books always promised they would help him regain the colour – as though the stories could somehow redeem things. But they never could. So he always had to read more and more books, just in case the next book was going to be the one that made the colours return. Thirteen. Which was when he'd started suffering from migraines. And he'd started putting on weight. And retreating. Into a sort of long insomnia. Which was why, ultimately, he was here. Nowhere. With the touch and the pause, awakening him again to grief.

'But how did he . . .' He was speaking, without even knowing he was speaking.

'It's . . .' began George. 'They're not sure at the moment.'

'Thou shalt not kill,' said old Mr Devine, shuffling under the rug.

'What?'

'Father! Sshh!' said George.

'The Lord does not abrogate His care over His elect,' mumbled Mr Devine.

'What?' said Israel, suddenly angry. 'What's he talking about?'

'It was an accident . . . Israel . . . I'm sorry.'

'Accident?'

'Killed hisself,' said old Mr Devine.

'What?' said Israel. What was this wretched man suggesting? 'What happened?'

'He seems to have been . . . I don't know. Some bookshelves, they . . .'

'What?'

'The bookshelves, they came down and . . .'

'Leonard Bast,' said Israel. He was clutching his head, as though in pain. 'Oh God.'

'Leonard Bast?'

'*Howards End*. Leonard Bast, he's . . . crushed.'

'*Howards End* by E. M. Forster?'

'Pearce mentioned it to me.' Israel's voice had become uneven, as though lacking air. 'I didn't think anything of it.' He felt as though he were choking. He felt like prostrating himself. 'He couldn't have . . .'

'It was an accident,' said George, reassuringly. 'It was definitely an accident.'

'He'll not get a burial if he killed hisself,' said Mr Devine.

'Father!' George was becoming exasperated.

'Speaking the truth,' said Mr Devine, apparently oblivious. '"Ye that fear the Lord, trust in the Lord. He is their help and their shield."'

'Anyway, he's at peace now,' said George.

'"And they that know thy name will put their trust in thee: for thou, Lord—'

'Will you shut up!' yelled George at old Mr Devine, unable to contain herself any more. 'You stupid, selfish man!' And as George screamed Israel recognised the emotion, which wasn't grief but rage, and the rage not just of today, but of years, and everywhere, and everything, the same rage he'd felt when his father died – the rage of being wounded, of being disgusted with himself, of being sacrificed by the dead to mourning. And he could suddenly see it in George too – having been sacrificed by her parents' death all those years ago. Hence her rage at Mr Devine. And 'Shut up!' she was yelling again at Mr Devine. 'Shut up! Shut up! Shut up!' and then she was banging her way out of the kitchen, with Israel hurrying out after her into the yard.

'George!' he called.

'Go away!' she screamed back, not turning, striding away from him, as if she were to blame.

'You want to be left alone?' called Israel.

'Yes,' she said. 'I want to be left alone!'

She didn't want to be left alone.

He left her alone.

He didn't want to be left alone. He found himself in the van, driving. Out of Tumdrum and down the coast road, remembering what Pearce had said: the best road in Europe. And then he was parking up down in Glenarm and taking the keys from the ignition and sitting there looking out to sea. And he could see nothing. Because there was nothing to see. And sitting and crying and shivering by himself. With nowhere to go. And nowhere to be. And nothing to think.

And then hours later, having disappeared into himself, in deep, pitiful mournful self-involvement, he was driving back, half dazed and despairing, to the Devines'. He needed to talk to someone.

He couldn't talk to George.

He couldn't talk to Gloria.

So there was no one to talk to.

Except perhaps the Reverend Roberts.

Lights were on in the manse, which was a two-bed semi inconveniently situated on a new-build estate just off the coast road. Tumdrum Presbyterian Church had sold the original – the real – manse many years before.

The original – the real – manse was a five-bedroom red-brick Victorian villa bang in the centre of town, with its own orchard and a walled garden, and a small housemaid's room, and a library, which had been home to generations of upright ministers and their uptight offspring, and which was now home to local pinstripe-jacket-and-tight-jeans-wearing businessman Martin Mortimer and his life partner Kevin, the hairdresser. Martin and Kevin were accepted, on the whole, in Tumdrum because, it was generally agreed, they were not 'flamboyant' and 'didn't rub your noses in it', and they had lavished time and money on the old manse and transformed it into a home of top-of-the-range chrome and mahogany fittings, with a wet room, and a lot of signature wallpaper, while the orchard had been sold and was now a development of – only three – executive-style town houses called 'The Orchard'. While in the new manse, the Reverend Roberts was living simply and quietly, lacking entirely Martin and Kevin's financial nous and interior design flair. The Reverend's possessions consisted almost exclusively of the clothes he wore, and a few Bible commentaries, and the furniture in the house consisted of the congregation's cast-offs: an outdoor plastic picnic table in the living room, which served as his desk, a straight-backed mock-velvet armchair, and no pictures on the wall, and no mess. The Reverend Roberts was someone who had somehow cleansed himself of the everyday mess of things, the detritus. He was not distracted. Which is probably what made him a great minister, and which is certainly why, when Israel could think of no one to turn to, he now answered the door wearing a faded blue towelling dressing gown that had once belonged to a member of the congregation. It was too short for him. He was wearing his glasses.

'Israel?' said the Reverend Roberts, peering into the darkness.

'I . . . just happened to be passing,' said Israel.

The Reverend Roberts double-checked his watch.

'At half past eleven on a Monday night?'

'Erm. Gosh. Is it? Sorry. I didn't realise. I'll—'

'No, no! Come on in,' said the Reverend England Roberts, reaching out and ushering Israel into the narrow hallway. 'It's fine. I was just making some coffee.'

'At half past eleven on a Monday night?'

'Come on. Come in.'

He led Israel into his kitchen, a room with old white melamine units and nothing else: it could have been the kitchen of a show-home.

'Well,' said the Reverend Roberts, as he busied himself with his coffee-making paraphernalia – the beans, the grinder, the silvery, screw-top, stove-top espresso pot. He didn't believe in skimping on coffee. It was his one luxury. Israel stood silently in the bright glare of the kitchen's downlighters. 'Everything all right?' the Reverend asked.

'Yeah,' said Israel, whose eyes were sore and puffy from tears. 'Yeah.'

'I was very sorry to hear about Pearce.'

'Yes.'

'I know that you were very close.'

'Well . . .'

'Very, very sad,' said the Reverend Roberts. 'He was a good man.' And then he added, reaching into the pocket of his dressing gown, 'Can I tempt you?' He produced a small white paper bag.

'What is it?'

'Crystallised ginger,' said the Reverend Roberts.

'You keep a bag of crystallised ginger in your dressing-gown pocket?'

'At all times,' said the Reverend Roberts. 'In case of emergencies.' He took a piece himself. 'It's very good. I get it from a shop in Derry. Vitelli's? Italians. Very good. They do amaretti biscuits as well, but I'm afraid I'm all out till next payday.'

'No, thanks, I'm OK.'

'Sure? You on a diet?'

'No.'

The Reverend Roberts reached into his other pocket.

'I have chocolate limes, if you'd prefer,' he said. He held out the bag. 'From the Sweetery. I've never known anyone refuse a chocolate lime.'

'No,' said Israel. 'Thanks anyway.'

'You sure?'

'Well,' said Israel, taking one. 'Maybe just one.'

'Good,' said the Reverend, as Israel unwrapped a chocolate lime. 'So, let's get our priorities right, shall we? You take the weight off your feet and I'll see to the coffee. Sit. Sit. Go on.' The Reverend set two stools incongruously either side of the oven, as though flanking a fireplace: Israel sat down and the Reverend Roberts busied himself with the grinding and brewing of the coffee.

'How's your chocolate lime?'

'Good,' said Israel, letting the taste fill his mouth.

'You ever try chocolate and champagne?' asked the Reverend Roberts.

'No, I don't think I have.'

'Oh, you must try it. The next time you're having chocolate and champagne.'

'Hmm.' Israel laughed.

'You let the chocolate – what would you call it? – the chocolate slime stick to the roof of your mouth, and then you drink champagne, and it washes it all away, cleansing your palate. Most extraordinary sensation. Wonderful.' He lit a flame under the coffee pot. 'There we are, then. Coffee's brewing.'

He sat himself down next to Israel on the other stool.

'So. It's always nice to see you, Israel. But I guess you didn't come here to drink coffee and eat my chocolate limes?' he said.

'No,' said Israel.

'Is it Pearce?'

'I suppose,' said Israel.

There was a long silence.

'Can I ask you a question?' asked Israel.

'Fire away,' said the Reverend Roberts.

'What does the Bible say about suicide?' asked Israel, eventually.

'Mmmm,' said the Reverend Roberts. 'The Bible . . .' He weighed his words very carefully. 'The Bible, Israel, is silent on a lot of things that we would like it to be clear about.'

'If Pearce did commit suicide—'

'Pearce?'

'Yes.'

'Oh!' boomed the Reverend Roberts. 'Pearce! I was worried for a moment you were talking about yourself there! Thank goodness!'

'Ah, right. Sorry.'

'That's OK! I'm delighted! I mean, not delighted about the whole situation.'

'No.'

'Obviously. But I don't think there's any suggestion of suicide, is there? It was an accident, is what I heard.'

'But Mr Devine was saying that he thought—'

'You shouldn't listen to everything Mr Devine says, Israel. You surely know that by now.'

'He's always quoting the Bible.'

'Never a good sign,' said the Reverend Roberts.

'But if he had . . .' Israel found it hard to say the word 'suicide'. 'If he'd . . . done it himself, would he still get a proper burial?'

'Well, that's a hypothetical question.'

'No,' said Israel. 'It's not.'

'Really?'

'Yes. It's just . . . Well, he mentioned to me—'

'Who mentioned to you?'

'Pearce, just before he died. He mentioned Leonard Bast.'

'*Howards End*?' said the Reverend Roberts.

'Do you know it?'

'I saw the film. Merchant Ivory. Excellent.'

'Exactly.'

'I don't see the connection, though, sorry.'

'Leonard Bast. He . . . died when the bookshelves came down on him.'

'I see.'

'And when I saw him, Pearce was scared of . . . dying, and demented, and he mentioned Leonard Bast . . . so . . .'

'So?'

'I think he probably pulled the bookshelves down on to himself.'

'I see.' The Reverend Roberts considered the facts. 'That does seem highly unlikely, Israel, if you don't mind me saying so. And even if he had, then—'

'But what does the Bible say about suicide?'

'The Bible doesn't really say anything about suicide, Israel.'

'But what do you think?' asked Israel.

'About suicide?'

'Yes.'

'Well,' said the Reverend Roberts. 'I know some Christians, who are good folk, find it hard to imagine that suicide could *not* be a sin. And that therefore . . . But, personally . . . I can see that sometimes suicide might seem like the only option.'

'Like for Samson,' said Israel.

'And Delilah?' said the Reverend Roberts.

'Him,' said Israel.

'He didn't commit suicide, I'm afraid, Israel.'

'Didn't he pull down the pillars on himself?'

'To gain vengeance against the Philistines,' said the Reverend Roberts. 'Samson was a kind of suicide bomber, if you like.'

'What?'

'You need to read your Old Testament, Israel. And not just your Old Testament, judging by your contribution to the Biblical Fish and Chip Night.'

'Hmm,' said Israel.

They sat again in silence. Apart from the sound of coffee brewing.

'You're going to miss Pearce,' said the Reverend Roberts.

'Yes,' agreed Israel. 'He was one of the only people here I could talk to.'

'You're talking to me,' said the Reverend Roberts.

'Yes, but that's not the same,' said Israel.

The Reverend Roberts laughed.

'No offence,' said Israel.

'No, none taken,' said the Reverend Roberts. 'I know what you mean.'

'Pearce was . . . I don't know. He reminded me of my father.'

'I see.'

'My father died when I was thirteen.'

The Reverend Roberts nodded.

'I felt I really lost my . . . I don't know. Ever since then I just feel . . . I'm getting nowhere.'

'And where would you like to be getting?'

'I don't know. Somewhere.'

The coffee was bubbling. 'Shall I be mother?' said the Reverend Roberts.

'Do you get lonely here?' said Israel, as the Reverend Roberts fetched some small espresso cups.

'Of course, Israel. Doesn't everyone feel lonely sometimes?'

'Yes. But I mean really, really . . .'

'If you're asking do I ever feel despair, then yes, I do.' The Reverend started to pour the thick black coffee into the cups. 'I don't know, but I suppose perhaps a little like you, I'm alone here, in Ireland. And sometimes it can be a very lonely job. People look up to you. They expect you to have the answer. Here. Coffee.' He handed Israel a cup. 'The sermons. Every week you have to write something that will mean something to them. Three thousand words a week.'

'That's a lot.'

'It is. And it's rare you're going to be inspired.'

'God.'

'Exactly. So sometimes one does feel a little . . . low. But, again, I think it's common. It's not unique.' He took a sip of his coffee. 'Milk?'

'No, thanks.'

'Sugar.'

'No. It's OK.'

'I do think,' continued the Reverend Roberts, 'that the state of being for Christians, and maybe for Jews as well, is a state of being banished, or exiled, "flung", if you like. That's certainly something we find in Scripture. So I always try to remember that when I have . . . low moods. I try not to be surprised.'

'And when people die?'

'People are dying all the time, Israel.'

'And doesn't it make you despair?'

The Reverend Roberts drank down the remainder of his coffee, and poured another cup. He sighed.

'Last month I had to conduct the funeral of a soldier.'

'Oh dear.'

'He was from Carnlough. 2 Para. He was killed by a suicide bomber in Afghanistan.'

'Oh God, yes. I read about that in the paper.'

'Yes.'

'That must have been difficult,' said Israel.

'Yes. It was. The family . . . Funerals certainly make you think about what you're doing and why you're doing it.'

'Does it strengthen your faith in God?'

'Not at all,' said the Reverend Roberts, laughing, bitterly. 'A God who could let this world be as it is. A soldier. Someone whose job it is to . . . And who is then himself killed? Monstrous. And then . . . a couple of years ago – before your time here – I did a joint funeral for a mother and her two young children, killed in a crash on the M2.'

'Oh God. That's awful.'

'She was driving home from visiting her own sick mother. Drunk driver crossed the central reservation.'

'God.'

'And last year, Johnny Fowler – you remember him?'

'No.'

'Kicked to death in a pub car park.'

'Oh God.'

'I probably shouldn't be telling you about these, Israel.'

'No, it's fine.'

'So, of course, that sort of thing makes you doubt. The mother and her children killed in the car crash? The other driver got a two-thousand-pound fine.'

'That's crazy.'

'It certainly makes you question the existence of a benevolent God.'

'I'll bet,' said Israel.

'Yes,' said the Reverend Roberts, meditatively.

'So what's the . . . point of being a minister?'

'Well . . . I think all we can really do is help one another as best we can to get through, isn't it? So. I am sorry about Pearce, Israel. But I don't have any answers, I'm afraid.'

'No. I understand.'

'More coffee?'

'No. Thanks. I should be going.'

'The hour is getting late,' said the Reverend Roberts, wistfully. 'You're very welcome to stay.'

'No, thanks. I need to get back.'

He got up and the Reverend Roberts led him towards the front door.

'You drive carefully on those roads,' said the Reverend Roberts.

'I will,' said Israel.

'And ring me any time if you need to,' said the Reverend Roberts.

'Yeah. Of course.'

Israel walked outside into the cold again, and got back in the van. His heart was beating fast. It felt as if he was anticipating something. Something that he knew would never happen. He couldn't bear the thought of returning to the chicken coop. So he drove back down the coast road. Down by the sign that said 'Try Your Brakes'. Down towards Ballintoy Harbour, the narrow windy road going down. There was a bright moon hanging in the sky. And he parked up at the bottom and looked out towards the sea. And after a while he went and lay down in the back of the van. He used last week's newspapers as a pillow. And used his duffel coat for a mattress, and wrapped the dog blanket around him for warmth. He lay with his eyes open for a long time.

12

He was awoken by the sound of banging. And it wasn't a headache.

'Who's there?' he said, turning over and opening one eye, his mind still fogged from bad dreams; dreams full of exits and entrances, about death and the dead. A dream in which he was a bird in a tree, not knowing which way to fly; a dream about a bed in which the sheets and blankets became bindings from which he could not escape. A dream in which his father came tapping at the window . . .

'It's the Tooth Fairy,' came the answer.

'What?' For one weird confused moment, in a half-dream-like state – during which he imagined himself briefly back at home as a child, tucked up safely in bed in suburban north London, his mother quietly slipping into his room, slipping fifty pence under his pillow and then quietly slipping out again – Israel considered the possibility that it was indeed the Tooth Fairy.

'And Santa!' called another voice. That broke the spell. The Tooth Fairy worked alone.

He lay there in a stupor. A kind of crushing hungover dullness descended upon him, weighing him down, a deep weariness – no, no, not weariness, ennui – overcoming him. He wondered whether he might need to spend a few more days in bed.

He started getting groggily to his feet, wrapping the dog blanket round his shoulders – even shabbier and more rumpled than usual. It felt like he was bruised around his ribs.

'Open up!' came the voice. 'Now!'

He was almost at the door when it was wrenched open. It wasn't the Tooth Fairy. Or Santa.

Israel found himself blinking into bright sunlight and the unsmiling face of his old friend Sergeant Friel looking in, moustache bristling, panting slightly from exertion and excitement. And out beyond Friel were the white limestone cliffs, and the dark volcanic basalt rocks of the harbour. And out to sea, guillemots, razorbills, kittiwakes, fulmars. Birds.

'What the hell are you doing!' said Israel. 'You've broken the bloody door!'

'Yes,' said Sergeant Friel, a 'yes' not of pleasant agreement but rather a 'yes' confirming a threat. Israel instinctively pulled the dog blanket a little tighter around his shoulders.

'But . . . look,' he said – to his shame – rather apologetically. The door hung limply from its hinges. 'The lock! You've broken the—'

'And a very good morning to you too, Mr Armstrong,'

171

said Friel, as he pushed past Israel on to the mobile library.

'But the door!' Israel repeated. 'Ted'll kill me!'

'Not if we do first,' said Friel.

'What?'

'Only joking. Have you lost weight?'

'What?'

'And the auld beard act as well, I see. Converted to Islam, have we?'

'What are you talking about?'

'Wouldn't be surprised. Mind if I come in?'

'You already are in,' said Israel.

'Yes. And how are we this morning then, Grizzly Adams?'

Israel groaned.

'Sleeping it off, are we?'

'Sorry,' said Israel. 'Sleeping what off?'

'Big night, was it, last night? Blocked, were we?'

'Blocked?'

'Drunk? Few too many?'

'No. No.' Israel rubbed his hands over his face, trying to clear his head. His chin felt bristly: he had forgotten he had a beard. And he had forgotten what exactly he was doing here. His body felt like a chair with the stuffing knocked out of it. 'No. No. I haven't been drinking. I don't know what you're—'

'She's not here, is she?' said Friel, looking around the inside of the van.

'Who?'

'You didn't have anyone staying with you overnight in your . . . love wagon here?'

'My love wagon?'

Following a recent unfortunate incident in which it had suffered an unauthorised and eccentric respray – it may have been the Delegates' Choice, but it was felt by the Mobile Library Steering Committee that it was not suitable for Tumdrum and District – the van had quickly been returned by Ted to its state of quite stunning faded glory. The interior was a riot of grey primer and non-slip vinyl flooring, the front chairs were as plastic as ever, the light casings as grey and as fly-filled. The exterior was back to its classic cream and red. The mobile library might be described as many things, but 'love wagon' was not one of them.

Sergeant Friel strode up and down the interior of the mobile library, peering at the shelves, as though they might reveal trapdoors or secret hiding places.

'Interesting,' he said.

'What are you doing?' said Israel.

'Just checking no one's here.'

'Why? Who are you looking for, Anne Frank?'

'Have you been drinking, Mr Armstrong?'

'No. I haven't been drinking.'

'Drugs?'

'No!'

'Well, we can always check later.'

'You won't need to check later. I'm perfectly sober and fit and . . .'

Actually, his body ached all over. This was when he could have done with his old layers of fat. It was as if he'd been wrestling all night long. He felt a little feverish. And he needed to use the toilet.

'Sorry. I need to use the toilet. Is that OK?'

'Is it en suite, then?'

'No. No. I mean, can I just nip outside for a . . .'

'Well.'

'I'll just be a minute.'

'I know you wouldn't be stupid enough to try anything, Mr Armstrong.'

'Try anything?'

'We wouldn't want any kind of incident.'

'No. No. Of course not. I just need to go and—'

'You go ahead there,' said Friel, with a wave of his hand.

Israel clambered down the steps. Imperious, was what it was, that wave of the hand. He had been trying to work out the word for it. Imperious was definitely it. As he clambered down the steps he saw the three other policemen standing outside, and two police cars. They seemed to tense as he appeared. Israel instinctively raised his arms.

'He's fine,' called Friel behind him. 'Call of nature.'

One of the policemen waved what looked like a crowbar in friendly acknowledgement.

Israel did his best to look calm and smiled and stood staring at Ballintoy Harbour. There were some mornings when you couldn't deny the beauty of where he was living. Some mornings when the sea was a rippling grey steel, and the sky was blue and the sun was golden, and the views out across the North Antrim coast took your breath away.

This was not one of the mornings. The sky was grey; the sea was squally; there was, as far as Israel could discern, no sun.

He'd suddenly lost the urge to go. He stood for a moment, not urinating into the ocean. And then he climbed back, defeated even by his own body, on to the mobile library.

Friel was browsing the biography section.

He waved a book at Israel. It was a book about a footballer.

'Any good?'

'It's OK. If you like that sort of thing.'

Israel hovered nervously by the issue desk.

'Take a seat,' said Friel. 'Make yourself at home.'

Israel sat down on what Ted called the 'kinder box', a wooden box containing children's books. *We're Going on a Bear Hunt*, *To Catch a Falling Star* and a Jan Pienkowski were sticking up uncomfortably. He stood up, neatly placed them in the correct height order, and sat down again.

'Sorry. I still don't quite understand what you're doing here,' he said.

'Well, I haven't seen you for a while, Mr Armstrong, and I just thought we might catch up. Maybe borrow some books.'

The last time they'd met up, Israel had been falsely accused of robbery. And the time before that he'd been accused of kidnap. And the time before that . . .

'Right. Well. It's always nice to see you, obviously, but the library's not open until—'

'I was joking, Mr Armstrong,' said Friel.

Someone should perhaps tell him his jokes weren't funny.

'Ah. Right,' said Israel. 'That renowned Northern Ireland sense of humour. Hilarious.'

'I'd think twice before taking a tone, Mr Armstrong.'

'I'm not "taking a tone".'

'Good.'

'So this is just a social call, then, is it?'

'Not exactly.'

'Right.'

'We're looking for a young girl.'

'Ah.'

Friel reached into his jacket pocket and produced a photograph and handed it to Israel. It was a schoolgirl. She was maybe twelve or thirteen. Blonde hair. Smiling. School uniform. Could have been any schoolgirl.

'Do you recognise her?'

'No. I don't think so,' said Israel, and went to hand the photo back.

'Could I just ask you to look again more carefully at the photo, sir.'

'Yes. Of course.' Israel scanned the photo with more care. She had a few freckles. Smile slightly lopsided. Hint of eyeshadow, perhaps. He took a few moments to consider.

'Take your time now,' said Friel.

Israel half huffed and looked again.

'No,' he said finally and definitively. 'That's definitely not someone I know.'

'Definitely not?' said Friel.

'Well, maybe not definitely, but I certainly don't recognise them.'

'What about if I told you she was in the library last week?'

'Really?'

'Yes.'

'Well, we get a lot of people on the library during the week, what with being open to the public and everything. So it's difficult to remember everyone who's—'

'I'm sure. Perhaps this photo might help.'

Friel then produced a piece of paper printed from an Internet site: the image showed what appeared to be a girl in her late teens, wearing black, in make-up. She was grinning at the camera, making a face.

'God. This is the same girl?'

'It is.'

'She looks different.'

'Indeed. Recognise her now, do we?'

'Well, she does look . . . familiar.'

'I see.'

'Is that . . . Maurice Morris's daughter?'

'Lyndsay Morris.'

'Yes. She was in at the end of last week.'

'Ah,' said Friel. 'So your memory's miraculously come back to you, has it?'

'Well. I mean . . . I've just remembered now.'

'I see. And I don't suppose you're suddenly going to remember seeing her since last week, are you?'

'No. No. Definitely not. She was just on the library, borrowing some books. I haven't seen her since.'

'Hmm. You're absolutely sure.'

'Definitely.'

'Well. You can perhaps see it might be difficult for me to take your word at face value now, Mr Armstrong, seeing as a few moments ago you lied about never having seen her before.'

'I didn't lie,' said Israel. 'I just forgot to . . . remember and then I just . . . remembered.'

'Really.'

'Yes. Really. And I definitely haven't seen her since.'

'So you said.'

Friel walked up and down the narrow space, hands behind his back, for all the world as though he were pacing in front of the fireplace in his own personal library.

'I don't really understand what this is all about, Sergeant—'

'Well, let me explain then, for your benefit. I think you'll agree it might seem just a wee bit odd that shortly after a young girl goes missing on our patch, you turn up, sleeping out in your van, tucked away, clearly emotional and upset.'

'I don't think it's odd,' replied Israel. 'And I'm not emotional and upset.'

'With a beard.'

'It's . . . just a coincidence.'

'The beard?'

'No, the whole thing.'

'A coincidence?'

'Yes.'

'I see. Well, perhaps you wouldn't mind telling me by what strange coincidence you're here, then?'

'Just. I had a bit of a shock yesterday—'

'Did you?'

'Yes.'

'Why don't you tell me all about it, Mr Armstrong?'

'Because it's . . . Well, it's private.'

'Well, you're among friends, Mr Armstrong.'

'I don't know if I'd—'

'And I'm sure you'd rather have it this way, Mr Armstrong, rather than accompanying me to the station, wouldn't you?'

Israel had absolutely no desire to revisit Rathkeltair police station.

Friel pulled up one of the metal tub steps and sat down.

'A nice cosy little chat. Just the two of us.'

'Cosy little chat?'

'That's right.'

'So I don't need a lawyer?'

'Only the guilty need a lawyer, Mr Armstrong,' said Friel, smiling, and showing his teeth.

'Erm. Actually, the last time we had a cosy little chat I was falsely accused and had to—'

'Ach,' said Friel, shaking his head, disappointedly. 'Let's not talk about the past, Mr Armstrong. That's all water under the bridge. Let's concentrate on the present, shall we?'

'Well . . .'

Friel produced his notebook.

'You're taking notes?' said Israel.

'That's right.'

'Of a cosy little chat?'

'Just so that we get an accurate record of our conversation.' He smiled again.

'Right.'

'So, why don't you tell me what happened?'

'What happened when?'

'From the beginning.'

'From the beginning of what?'

'I don't know. You're what? Early thirties, Mr Armstrong—'

'I'm still in my twenties, actually. It's my birthday next—'

'And you're not married?'

'No.'

'And have you got a girlfriend?'

'I don't see why that's relevant.'

'Just asking.'

'Well,' said Israel. 'Yes, I do have a girlfriend, actually. Or, no. I mean, I *did* have a girlfriend, until recently, we . . . split up.'

'On the rebound, then, are we?'

'Sorry?'

'Looking for someone to share our little secrets with?'

'I don't know what you're implying—'

'I'm not implying anything, Mr Armstrong. I'm just thinking aloud here. Trying to piece things together.'

Israel had the feeling that the conversation was being pieced together in a way that was not advantageous to him. And that it was about to be made into a very unpleasant jigsaw.

'Where were you last night, Mr Armstrong?'

'Erm. I was here. In the van.'

'And you make a habit of sleeping in the mobile library, do ye?'

'No. It was just—'

'A sort of secret meeting place for you, is it?'

'No.'

'Somewhere to entertain?'

'No! Nothing like that.'

'So did you see anyone last night?'

'Yes,' said Israel. 'I did. Yes. I saw the Reverend Roberts, actually.'

'And what time would that have been?'

'At about eleven o'clock.'

'That's the Reverend Roberts of First Presbyterian Church in Tumdrum?'

'That's right.'

'And you were entertaining him on the van?'

'No, I wasn't entertaining him anywhere. I visited him at the manse, up in town.'

'I see. And you make a habit of dropping in around eleven to see him every night, do you?'

'No. It's just—'

'You have a close relationship, you and the Reverend Roberts?'

'No! I'm not . . . What are you suggesting?'

'I'm not suggesting anything, Mr Armstrong. It's obviously your business who you visit late at night—'

'Look. I'm not—'

'What, Mr Armstrong?'

'I'm a perfectly . . . normal . . . red-blooded heterosexual, if that's what you're implying.'

'I see,' said Friel.

'I was . . . just upset . . .'

'I see. And you'd often go to your friend the Reverend Roberts if you're "upset", would you?'

'No, not really. I just . . . He's a friend. You can ask him.'

'Oh, we will be asking him, Mr Armstrong, don't you worry about that.'

Israel could feel all the early warning signs of a migraine coming on.

'And before you visited the Reverend Roberts, Mr Armstrong. Can I ask where you were before that?'

'Before that? Erm. I was at the Devines'. You can ask them as well.'

'Good. Thank you. We will.'

'And before that I was—'

'OK, thank you. That's enough for the moment. You certainly seem to have your alibi all worked out.'

'Alibi! What do you mean, alibi? It's not an alibi! It's the truth. An alibi is when you . . . try and prove that you didn't do something—'

'That's right,' said Friel.

'So it's not an alibi,' said Israel.

'We'll be the judge of that, shall we, Mr Armstrong?'

At which, he got up and started to walk towards the door.

'Hang on,' said Israel. 'Where are you going?'

'I have no further questions for you at the moment, Mr Armstrong.'

'Well, you can't just leave, having suggested I've concocted some sort of alibi for something I don't know I'm supposed to have done.'

'I just want to make sure we all lay our cards on the table, Mr Armstrong. If you cooperate with us I'm sure we'll get to the bottom of things very quickly and easily.'

'Yes. Right,' said Israel, unconvinced. 'You don't seriously think I've got anything to do with this girl's disappearance, do you?'

'Actually, to be honest, Mr Armstrong, on this occasion . . .' And Friel paused for what seemed like an eternity. 'No, I don't think you have anything to do with the disappearance.'

'Oh, thank goodness,' said Israel.

'But we do have to ask, you understand.'

'Yes, of course.'

'No stone unturned.'

'Absolutely.'

'But,' said Friel, at the door.

'There's a but?'

'There's always a but, Mr Armstrong. I don't think you had anything personally to do with her disappearance – not really your style, is it?'

'My style?'

'Violence. Kidnapping.'

'What? She's been kidnapped?'

'We're keeping our lines of enquiry open at this time,' said Friel, looking Israel up and down. 'But not your style.'

'Of course it's not my style! I'm a librarian! I'm a pacifist! I—'

'I'm sure, Mr Armstrong. It's just I have a wee hunch, that tells me that you might be able to tell us something about the disappearance.'

183

'I don't know anything about it,' said Israel.

'Nothing at all?'

'No. Nothing.'

'Fine. If you want to stick with that story.' He turned his back again, as if to leave.

'It's not a story! It's the truth!' said Israel.

'The whole truth and nothing but the truth?' said Friel.

'Yes. And I'd swear it on the Bible, if we had a . . . Bible in here.'

'Have you got a Bible in here?' said Friel.

'Well, we've got a reference copy.' Israel made to get up and retrieve the Bible from its shelf. 'That'd do, wouldn't it—'

'I'm joking, Mr Armstrong.'

'Oh.'

'There's no need for swearing on Bibles at the moment, thank you. Plenty of time for that later.'

'I'm telling you the truth,' said Israel.

'Hmm,' said Friel.

'What's that supposed to mean?'

'What?'

'The "hmm".'

'It's just putting all the pieces together, Mr Armstrong.'

'Like a puzzle,' said Israel.

'If you like. And there's just one other piece of the puzzle you might be able to help us with.'

'Of course.'

'Good. Why don't you tell us about the Unshelved, Mr Armstrong?'

'The Unshelved?'

'Yes.'

'What do the Unshelved have to do with anything?'

'Why don't you leave the questions to me, Mr Armstrong? That's my job.'

'Right. Fine.'

'So? The Unshelved.'

'Yeah. Do you want me to show you?'

'That might be good, yes.'

Israel went over to the issue counter behind the driver's seat. He reached down underneath and started pulling out the current Unshelved, laying them on the counter. *A Clockwork Orange. The Anarchist Cookbook. As I Lay Dying. Asking about Sex and Growing Up. Brave New World. Bridge to Terabitha. Carrie. Catch-22. The Chocolate War. The Handmaid's Tale. One Flew over the Cuckoo's Nest. Slaughterhouse-Five.* And a book called *What's Happening to My Body*?

'The Unshelved,' he said, when he'd piled them all up.

'That's it?'

'That's what's currently not on loan.'

'And what are they exactly?'

'Well, the Unshelved are books that the mobile library steering committee believes – in its wisdom – to be unsuitable for young people to read.'

'I see. So they're kept under the counter?'

'That's right.'

'Actually under the counter,' said Friel, peering under.

'Yes. So that no one can see them. In case it might corrupt innocent minds.'

'But nonetheless you allow young people to read them.'

'Yes, well, if they ask.'

'And is that library policy, or is that just your own personal decision?'

'Well, there's no real policy as such. It's a slightly grey area. It's sort of left to our discretion.'

'I see. And your discretion, Mr Armstrong?'

'What?'

'Allows you to lend the books to anyone?'

'Well. Yes. I suppose.'

'Not very discreet, then, your discretion?'

'Well. I just . . . I think everyone should be allowed to read these books. Look.' He picked up Graham Greene's *Brighton Rock*. 'What's wrong with that?'

'You'd have no problem issuing that book to a child?'

'Children don't tend to want to borrow Graham Greene, on the whole. But young teenagers, I suppose. I'd have no problem with that really.'

'I see. And these books contain descriptions of violence and sex?'

'Some of them. But they're mostly about what all books are about.'

'Which is?'

'I don't know. What all books are about: the glory and . . . misery of being human.'

Friel wrote down what Israel had said, looking rather doubtful.

'So you have no problem with lending young people that sort of material?'

'What sort of material?'

'This sort of material: the Unshelved.'

'Well, some of it, maybe, but not really. It's all different.'

'But you just said all books were about the same thing.'

'Well, yes, they are and they aren't.'

'Some of them more disturbing than others perhaps?'

'Of course.'

'And the more disturbing material, you're happy to lend out?'

'Well, look, they're all on MySpace, and file-sharing, and YouTube, and goodness knows what. So what's the problem with them borrowing a Nabokov?'

'Is that a book?'

'That's an author.'

'I see,' said Friel. 'And how are you spelling that?'

Israel spelt it. Friel wrote it down, and ominously closed his notebook.

'Is that it, then?' said Israel. 'You've finished with our cosy little chat?'

'Yes. I think so,' said Friel.

'Good,' said Israel, relieved.

'I just need you now to accompany me to the station, Mr Armstrong.'

'What? You said—'

'I'd just like you to clarify a few points for us. On the record.'

'Oh no. No. I'm not—'

'It's not really a request, Mr Armstrong.'

'No. Please. I thought you said that I didn't have to come to the station. Don't make me—'

'I'm not going to make you do anything, Mr Armstrong. I believe in the force of argument. But, alas, my colleagues' – and here Friel nodded towards the other policemen gathered outside the van – 'tend to believe in the argument of force.'

'Oh God.'

'Good. You can drive the van to the station. I hardly think you're going to make a dash for freedom, are you?'

'What?'

'Good. If you follow my vehicle, and we'll have another car behind, just to make sure.'

So, just as he'd driven into Ballintoy Harbour last night under a cloud of despair, Israel now drove back up the winding hill, under a cloud of suspicion.

13

'I'll tell ye what, ye don't want to be making a habit of this,' said Ted, as Israel emerged from Rathkeltair police station into the rain some hours later.

'I have no intention of making a habit of this, Ted, believe me.'

'Getting caught up with police investigitations. It looks bad.'

'I know it looks bad.'

'Bad,' repeated Ted.

'Yes, I know. I haven't got anything to do with it, though, you know.'

'Aye, well. I know that, ye eejit.'

'Thank you.'

'Not even ye'd be stupit enough to—'

'Yes, all right, thank you, Ted. I appreciate your support.'

'Trouble is, try telling them that.'

'Who?'

'Come under the umbrella here,' said Ted. 'Quick.'

Israel obediently leant down under the umbrella – a vast golfing-type umbrella, advertising Maurice Morris's financial consultancy.

'We need to get you away, son.'

'Why?' said Israel, as he huddled under the umbrella with Ted, striding away from the station.

'The media,' said Ted.

'Why are they here?' said Israel.

'What? Young girl goes missing? Librarian being questioned? Wise up, Israel! Why do you think? You need to lie low.'

'Oh God.'

'And save yer prayers. Round the corner and we're into the home stretch. I've the taxi parked just there.'

They walked quickly down Rathkeltair's notoriously cracked pavements – subject of more than one minor injury claim against the council. The air around them smelt of rain, and cat piss, and potatoes; somehow Rathkeltair always smelt of potatoes. Rathkeltair was the kind of place that smelt as though someone had always just cooked dinner.

As they rounded the corner there was the ominous sound of running behind them.

'Israel! Israel!' came a voice.

'Ye've got company,' said Ted. 'Come on. Don't stop. Don't turn around. And don't show 'em yer face.'

They started walking even more quickly, and whoever it was started walking more quickly also. In heels.

190

'Israel, wait, wait!'

'I think I know who it is,' Israel said to Ted.

'I don't care who it is.'

'I think it's Veronica.'

'What?' said Ted.

'Veronica Byrd.'

'Ach. The wee hasky bitch from the *Impartial Recorder*? I might have guessed.'

Veronica caught them as they reached the cab. She was wearing a red raincoat that looked as though it had recently been poured from a sauce bottle; her blonde hair was swept back into a bun, held in place by a shining tortoiseshell comb; and she wore shoes that would surely have made any kind of reporting difficult.

'Hello, Israel,' she said, as Ted lowered the umbrella and went round to open the driver's side.

'Hello,' said Israel, rather shyly.

'I knew it was you!' she said.

'How?'

'Your cords,' she said.

'Ah,' said Israel. 'Betrayed by the cords.'

'Indeed,' she said, cocking her head slightly. 'So?' she said.

'So?' said Israel.

'Come on,' said Ted, who had opened up the passenger car door.

'How did you get mixed up in this one, Israel?' She spoke in a tone of good-natured reproach, and when she spoke, you noticed her cheekbones – or, at least, Israel noticed her cheekbones. They were reproachful cheekbones.

'Well, I'm not really mixed up in it, to be honest. Whatever *this* is.'

'Come on!' said Ted. 'In.'

'Look, it's nice to see you, Veronica, but I have to—'

'No, no,' she said, standing in front of the open door. 'Don't be rushing off when we've only just said hello.'

'Sorry. I have to.' Israel went to reach round her to get into the car. Veronica pushed him back and shut the car door with her hip.

'We're old friends, Israel, aren't we?'

Israel hesitated.

'And I'm sure you could use a friend at the moment, couldn't you?' she asked.

'He's got a friend,' said Ted, who had leaned across and opened the passenger door again from the inside. 'You!' he said, addressing Israel. 'In!' And then 'You!', addressing Veronica. 'Run along there.'

'Yeah!' Veronica laughed. 'Right. In these shoes? Come on, Israel,' she said, with authoritative boldness. 'I'll buy you a drink.'

'No, thanks,' said Israel. 'I don't drink at lunchtimes.'

'Oh, go on.'

'Into the cab,' said Ted. 'Now!'

'Come on,' she said. 'You can catch up with Lurch later.'

'In!' said Ted.

'Come on, Israel. Please.' She fixed him with her pale, piercing blue eyes. 'Give a girl a break.'

Israel stood and looked at her. He'd always liked her.

He liked her because she talked as if she were in a film starring Peter Lorre and Edward G. Robinson. And he liked her because she always talked as if the world was in jeopardy but that she alone could somehow sort things out.

'Give a girl a break,' he repeated.

'Yeah. Go on.'

'You!' shouted Ted. 'In! Now!'

Israel hesitated. Fatally.

'Ted. I'll be fine,' he said.

'You'll be flippin' eaten alive, ye eejit! Now!'

'Come on, then. I'll buy you lunch,' said Veronica.

He certainly did need a friend.

'Come on, I think I can help you,' said Veronica. Her voice had always had a slightly breathless quality. And her wide blue eyes – enhanced by coloured contact lenses? – and her open, trusting face, and the determined jut of the chin.

'Nice raincoat,' said Israel.

'You auld flatterer!' she said. 'Now are you going to let me buy you lunch, or not?'

'All right,' said Israel, his defences having been quickly broken down.

'Come on, let's go,' she said. And she took Israel by the hand and started walking briskly and triumphantly away from Ted's cab.

'Hey!' said Ted, emerging from the cab. 'What are ye doin'?'

'I'm just going to get some lunch here, Ted. OK?' said Israel, shouting back. 'I'll see you later.'

Ted shook his head.

'Well, don't say I didn't warn you,' he bellowed.

Veronica glanced behind her and smiled.

'Bye-bye now!' she called. 'Don't wait up!'

'Where are we going, then?' said Israel.

'There's a little bistro I know.'

'A bistro?' said Israel.

'Yes.'

'In Rathkeltair?'

'Yes.'

'You're kidding?'

'No. Why? Do you have a problem with bistros?'

'No, I have no problem with bistros whatsoever.'

'Good.'

The bistro was just off Main Street, so it was called, naturally, Off Main Street, in case you forgot. Rathkeltair, as a town, was just a cut above Tumdrum, and so the Main Street in Rathkeltair was not merely different in degree to the Main Street of Tumdrum, it was different in kind. And Off Main Street was correspondingly a cut above anything off Main Street in Tumdrum: the menus, for example, weren't laminated. Israel couldn't remember the last time he'd seen a non-laminate menu. It was like holding the Torah scrolls. Off Main Street was decorated in a kind of cheap IKEA fantasy of a cosmopolitan loft apartment. There was a lot of exposed brickwork, and abstract art. Huge wineglasses. Café-style chairs. Dim lighting. Slightly noirish film-score-type music just a little too loud, as though you were in Berlin, or *The Bourne Ultimatum*.

With Gloria, back home in London, Israel used to
eat out at least once a week, in cheap Italians or
Indians or Chinese restaurants round by where they
lived, or he would go up and meet Gloria in town
and they'd find somewhere different and new and
exciting. There was this vegetarian restaurant they
liked up round by Old Street, where they served
saffron lasagne with pistachio and ginger and it was all
scrubbed wooden tables and body-pierced Australian
waitresses. That was a great restaurant. He'd never
really enjoyed eating out since he'd been living in
Tumdrum: a meal out in Tumdrum invariably came
with a side order of chips or champ, and the local
chefs and restaurateurs seemed long ago to have
abandoned any idea of flavour, or texture, or indeed
portion control, and gone flat out for bulk. In compar-
ison to eating out in Tumdrum, dining out in
Rathkeltair was like walking into a 3-D Michelin
restaurant guide. This lunchtime there were half a
dozen people already seated, men in suits mostly, and
middle-aged women in make-up. Civil servants, probably. On flexitime. But they might as well have been
Cary Grant and Lauren Bacall as far as Israel was
concerned.

He sat there, mesmerised by the non-laminate menu,
which promised crostini; and beet-and-goat-cheese
salad; and *moules du jour*; and red snapper fillet; ginger-
yogurt cheesecake. He ran his fingers over the paper,
as though checking the weave.

'Wow,' he said. And then, looking at the prices,
'Wow,' he said again.

'It's my treat,' said Veronica.

'On expenses, then?' said Israel.

'Still my treat,' she said, smiling.

He remembered the very first meal out he and Gloria had ever had. He could see it now, in his mind's eye, as clear as – if not clearer than – he could see Veronica before him now, placing a finger on her lips and gazing at the menu. It was a Greek restaurant, somewhere around Palmers Green. There was ornamental trellis-work and a big amateur sky-blue mural, and the cutlery glistening, the plates white. They ate vegetable kebabs and drank retsina poured from big copper jugs and pulled faces at the taste, and they held hands. And all to the accompaniment of the theme tune to *Zorba the Greek*.

'What do you think?' said Veronica.

'It's OK,' said Israel. 'Did you ever see *Zorba the Greek*?'

'Is that a film?'

'Yeah.'

'No.'

'Oh.'

He and Veronica had never had that much in common.

'This used to be a wine bar,' Veronica was saying. 'Back in the nineties.'

'Right.'

'But they've really transformed it, haven't they? I like all these little accents.'

'Accents?' said Israel.

'The little Chinese-lacquer red bowls and everything.'

'Right,' said Israel. 'Yes. Nice.'

'The chef's from here, but his wife's Polish,' said Veronica.

'Really?'

'Cosmopolitan, you see. International. I like it because it reminds me of London.'

'Yeah,' said Israel. 'Kind of.'

A waiter stood beside them. He was wearing a black silk shirt – always a bad sign in a waiter.

'Would you like some wine with your meal?'

'Why not?' said Israel.

'Red or white?' said Veronica.

'White,' said Israel.

'I thought you drank red?'

'It stains.'

'You're meant to drink it, Israel, not spill it. We'll take a bottle of house white,' said Veronica, without consulting further.

'What is the house white?' said Israel.

'It's a quirky New World wine,' said the waiter.

'What?'

'It's a Riesling.'

'Hmm. A quirky New World Riesling?'

'Yes.'

'Really? OK. And what have you got that's French?' asked Israel.

'Since when did you take an interest in wine?' said Veronica.

'I . . . just . . . You know. I find there's a lack of character and vibrancy in a lot of the New Worlds, for my liking. I prefer something with more freshness.'

'OK,' said Veronica. 'You're going to be telling me you can cook and clean next, are you?'

'I like to think I can look after myself,' said Israel. Which was a lie.

'You want to snap him up before someone else does,' said the waiter.

'We'll see,' said Veronica. 'I need to road-test him first.'

Israel blushed.

'So?' said the waiter.

Israel was still scanning the wine list.

'Actually, why don't we go for a Riesling from its spiritual home?' he said.

'Right,' said Veronica. 'Sounds fine.'

'We'll go for the Markus Molitor, then, please.'

'At £29.95 a bottle?' said Veronica, seizing a menu.

'I'm buying the wine,' said Israel.

'Oh, well, in that case.'

'Very good, sir. Madame,' said the waiter, smiling, unconvincingly – 'Madame' spoken with a Northern Irish accent sounding suspiciously like an insult – and walking away.

'I am impressed,' said Veronica. 'So, what have you been doing in that coop of yours? Sitting around reading wine encyclopedias?'

'Not exactly. Pearce taught me, actually.'

'Pearce Pyper?'

'Yeah.'

'You have heard, have you?'

'Yes,' said Israel, sadly. 'I have.'

'I'm meant to be doing the obit later this week. I don't know where to start.'

Israel laughed.

'What?'

'Where to start with Pearce, that's a good question.'

'You knew him quite well, didn't you?' said Veronica.

'Yes,' said Israel. 'I do. I mean, I did.'

The waiter reappeared with the wine, Israel approved it – and they raised their glasses.

'Cheers,' said Veronica.

'*L'chaim*,' said Israel.

'Whatever. Are you ready to order?'

'I might just need a few more minutes,' said Israel.

'Of course,' said the waiter, raising his eyes to heaven, and wandering off.

'Anyway,' said Veronica. 'You're looking well.'

'Right,' said Israel.

'Seriously, though,' said Veronica. 'Have you been working out?'

'No!' said Israel. 'Just—'

'You're not on a diet, are you?'

'No, not really.'

'Have you been going to the gym?'

'Do I look like I've been going to the gym?'

'Yes, actually. And the beard?'

'Yes,' said Israel. 'What do you think?'

'I'm not sure about the beard,' she said. 'What's that all about?'

'I'm . . . cultivating my mind,' said Israel.

'Well,' said Veronica, 'that doesn't necessarily mean

you have to be cultivating your beard at the same time, does it?'

Israel took the opportunity to draw Veronica's attention to the venerable history of learned beards, arguing that it was in fact only a recent twentieth-century phenomenon that sophistication should be associated with beardlessness: shaving, he argued, being merely a sign of a male vanity that is directly linked to the West's military-industrial-puritan complex.

'My brother Esau is an hairy man, but I am a smooth man!' he said.

'Whatever,' said Veronica.

There was a silence, as they looked at each other.

'This is where you're supposed to compliment me on how I'm looking,' said Veronica.

'Gosh. Sorry,' said Israel. 'I mean, of course you're looking well.' Veronica looked more than well.

'Well, thank you. We do our best,' she said.

The reason Israel liked Veronica was because she was so candid. She was the sort of person who cut to the chase.

She cut to the chase.

'So do you want to talk business or pleasure first?'

'Erm,' said Israel. 'Can we order first?'

'Oh, yes, of course. Silly me. What are you going to have?'

'I can't decide,' said Israel.

'I'm having the Caesar salad,' said Veronica.

'Oh,' said Israel, slightly disappointed.

'What?'

'Ladies always have Caesar salad.'

'We have to think of our figures.'

'Right.'

'Don't let that stop you having something else. The steak's good.'

'I'm vegetarian.'

'Oh, I forgot.' And then, without waiting further for Israel, she called over the waiter and ordered her Caesar salad. Israel, under pressure, went for what looked like the least-worst option – the vegetarian lasagne.

'So, shall we get down to business?' said Veronica.

'Here?' said Israel, who'd been rather buoyed by Veronica's compliments about his new-found svelte figure. He decided he rather liked it here. He had an unusual sense of ease. Glass of wine in hand. Beautiful woman paying him compliments. He felt dangerously wonderful and alive.

'Not that sort of business, Armstrong,' said Veronica.

'Sorry,' he said.

'So?' she said.

'What?'

'Do you want to tell me all about it?'

'About what?'

'Israel! About the police investigation into the disappearance of Lyndsay Morris, of course!'

'Well, I don't know. I don't really know anything about it. I don't have anything to do with it, obviously,' said Israel.

'Obviously!' said Veronica, in a way that suggested not so much Israel's welcome innocence as that he was clearly destined to be only a bit-part player in the theatre of life, and so was incapable of being responsible for any action, good or bad.

'Oh God, what's this music?' Veronica said, suddenly.

'I don't know,' said Israel.

'You do, you do. It's the Kings of Leon! I love the Kings of Leon.'

Israel felt very much his almost-thirty.

'I saw them at Glastonbury,' said Veronica. 'They were fantastic!' She looked Israel in the eye. 'Can I be honest with you, Israel, as a friend?'

'Yes, of course.'

'I need this story,' she said.

'What story?'

'The Lyndsay Morris story.'

'The Lyndsay Morris story? It's hardly a story, is it? She's a young girl who's—'

'Everything's a story, Israel.'

'Right. Well.'

'And I need your help.'

'Well, I don't know how I can help, but of course if I can—'

'I need to know everything the police told you.'

'They didn't tell me anything really,' said Israel, swirling the wine around in his glass. 'Anyway, how have you been? What have you been up to?'

'No, Israel. Concentrate.'

'I am concentrating.' He was concentrating for that moment on her pretty face and her lips.

'I need this story,' she was saying. 'I *really* need this story.'

She suddenly reached down under the table. Israel

wondered what was happening. She pulled her handbag up on to her lap. There was a book poking out the top.

'What are you reading?' said Israel.

She pulled out a copy of *The Alchemist*, by Paulo Coelho.

'Oh,' he said, involuntarily.

'What?'

'Paulo Coelho.' He pronounced it 'Co-el-you'.

'Is that how you pronounce it?'

'I think so.'

'I love Paulo Coelho.' She pronounced it 'Coal-Ho'. 'Have you read any?'

'God, no. It's shit.'

'It's not shit, actually, Israel. You just don't like it.'

'Well, there are objective critical standards.'

'Yeah, sure, if they're yours.'

'Not just if they're mine. Lots of people think Paulo Coelho is shit.'

'Look.' Veronica pointed the book out to him. 'It says on the back here that the book has been translated into sixty-four languages and sold twenty million copies worldwide.'

'That still doesn't mean it's not shit. Hitler was pretty popular too.'

Veronica tutted.

'Israel! Anyway. I was going to show you this. Here.' She pulled a newspaper from her bag, flicked through, and pointed to a page. It was a copy of last week's *Impartial Recorder*.

'What?' said Israel. He read the headline. '"Solar Heating Firm Wins Prestigious Award". So?'

'What's the byline?'

'"By Our Reporter".'

'That's me.'

'Uh-huh,' said Israel, not understanding.

'What about that one?' She pointed to another story.

'"Local Dairy Export Farm Praised for Its Marketing".'

'Guess who?'

'You?'

'Correct.'

Israel flicked through the rest of the paper – the birth of a very large pig, a school recycling art project, and twelve jobs saved at the local meat-wrapping plant.

'So?'

'Israel. I am twenty-eight years old. I have been working on this newspaper for almost ten years. I have no intention of working on this paper for the next ten years. I need this story.'

'Well, you're a journalist, can't you—'

'I need *this* big story.'

'Right. Well, can't you just sort of write it up, or whatever you usually do.'

'I don't have any source or any inside information.'

'Ah.'

'Which is where you come in. You're the closest thing I've got to a source.'

'Me?'

'Yes.'

'Oh.'

'So what do you say?'

'No, sorry. I don't really see how I can—'

'Israel,' she said, putting her hand out and placing it on his. He noticed her nails. She had soft hands. 'I don't believe for one moment that you're involved in this.'

'Good.'

'And it's as a friend that I'm asking you to help me with this.'

'Yes, I know.'

'I value our friendship very much, Israel.'

'So do I,' said Israel. 'But there's really nothing to tell.'

'Israel.' She picked up her glass of wine and took a small sip. 'I really think you should help me.'

'Why?'

'Because . . .' She took another, longer sip of wine. 'There's no easy way to put this. If you don't, Israel, I'm going to have to report it in the paper anyway.'

'Report what?'

'Well, I don't know. Something like "A thirty-something English man has been helping police with their enquiries".'

'I'm not thirty-something!'

'I thought you were.'

'Why does everyone think I'm thirty already?'

'I don't know.'

'I'm not thirty . . . until next week.'

'Sorry.'

'But why would you write that?'

'Why not? It's within legal limits. And the *Impartial Recorder* is a journal of record.'

205

'*The Impartial Recorder*?'

'Yes, actually.'

'But there'd be a witch-hunt. People would think I had something to do with her disappearance. They'd send out a lynch mob.'

'I doubt it,' said Veronica. 'Not a lynch mob as such. People might start asking questions, though, I suppose. You know what they're like round here. "There's no smoke without fire," they might say.'

'Exactly!'

'People will assume that just because you've been interviewed and it's been reported in the paper, that you must have something to do with it.'

'But I don't.'

'Of course not. And certainly none of us want to see an innocent man in court.'

'I'm not going to court!' said Israel.

'No, you're not. That's exactly what we want to avoid happening, Israel. Which is why I want to help you.'

'I thought you said it was me helping you?'

'We'd be helping each other,' said Veronica.

'That's blackmail,' said Israel.

'Don't be silly! That's not blackmail, Israel. It's how business works. It's just a suggestion as to how we might come to an arrangement to our mutual benefit.'

'No,' said Israel, 'sorry.'

'I'm sure if you help me, there are lots of ways I could help you.'

She looked Israel up and down.

'Erm.' Israel looked shyly away. And then he looked

less shyly back at her. He had rather missed female company.

'Well,' he said.

'I don't mean like that, Israel,' said Veronica.

'Oh. Sorry. I just thought you . . .'

'Israel. This is not like the last time.'

'When?' said Israel, innocently.

'When Mr Dixon disappeared. That was different.'

'Why?' said Israel.

'Well, he was a silly old fool. This is a young girl who's gone missing.'

'Yes,' he said. 'Of course.'

'So,' she said, leaning forward. 'Just to be clear. What happened between us before—'

'Yes?'

'Was a terrible mistake.'

'Ah,' said Israel. 'Yes.'

'So long as you're clear about that.'

'Yes.'

'Good.' She straightened out her skirt, and took a sip of her wine. 'Look at us!' she said, laughing.

'Yes!' said Israel, sadly. 'Look at us.'

'Like old friends!'

Israel thought about Gloria again.

'So, do we have a deal?'

'Do I have a choice?' said Israel.

'Not really,' said Veronica. 'No.'

'Well, then.'

She put out her hand.

'So we're in business?'

'I suppose,' said Israel.

'Good.' She took a napkin and a pen.

'You can't write on the napkin!'

'At these prices, Israel, I can write on the walls.'

Veronica started making shapes and doodles on the napkin.

'What are you doing?'

'I'm mind-mapping.'

'You're what?'

'Mind-mapping? Tony Buzan. It's a good way of problem-solving.'

'Like brainstorming?'

'Kind of. What we need to do is build up a complete picture of Lyndsay's friends, her social circle. We need to think laterally.'

'We should try and get Ted on board,' said Israel.

'On board?'

'With the mission,' said Israel.

'Yeah, well, I'll leave that to you. Good luck with that. We'll need to talk to her parents, of course.'

'I can't do that,' said Israel.

'Why not?'

'Well, we've had a little bit of a history, me and Maurice Morris.'

'Fine. I'll do him. You can do the mother. What else do we know about Lyndsay?'

'She borrowed books from the library.'

'Apart from that.'

'She was at school.'

'What else? Clubs? Hobbies?'

'No idea.'

'She worked sometimes at weekends in the fish and

chip shop at the bottom of High Street in Tumdrum.'

'The Venice Fish Bar?' said Israel.

'That's the one.'

'Why is it called the Venice Fish Bar? I've always wondered.'

'I don't know.'

'Why did she work there?'

'I'm guessing her father wanted to teach her the value of hard work. You know what wealthy parents are like. Listen, if you're going back to Tumdrum, why don't you check that out, and I'll look into any other hobbies or interests that might be a lead?'

Veronica's phone rang. Her phone had the theme tune to *Mission Impossible*.

She answered it, naturally.

'Yes,' she said. And 'No!' And 'I don't believe you!'

Israel smiled at her understandingly.

She held the phone away from her mouth for a moment.

'Sorry,' she said. 'I just need to take this.'

'Sure,' said Israel.

She got up and strode out of the restaurant. Israel watched her go.

A few moments later the waiter appeared with their lunch.

Israel sat and waited. And waited.

He poured himself another glass of Riesling.

And then another. It was good.

He ate his vegetarian lasagne.

It was OK.

He ordered dessert.

Key lime pie.

It was OK.

And coffee.

When Veronica eventually walked back in she was looking thrilled. And unapologetic.

'Have you eaten?' she said.

'Yes,' said Israel. 'Sorry.'

'No, no, that's all right. Listen, I've managed to set up an interview with Maurice Morris.'

'Great.'

'Now. So I need to dash – would you mind settling up?'

'Erm . . . Yeah. But . . .'

'Thanks, Israel.' She leant forward and pecked him on the cheek. 'I'll be in touch, OK?'

'You'll be in touch,' repeated Israel. 'Right.'

'You're going to the fish and chip shop.'

'OK.'

'Any time today would be good. We need to stay on top of this.'

'Right.'

'You can report back later.'

'OK.'

'Ciao!' said Veronica, sashaying out the door.

'Bye,' said Israel.

'The bill, sir?' said the waiter.

'I suppose,' said Israel.

'Your treat?'

'Clearly.'

14

That evening Israel stood in the queue at the Venice Fish Bar, his vegetarian lasagne lying heavily in his stomach. The rain had kept on all afternoon: it was turning into one of those classic Tumdrum long, damp days. Fortunately, the Riesling kept him warm.

It was a long queue but a small shop, and as he waited outside in the rain, his duffel-coat hood pulled up tight around him, Israel looked in through the window. Even from outside you could tell that it wasn't exactly what you'd call spotless. The tiled floor was cracked in places, and the brown-spotted pale yellow walls looked as though they might have once been white, and there was an old TV mounted on a shelf up high in the corner, the volume turned up so loud that you could hear it outside, even in the rain; it was a repeat of *Buffy the Vampire Slayer*. Israel stood staring blankly as Sarah Michelle Gellar raced around, skimpily, warding off evil. He only wished he was Anthony Head as Giles the Watcher. *Buffy* was probably one of the things that had made him want to become a librarian in the first place. That, and the fact that he was a mournful, withdrawn, unhappy individual who preferred books to people.

Through the window he studied blurrily the big plastic signboard above the counter. The Venice Fish Bar was the kind of fish and chip shop where fish and chips were just the beginning, the prelude to a big *concerto grosso* of battered fish and fast foods. As well as fish and chips it did burgers, pizzas, kebabs and curries. Basically, if it was bad for you, the Venice Fish Bar did it: if you could batter crack cocaine, or just deep-fry, salt and sell it, then the Venice Fish Bar would have done it. This was not Off Main Street.

He watched the women inside, serving. They wore red baseball caps and red polo shirts and they were all pale white, discoloured by the exposure to spitting fat, and they looked bored almost to the point of self-destruction, as though they had become their baseball caps and red polo shirts, mere chip shop automatons, like machines assembling food, moving slowly from the counter to the cash register, and from the deep fat fryers to the griddles. It was not a happy sight. Israel felt depressed just watching it.

He made it in through the door as a couple were making their way out.

'Smell that,' said the man, opening up a grease-stained brown bag with an incongruous image of a gondola crudely printed on it, the grease seeping through like

212

flood water. The woman with him obediently sniffed the contents.

'Mmm,' she said.

'Beautiful, that is,' said the man. 'Hawaiian burger.'

The fumes were like those from a particularly fruity air freshener; like a meat-based fruity air freshener. Fructified manure. Israel quietly gagged, huffed, puffed out his cheeks, and queasily waited his turn.

Finally, there was just one more person in the queue in front of him, a woman with hair so shiny and so straight it had the appearance of man-made fibres. She ordered a cod supper and a Coke.

'No Coke, only Pepsi,' said the baseball cap behind the counter. But the straight-haired woman was wearing headphones, so she couldn't hear.

'No Coke, only Pepsi,' repeated the baseball cap.

Israel tapped the straight-haired woman in front of him on the shoulder, and she turned round, her hair swaying, her face stony. A face that may have been eighteen. Or may have been thirty. A fast-food-preserved face; a face that had temporarily postponed the consequences.

'What?' she said.

Israel motioned for her to remove her earphones.

'Sorry,' he said, pointing to the woman behind the counter. 'Just, the lady was saying there's no Coke, only Pepsi.'

'Pepsi'll do,' said the straight-haired woman, putting her earphones back in, and turning her back on Israel.

When the woman handed over the Pepsi it was a litre bottle. The woman staggered out.

Just to his right a man and a woman sat in a booth with their daughter, who was perhaps four or five years old. She was lying down on the wooden bench.

'Get up,' said the man. The girl got up quickly and proceeded to nibble at the plastic clamshell of chicken nuggets set before her.

'Can I eat it on the way home, Mummy?'

'No,' said the man.

'Your daddy says no,' said the woman. 'Eat it now.'

'But Mummy, I want to save it for home.'

'No. Your daddy says you can't. Eat it now.'

'Daddy . . .'

'Shut up and eat it or you'll get a slap round the head,' said the man.

Israel concentrated again on the menu board.

'Who's next?' said the baseball-becapped young woman behind the counter.

'Oh, I think I am. Erm,' said Israel.

He gazed up.

'Yes?'

'Erm . . .'

'Yes?'

'Just a portion of chips, er, please,' said Israel.

'Regular or large?'

'Regular, please.'

'That all?'

'Yes, thanks.'

'That's £1.70 please,' she said.

Israel handed over the money.

The young woman walked over to a brightly lit metal container full of chips and with one hand scooped a metal shovelful into one of the plastic clamshell containers. And then she walked back and handed over the chips.

'Thank you,' said Israel.

'Who's next?' said the woman.

A man behind Israel started jostling to get past him. But Israel stood his ground at the counter, spreading his arms slightly to prevent the man coming forward.

'Erm. Actually, I wanted to ask you about Lyndsay Morris?' he said.

The young girl looked at him.

'Are you the police?'

'No, I'm not the police.'

'Are you a journalist?'

'No, I'm not a journalist.'

'Who are you, then?'

'You done?' said the man in the queue behind Israel.

'Yes,' said Israel, turning round. 'Just one moment, please. I just really need to speak to someone about Lyndsay.'

'There's people queuing here,' said the man behind Israel.

'Please,' said Israel to the girl behind the counter.

'Ask Katrina,' said the girl.

'Right. Thanks,' said Israel.

'Oi,' said the man. 'It's not a talking shop, it's a fish and chip shop. Come on.'

'And where would I find Katrina?' persisted Israel.

'Go out and up the stairs,' she said. 'Yes, love?' she said to the man who had pushed past Israel. 'What can I get yous?'

Israel walked triumphantly from the shop, and dumped the chips in the nearest bin.

Immediately outside the shop and to the right there was an open stairway, filled with rubbish – the remains mostly of the Venice Fish Bar meals, both the meals themselves and the wrappings, along with plastic knives and forks smeared with ketchup, like elaborate place settings for a rats' tea party.

Israel kicked his way gingerly through the rats' place settings and walked up the stairs. At the top was a steel door.

He knocked. There was no reply.

He knocked again.

'Yes?' said a voice from inside.

'Katrina?' said Israel.

'Yes,' said the voice.

'The lady downstairs sent me up to see you. I'm looking for Katrina.'

'Are you the police?'

'No. I'm a librarian.'

This was Israel's trump card.

'What?'

No one wanted to turn away a librarian. It would be like turning away the postman, or Jimmy Stewart. It wouldn't have seemed right.

'A librarian?' said the woman.

'Yes,' repeated Israel.

And as usual, it worked its magic: it was just a pity the same trick didn't work on more romantic and intimate occasions.

The heavy steel door was heaved open.

'A librarian?' said the woman, as Israel stepped over the threshold.

'Katrina,' he said. 'I should introduce myself,' he said. 'I'm—'

'A librarian,' she repeated

'Yes, and I just wanted to ask about . . .'

As he spoke Israel's eye wandered slowly from Katrina to the room in which he now found himself. Like the staff downstairs, Katrina was wearing a red polo shirt and red baseball cap – dyed blonde hair poked out the back. She wore powder-blue eye-shadow. And the room he was standing in seemed to be her bedroom. There was a low, thin, sick sofa in brown Dralon pressed up against the left wall, a chipped and clawed white melamine wardrobe next to it. Big empty metal cans that had once contained cooking oil seemed to double up as furniture, with clothes slung on them, plates stacked up. The place stank of smoke and fat. In the middle of the room was a single bed with a faded purple padded head-board that people seemed to have been using for some time to stub out their cigarettes. A young man wearing a white tracksuit and a white baseball cap lay on the bed on a yellow blanket. A TV in the corner of the room was showing what appeared to be a zombie film, in which corpse-like individuals in tattered clothing lurched, moaned and grunted in a swaying crowd through a shopping mall.

'This is . . . very cosy,' said Israel. 'This is your . . . recreation area, is it?'

'Recreation area!' Katrina laughed.

'Well, I mean, where you all congregate for . . .'

'We live here.'

'Do you?'

'Yes.'

'And you work downstairs?'

'Yes. We work downstairs and live here.'

'That's . . . handy, for work, then,' said Israel.

'You want to live on a chip shop?'

'No, not really,' said Israel.

She gestured forlornly around her.

'For this, we pay one hundred pounds,' she said.

'A month?'

'Week.'

'One hundred pounds a week!'

'Five of us living here. When it rains . . .' She pointed up at a cracked plastic skylight, which had been patched together with masking tape and Sellotape.

'Water. Falls down,' she said.

'That's terrible.'

'Yes,' she agreed. 'But so?'

'Who is he?' said the man on the bed.

'A librarian,' said Katrina.

'Librarian?' said the man. 'You are going in the library?'

'No,' said Katrina.

'So why is he here?'

'Erm. Let me explain. I'm just . . . I wondered if you'd seen Lyndsay Morris lately?'

The man snorted, dismissively.

Israel thought he might try another tack.

'Where are you from? Poland?' He'd got to know some of the Poles working on the local farms. They walked up and down the coast road to and from work, wearing bulging fluorescent coats. He sometimes gave them a lift in the mobile library into Tumdrum, and he'd try to have conversations with them, the kind of conversation conducted in the abstract, consisting largely of questions such as 'You like Northern Ireland?' and 'How long have you been here?' And when they answered, the Poles had a faraway look in their eyes, like people who had lost something, or had something taken away from them; it was an expression he recognised from the photographs in the silver frames of his parents, back home in London.

'I'd love to visit Poland,' said Israel.

'It's very beautiful,' agreed the woman. 'Cigarette?'

'No,' said Israel. 'In Poland, everybody still smokes, don't they? It's normal.'

'I don't know,' said Katrina. 'I'm from Romania.'

'Ah,' said Israel, slightly stumped. 'Sorry. I thought you said you were from Poland?'

'You said I was from Poland.'

'Ah. Right. Sorry. And where are you from in Romania?'

'You know Romania?'

'No.'

'So why do you ask?'

'I just . . . Anyway.'

'Where are you from?' said Katrina.

'London,' said Israel.

'London!' She laughed.

'Yes,' said Israel.

'I've been to London,' said Katrina.

'Oh, have you?'

'It's like a big rubbish bin,' she said.

'Well. Parts of it could certainly do with a bit of a—'

'Too many immigrants,' said the man on the bed, as the zombies continued to roam abroad in search of human flesh.

'Well, that's certainly one way of looking at things . . . So how long have you been over here?'

'You ask a lot of questions.'

'Yes. Sorry.'

'I thought you want to ask about Lyndsay?'

'Yes. Yes. I do. I just wondered how long you'd known her.'

'As long as we live here.'

'Right.'

'Not long.'

'And how did you—'

'I come here to study English,' she said.

'Your English is very good.'

'Ha!' She laughed. 'Everybody says that, and then they laugh when you speak a mistake.'

'No. No. I'm sure that's not right. Your English is really very good.'

She smiled as though it was a great sadness.

'So. Lyndsay? You know her quite well?'

'I know her. She is my friend.'

The man on the bed had sat up. His arms were burnt up to the elbows from the chip fat and frying.

'How long have you worked here?'

'Six month.'

'And you got to know Lyndsay while working here?'

'Yes. She is a good person.'

'Right.'

'She helps me find babysitting.'

'I see. You do babysitting as well as—'

'I work here in evenings. And bar at night. During the day I clean. Day off, I do babysitting.' She counted the jobs off on her fingers.

'Wow. That's—'

'I don't like babysitting.'

'Oh.'

'It's worst.'

'I would have thought—'

'Most don't ask my name. They don't look at me. They don't care. I could be anybody!' She laughed again. 'They don't know my name. And I am looking after your kids. There, in the house.'

'Well,' said Israel.

'In Romania, where I am from, your parents, to look after your children. If you are going out. Always. A relative. Or a friend. Not stranger. Never.'

'Yes, I agree,' said Israel. 'That certainly sounds more sensible.'

'Bad job,' said Katrina.

'Well, I'm sorry to—'

'And the men, they do not pay.'

'Do they not?'

'Of course. Sometimes. We agree price. They come

back – they're eating dinner, or drinking – and the man asks me how much money. And I say we agree twenty pounds, twenty-five pounds. For looking after their children! But he does not want to pay. And even after midnight when it is more money. And he gets—' She indicated something with her fingers.

'Calculator,' said Israel.

'Yes. Calculator. And the wife, she is gone. In bed. And the man says he will pay me ten pounds.'

'I see.'

'Or he says he will pay twenty pounds, but I have to do something for him.'

'What?'

'Sex!' The man on the bed laughs.

'Yes,' agreed Katrina. 'He means sex with him.'

'Oh God.'

'His wife is bed, upstairs,' said Katrina.

'That's terrible,' said Israel. 'I'm so sorry.'

She blew smoke up towards the ceiling. 'Is not your fault.'

'No, but . . .'

'What do you want to know about Lyndsay?'

'Well, I don't really . . . Anything, really.'

'She was nice.'

The man on the bed nodded his head in agreement. 'I like her. She help me with things.'

'And did she have any boyfriends, or . . .'

'Yes, of course. Boyfriends. She is pretty.'

'Yes. Anyone in particular?'

Katrina looked at the man. The man looked back.

'You don't know anybody we know this.'

'No. No. Of course.'

'We think Gerry.'

'Gerry who?'

'The boss.'

'She was friendly with the boss?'

'Yes. He used to give her a lift home.'

'I see.'

'In his Mercedes.'

'Oh.'

'He pick her up, night she disappear.'

'In his Mercedes?'

'Yes.'

'You saw him pick her up?'

'I see the car,' said the man on the bed.

'Are you sure?'

'Mercedes.' The man nodded his head.

'Did you tell the police?'

'No.'

'Why not?'

'I don't want to lose my job.'

'But what if Lyndsay's been . . .'

'What can I do?' said the young man.

'What's he like, this Gerry?'

Katrina hesitated before answering.

'He's a bad man.'

'Really?'

'*Bad*,' piped up the young man on the bed.

'I see.'

'DVDs. Computer things. His other business. Illegal.

Friend of ours. He was caught by police. He go back to Romania.'

'That's terrible. Did you tell the police?'

Katrina laughed.

'We're just immigrants.'

'And you're a librarian!' said the man on the bed, laughing.

'In Romania, I study literature,' said Katrina. 'One day, I think I believe I will become great playwright! Like Ionesco. And look! Here I am! You know Ionesco?'

'No. Not really. I mean, I know—'

'*Rhinoceros*? Everybody knows *Rhinoceros*.'

'In Romania, everybody knows *Rhinoceros*,' echoed the man on the bed. 'Schoolboys!'

'Here,' said Katrina, 'nobody knows nothing.'

'Anything,' said Israel.

'What?'

'Nobody knows anything, that's the . . .'

'Nobody knows anything!'

'Yes. Well, thanks.'

'Nobody knows anything! *Les morts sont plus nombreux que les vivants. Leur nombre augmente. Les vivants sont rares*,' said Katrina.

'Yes,' agreed Israel, assuming that she'd told him a joke. 'Very good.'

As he left the building he could still hear them laughing.

He returned to his chicken coop.

Rang Gloria.

No reply.

Lay on his bed.
Wept.
Decided it was time to go and see a doctor.

15

While Israel was doing his best for the cause of international relations, Veronica was doing her best with Tumdrum's Independent Unionist candidate for MLA, Maurice Morris.

Maurice's constituency office was on the High Street, in Rathkeltair, a street that boasted more clubs and takeaways than any other comparable small town in the north of the county. Which was quite a claim to fame. High Street had helped transform Rathkeltair into a weekend mecca for the young and hungry and thirsty of the north of the north of Ireland. On High Street, in the course of just a few hundred yards, you could sample the culinary delights of pizzas, kebabs, chips, Chinese and Indian food, some of it actually cooked by people from China, and India, or countries thereabouts. Stumbling out of, or into, one of the town's renowned clubs – Club Foot, the Waterfront or the Destination – you could choose to eat in, or out, at the Great Wall, or the Pooh Ping Palace, or Yum Yums, or in Billy's Fat Subs, the Bakehole, Gobble and Go, Nachos, Little India, Taste of the Taj, or half a dozen others of lesser renown. Indeed, some young people took it as a challenge on a Friday or Saturday night to eat in *all* of Rathkeltair's popular eateries, often ending up in the Thai Tanic, a Thai restaurant and karaoke bar with a *Titanic* theme, which served, it was said, the best Thai curry chip in the whole of Ireland – evidence of such being often available on Saturday and Sunday mornings, before the road-sweepers got to work clearing last night's fun.

Maurice's office was up at the untakeaway end of the street, above Dennis McIlhone's, the podiatrist – who advertised his business with a large pair of plaster-of-Paris feet in the window, and below Alison Arden, the dentist – who advertised her business with a banner showing a blonde, lipsticked woman smiling with perfect white teeth. Maurice had chosen as his party symbol a heart, which had been produced in large sticky graphics and pasted up on the window. The building looked like a bizarre art installation.

The big heart had been Maurice's idea. As an Independent Unionist, according to his campaign literature, Maurice believed in Strong and Safe Communities, and in Quality Public Services, and Protecting the Environment and Maintaining the Union. But above all, Maurice believed in people. Or rather, Believed in People. And he had A Big Heart for the people of Rathkeltair and Tumdrum and county.

In the reception area of Maurice Morris's office (open 8.30–4.30 Monday to Friday) there were fluorescent and halogen lamps, beech-effect filing cabinets, a large, wall-mounted plasma-screen TV set on the usual magnolia walls, a vase containing some sad little drooping tulips, a laptop computer, a printer and a shredding machine set up on furniture that looked as if it had been bought yesterday from a catalogue – it had little tufts of plastic in hard-to-get-at corners. There were certificates and photographs on the wall, and a map of the area with ominous-looking Post-it notes attached.

Veronica was sitting on a bright blue office chair. Next to her – worryingly close to her – was Micky Highsmith, a small, stout, tense man, with an uneven moustache, prominent bulging eyes and the active hand movements of an ex-smoker, who was Maurice Morris's election agent and handler. He was briefing her.

'Now, before you go in, you understand that this interview with Mr Morris is a feature piece?' he said, his moustache bristling wonkily.

'Sure,' said Veronica.

'You're in no doubt about that.'

'None at all,' said Veronica.

'You're going to keep it fairly light.'

'Of course.'

'Not funny, though. You're not going to try and be funny.'

'I don't do funny, Mr Highsmith.'

'Good. Maurice Morris doesn't like journalism that's more about the interviewer than the interviewee.'

'Me neither,' she lied.

'So no questions about . . . economics.'

'Fine.' She didn't have a clue about economics.

'Or the War on Terror.' It was difficult to see what she might ask Maurice Morris about the War on Terror.

'You're not recording this, are you?' asked Micky.

'You don't want me to record it?'

'Definitely not!' said Highsmith. 'When I spoke to the paper, I said—'

'I'm not recording it,' said Veronica.

'Good. No recording devices on you?'

'No. I'm going to use . . .' She held a spiral-bound reporter's notebook. 'This.'

'OK. Oh. Here.' Highsmith produced from his pocket a ballpoint emblazoned with the words 'Maurice Morris: The People's Choice'.

'Thank you so much. I'll . . . treasure it.'

'You're going to be focusing more on his personal life.'

'Sure,' said Veronica, flashing her most winning smile, in a way that suggested not merely a quiescence but a supine obedience; it was this smile, one might argue, and this smile alone, which had ensured that she was one of the *Impartial Recorder*'s most successful reporters. It was her ticket out of here.

Highsmith looked at her, with a middle-aged man's look between lust and contempt: her clingy dress, her high heels. She did not seem to him to be dressed so much for a serious political interview as for a cocktail party covered by the *Ulster Tatler*. She did not look serious. She was perfect as an interviewer for Maurice Morris.

Highsmith looked at his watch.

'You're only going to get about fifteen minutes, OK?'

'That's fine. That's plenty.'

'May I look at your questions?' he asked.

'Oh, no,' she said. 'I'm sorry, I haven't got anything written down.'

Highsmith viewed her up and down. She looked too stupid to do any serious damage.

'Wait here, I'll see if he's ready to see you.' He knocked on the door of the inner sanctum, waited, and then entered, closing the thin wood-effect door carefully behind him.

She glanced around at the black-framed certificates and photographs on the wall – certificate for this, certificate for that, Maurice Morris emerging from the sea, his body surprisingly lean for a man in his fifties. And his wife and daughter, of course. The wife – she'd always struck her as a little bohemian looking.

Highsmith returned and ushered her in.

She had of course interviewed politicians before, but not often, and always at press conferences, or local ceremonies and events; public occasions. This was the first time she'd secured a one-to-one. And she had to admit, she was excited. Previously she'd always been separated from them by a certain distance. Even then, she could feel it, although exactly what the 'it' was she wasn't entirely sure. It wasn't exactly charisma, though some of them certainly had that. It was something else, though, something that made you look at them, watch them. Maybe it was power, pure and simple – like being in thrall to an animal, the thrill of some non-human thing.

Maurice Morris was taking her hand in front of a large mahogany desk and leading her to a seat. How old was he? Forty-five? Fifty? Fifty-five? It was difficult to tell. His hair was beginning to grey around the temples, but he was still attractive. Two words sprang into her mind. George. And Clooney. And then another two.

'So. Miss – it is Miss?'

'Yes.' She blushed through her blushes.

'Tell me about yourself. How long have you been with the paper?'

Within ten minutes Veronica seemed to have told Maurice Morris her entire life story; her hopes, her dreams. She told him all about growing up in Tumdrum, the daughter of the owner of the grocery store, how she'd worked there helping her father after her mother had died, and had given up her dreams of going to university in order to pursue a career in journalism which would allow her to assist her father. He smiled serenely and nodded. It was like talking to her father, except Maurice was better looking, with white teeth, and hair, and no paunch.

'Well, let me wish you all the best in your career,' said Maurice Morris, in the tone of someone wrapping up the interview.

'Actually, sorry. I do have some questions.'

'I'm sure you do,' he said.

There was a knock at the door and Highsmith entered.

'Time's up,' he said.

'Oh, no. What a shame!' said Maurice. 'That's our time up. I'm so sorry.'

'But I haven't had time to ask all my questions,' said Veronica, 'for the profile.'

'Ah. I think we maybe need a little more time together, don't we, Veronica?' said Maurice. 'Could you give us five minutes, Micky?'

Micky nodded and silently exited.

'Thanks so much,' said Veronica.

'No problem,' said Maurice Morris. 'You've some more questions?'

'Yes, I wanted to ask you about your daughter, if that's OK?'

'Well, yes.' Maurice looked down. Tears sprang instantly to his eyes.

'This must be a very difficult time for you,' began Veronica.

'Yes. It is. It's . . . awful. It's very difficult for me to talk about this. Particularly with the election so close. I don't want the focus to be on me. I want the focus to remain on policy issues.'

'Of course,' said Veronica. 'But your daughter's disappearance must be a terrible worry and a burden to you.'

'Yes, it is.'

'I wonder if you wouldn't mind telling me a little bit about your daughter, and your relationship with her?'

Which Maurice Morris gladly did.

*　　*　　*

232

'That's all now,' said Highsmith, reappearing five minutes later.

'That's such a shame,' said Maurice. 'Perhaps we could meet up for an informal chat,' he said, 'over coffee?'

'Well, that would be . . .'

'Here's my card,' said Maurice. 'Call me any time. If there's anything I can help you with.'

16

Israel managed to get an early morning cancellation with a doctor in Tumdrum's purpose-built, state-of-the-art Health Centre out on the main road going up towards Coleraine.

The Health Centre looked like something designed by dreamy Finns and built by Australians in a screaming hurry, a kind of cross between an Alvar Aalto and a woolshed in New South Wales, with a lot of ambitious angles and exposed wood and steel frames and corrugated-iron cladding in bright blue and red, and with a big black roof like a butterfly straining to take off from its mounting board. Yard upon yard of thick red plastic guttering spewed rain into downpipes, as if the building itself had realised its mistake and had slit its veins and was slowly bleeding to death into Tumdrum's bitter ground. There was what appeared to be a cattle ramp – a long, high-sided yellow platform bridge, the yellow of an old French postal van, like a long, sickly unrolling tongue glistening with saliva – leading from the car park to a deep, shady veranda stretching along the whole front of the building, set with low steel benches on which sat disconsolate smokers, people shamed and condemned by their own families and contemporaries, who sat inside staring out at the backs of them through the floor-to-ceiling windows. The building would probably have worked in Helsinki, or Sydney, and may even have won prizes, but in Tumdrum it was a sick joke, as if an architectural prankster had dumped it off the back of a truck and driven away at high speed: the iron parts were rusting, the wood cladding was rotting into a sickly shade of green, the miserable phormiums planted up all around it looked as though they'd been chewed at by hungry hounds, and the acres of glass were not a good idea in Ireland, thought Israel, as he sat and waited to see the doctor, the whole building thrumming with the sound of rain, and the big windows streaked as if they themselves were downpouring. He closed his eyes and tried to imagine that he was elsewhere.

It didn't work.

Eventually, he was buzzed through to his appointment with Dr Withers.

'Yes?' asked Dr Withers, as though Israel had arrived unexpectedly to clean the room.

'Dr Withers?'

'Yes?'

'I'm Israel Armstrong.'

'Israel Armstrong,' repeated the doctor. 'I see.'

Israel hovered nervously by the door.

'Come in and sit down.'

Israel came in and sat down, and 'Yes?' said Dr Withers again. He was hoping for a hiatus hernia. 'How can we help you?'

'I need a sick note,' said Israel.

'I see,' said Dr Withers. They all needed sick notes. 'What seems to be the problem?'

Israel listed his symptoms: exhaustion; vomiting; weight loss; sleeplessness; anxiety.

'Yes,' said Dr Withers, disappointed, when Israel took a pause for breath. He eyed the Jack B. Yeats print he'd recently rehung on the other side of the room, to give him something interesting to ponder when pretending to listen to his patients. He had an original Paul Henry at home. He'd not had a hiatus hernia for a while.

Withers was a jowly man with a funereal manner who had pure white hair and wore dark suits, and who had his glasses – little half-moon glasses – on a small golden chain around his neck, making him look more like a magistrate, or a mayor, than a man of medicine. He looked like a hanging judge. With his glasses off you could see clearly his hard, unforgiving eyes, eyes that had all the assurance of a man who was comfortable in his knowledge of his own body, and who was more than happy to point out the faults in others'. At weekends, it was said, Dr Withers played the bassoon and wore a hat, and cultivated his interest in art, and in poetry, and in music, and attempted to bully his obstinate and determinedly independent wife, a woman who preferred the Beatles to Beethoven, and who was unimpressed by her husband's moods and his Wagner. They often visited Dublin, the Witherses, and they had a second home in Donegal; they were perfectly self-satisfied. Dr Withers was not the kind of man you could imagine either young or happy, and his patients provoked in him only the occasional pity, at best.

'They're my symptoms,' said Israel.

'Yes,' said Dr Withers.

'I've not been feeling very well.'

'Not very well.' None of them took any responsibility for their lives, that was the problem. Working classes. Middle classes. They were all the same. 'I see. And how long have you been off?'

'I was off for a week. My boss says I need a sick note.'

'I see. Any other symptoms? Or is that it?'

'I think that's it,' said Israel, wishing he had something astonishing up his sleeve. 'Actually, no,' he added. 'I suffer from migraines.'

'Migraines,' said Dr Withers, unimpressed. Migraines. Dispensing for migraines was not what you became a doctor for. 'And what are your migraine symptoms?'

'Well, just the usual, I suppose. Headache. Nausea. Flashing lights sometimes.'

'And you take medication for these symptoms?'

'Mostly Nurofen.'

'Hm. And anything else? Maxolon, or Migramax?'

'I've tried different things. I saw you, about a year ago?'

'I see.'

'But I'm not taking any medication at the moment, no.'

'I see. And how long have you been suffering these other symptoms?'

'I don't know. A few months.'

'A few months.' If he repeated what the patient said often enough, it appeared as though he was listening. His wife didn't allow him to do it at home; she'd rumbled the trick years ago. 'Can I ask what do you for a living, Mr Armstrong?' He always wondered what they did for a living, the patients. He was always looking for one of them to surprise him: a concert pianist perhaps. Or a rodeo rider. Something a little out of the ordinary. But they were always the same. On the social. Or on the sick. Working for the council. Work-shy malingerers, most of them.

'I'm a librarian,' said Israel.

'A librarian,' said Dr Withers. Better than nothing. 'Life of the mind.'

'Well, it's physical as well as mental,' said Israel. 'Because of all the driving.'

'The driving.'

'Yes.'

'You drive to work?'

'No. I drive *in* work: it's the mobile library.'

'Ah,' said Dr Withers, displaying exactly the kind of response that most people had to the mention of the mobile library, as though the fact of its being mobile made it less of a library, as though it were in some way lacking.

'And did you say you're not sleeping?'

'That's right,' said Israel. He wasn't sleeping because

of the dreams. Every night, the same vivid, troubling dreams. Often he would wake with a jolt, as though a vast electrical current had passed through him. One dream: he's in a hotel and has lost everything. The only thing he has is a pair of shoes. His choice is to stay in the hotel room, waiting for someone to come, or leave and walk the streets only in his shoes.

'I see.' Dr Withers always hated this bit of the consultation. It always came to this: confessions of hopelessness and helplessness. People wallowing in their human weakness. But he had to ask; he was supposed to ask. 'And are you feeling depressed at all?'

'Yes,' admitted Israel. 'I suppose I am.'

'I see. And are you getting any exercise?'

'I . . . well, not really, no.'

'I see. And have you ever taken anything for your depression before?'

'No.'

'And have you had counselling' – or, rather, *counselling*, he said, *'counselling'* – 'or therapy?'

'No.'

'No. Well, what I'm going to suggest, Mr Armstrong, is that we prescribe you a mild antidepressant and refer you to one of the counsellors here in the Centre.'

'Oh. I don't know if I . . .'

This is what always happened. They always resisted when you prescribed the cure. Anyone would think they wanted to be depressed. Snivellers.

'What I'm prescribing is known as an SSRI. It'll treat your symptoms and then the counselling should deal with the underlying causes of your problems.' He typed into his computer, pressed PRINT, and the prescription printed.

'Well, I'm not sure that—'

'There should be no problem with you continuing taking ibuprofen. Some patients, however, can experience a temporary increase in anxiety when using SSRIs,' said Dr Withers.

'Increase?'

'That's correct. But often that's a good sign that the treatment is going to be effective.'

'It gets worse before it gets better?'

'Yes. So.' He handed Israel a prescription. 'And there's nothing else?' The old catch question: you treated the first set of symptoms, and then they revealed the lump in the breast.

Nothing else? Where to begin?

The fact that he was nearly thirty?

Or that his girlfriend had left him and he was alone in Tumdrum, adrift without purpose or destination?

Or that being on the library made him feel sick – all that knowledge, pretend knowledge, looking down on him, mocking him, speaking to him of his wasted opportunities?

The accumulated weight of all the years, and the books, all that acid in them, digesting themselves and him with them?

'No,' said Israel. 'Just the sick note. Which is what I really came for.'

'Ah, yes,' said Dr Withers. 'The sick note.' He typed again, pressed PRINT again. The sick note printed.

'There we are. That's us, then, I think, Mr Armstrong?'

'Yes. Right. Thank you, goodbye.'

Israel got up and left, with his sick note, and his prescription. Dr Withers looked at his watch. Only another seven hours to go. He flicked open the latest issue of the *British Journal of Psychiatry*. That was always good for a laugh.

17

While he drove to pick up Ted, Israel listened, as he always listened, to the news on BBC Radio Ulster. And, as always, it made no real sense to him: it was like news from some pointless elsewhere.

Except, alas, this pointless elsewhere was here.

'I was ten months pregnant,' a woman was saying.

'Ten months pregnant?' said Israel back to the radio.

'And I'm standing there, ten months pregnant, crying and gurning,' continued the woman, 'and the traffic warden was horrible to me, so he was. I had to ring my mummy and she had to come and get me. And me ten months pregnant. It's a disgrace, so it is.'

'And now the farming update,' said the presenter. 'Charolais are up. Hoggets are down—'

'Oh God,' said Israel, to no one.

*   *   *

He drove as quickly as he could round the coast road to Ted's house, which sat looking out to sea, and the A2. He parked, took a deep breath, and knocked at the door.

When Ted eventually opened the door, Israel was surprised by a strong waft of . . . what seemed to be curry. Which was not a smell he associated with Ted. It was not at all an unpleasant smell. In fact – since he'd rather got into the habit of skipping breakfast – Israel found the smell rather piqued his morning appetite.

'Mmm,' he said.

'What do ye want?' said the curiously currified Ted, who was wearing his apron. He had a tea towel over his shoulder, and his Jack Russell terrier at his feet.

'Woof!' said the dog.

'Quiet,' said Ted.

'What are you cooking?' asked Israel. 'It smells like—'

'Curry,' said Ted. 'You've had enough of yer lady friend, then, have ye?'

'Yes, thank you,' said Israel.

'Ach, she's a false face if ever there was one.'

'Do you think?'

'Ach. Wise up. Ye wouldnae trust her with one half of a bad potato.'

'Well, no one's asking you to trust her with a half of a bad potato.'

'Good. Because I wouldn't,' said Ted.

'Fine.'

'Not even one half of a half.'

'A quarter,' said Israel.

'Exactly,' said Ted.

'Anyway,' said Israel. 'Lovely to see you. As always. Are you ready?'

'For what?'

'For work.'

'Aye, well,' said Ted, 'ye were that late I'd given up on ye. Thought ye'd mebbe decided to take to your sickbed again.'

'Sorry,' said Israel. 'I was at the doctor's.'

'The doctor's?'

'Yes.'

'What in God's name were ye doing at the doctor's?'

'I had to get a sick note for Linda.'

'Why?' said Ted. 'Is she not well?'

'No, for me.'

'Aye. Right. What, ye looking to swing the leg again, are ye?'

'No,' said Israel. 'I need a sick note for when I was off last week.'

'Ah, well. Where'd ye go? The Health Centre?'

'Yes.'

'Who'd ye see?'

'Dr Withers?'

'Ach, for goodness' sake. What d'ye go and see him for?'

'I didn't have a choice.'

'He's a complete header.'

'Really?'

'Aye. Of course. They're all the same. He give you anything for it?'

'For what?'

'For the stress and strain of being Israel Armstrong?'

'Yes, he did actually.'

'Good. Mind ye, much longer ye won't be in need of it.'

'Why not?'

''Cause ye'll have disappeared completely. Sight of ye! Good feed's what ye need, never mind medicine.'

'Anyway,' said Israel. 'Much as I enjoy your hilarious craic and banter, Ted, shall we go? Are you ready?'

'Do I look ready?' said Ted, indicating his apron and tea towel.

'No . . . Not really.'

'Well then. I need to turn off my curry.'

'Shall I come in and wait?' asked Israel.

Ted huffed.

'It is quite cold out here, actually,' said Israel, putting on his best shivery face.

Ted huffed again, but allowed him to enter.

'Mmm,' said Israel, as he stepped across the threshold and the curry wafts became all-embracing waves. 'That really is curry.'

'Aye,' said Ted. 'And what's wrong with curry?'

'Nothing. I like curry.'

'Good. Because you're not having any.'

'No, I don't want any, it's fine,' said Israel. 'But do you often have curry for breakfast?'

'It's for my tea, ye eejit. D'ye not plan ahead?'

Israel didn't, actually, plan ahead at all. Gloria had always planned ahead. She worked out everything in accordance with a great scheme – as if she had been born with a ready reckoner in one hand and a five-year day-to-view diary in the other. Gloria planned not just weeks or months but years in advance. If she wanted to be doing something in, say, two years' time she simply worked backwards, step by step, to the present, and worked it into a grid. It was like the mind of God. If God was a highly organised young lawyer. Which, clearly, He wasn't. What God needed was a wife. God needed Gloria. So did Israel. If he'd planned ahead properly he'd be living in a brownstone in Brooklyn, going for breakfast with Paul Auster. He certainly wouldn't be picking up Ted in a mobile library van in the middle of the middle of nowhere and discussing his curry-making.

'Good idea,' he said, wistfully. 'Planning ahead.'

'It's not exactly rocket science,' said Ted.

'No,' said Israel. 'I didn't really have you down as a curry kind of a man, though.'

'Aye, well. You might want to re-examine your prejudices, then, eh?'

Ted disappeared into his kitchen. Israel followed. The kitchen was spotless, and ancient: a shrine to wipe-clean Formica. There was a small table in the middle of the room, set neatly with breakfast things: a loaf of bread, butter, jam, a brown teapot.

'Sorry to hear about yer man Pearce,' said Ted, dessert-spooning up a testing mouthful of curry.

'Yes,' said Israel.

'When's the funeral?' said Ted, shaking corrective pepper into the pot.

'Friday, I think.'

'Is the house open?'

'How do you mean?'

'So people can call in and pay their respects.'

'I don't know,' said Israel.

'I tell ye what,' said Ted, spooning a second testing mouthful of curry.

'What?' said Israel.

'Perfect!' said Ted, referring to the curry. 'It's a reminder to us all, isn't it?'

'What is?'

'Yer man, Pearce. If ye can put yer elbows out in the morning and ye don't touch wood, ye're doing OK.'

'What?'

'If ye . . . Never mind. Anyway,' said Ted. 'While I get myself ready, could ye—'

But Israel was over at the stove inspecting the curry.

'The smell's lovely,' he said. 'How do you make your curry?'

'How do ye think?' said Ted.

'I don't know. I've never made curry,' said Israel.

'Never made curry.' Ted shook his head, as though this confession was tantamount to admitting to never having had a bath. Israel hadn't had a bath recently either, actually.

'Do you have a recipe?'

'I do not,' said Ted, appalled.

'Is it lamb?' said Israel, peering in.

'Mince,' said Ted. 'Half a pound of mince, some carrots, some onions. Potatoes.'

'Really?'

'Aye.'

247

'It doesn't sound like curry, actually,' said Israel.

'Does it not?'

'No,' said Israel. 'That sounds more like shepherd's pie.'

'And then I add some curry powder,' said Ted.

'Ah.'

'Curry,' said Ted, decisively, turning off the heat, and putting a lid over the saucepan.

Before his recent listlessness Israel's repertoire had been slowly expanding. He had perfected a number of simple recipes: sautéed mushrooms on toast; tomatoes on toast; cheese on toast; cream cheese on toast; beans on toast. He was particularly fond of toast flavoured lightly with salt and pepper. It was, admittedly, a largely toast-based repertoire, but it served its purpose. It was all going well until the toaster broke: it was a blow to him. There was a burning smell and the toaster stopped working. He'd changed the fuse. No good. It must have been the element. He didn't know how to fix the element.

Thinking about his recipes, and smelling the curry, his appetite was now well and truly whetted: he felt like Winnie the Pooh faced with a honeypot. He found himself helplessly eyeing up the breakfast things set on the kitchen table.

'So,' Ted was saying, 'I take it you've sorted this trouble with the Morris girl, then?'

'Not exactly,' said Israel, distractedly.

'No?' said Ted. 'It was on the news earlier.'

'Was it?'

'Aye. A twenty-nine-year-old man is helping police with their enquiries, apparently.'

'That'd be me,' said Israel, wrenching his thoughts and his gaze away from breakfast. 'Do they have to tell people your age?'

'And how are the police enquiries going?' said Ted.

'I have no idea,' said Israel. 'I'm sort of working on the case myself now.'

'Working on the case yourself?'

'Yeah.'

'Aye, right, Columbo,' said Ted. 'That woman put you up to it, did she?'

'What woman?'

'Flashy Annie, yer journalist?'

'No,' said Israel.

'I'll bet she did,' said Ted. 'Sticking her . . . bits in where they don't belong. No good'll come of it, if you ask me.'

'Ah, well, funnily enough,' said Israel, 'I was going to ask you, actually.'

'No!' said Ted.

'Hold on, I haven't—'

'The answer's no,' said Ted.

'I haven't asked you yet!'

'Well, whatever you're asking, the answer's no,' said Ted.

'What, you're not going to help me out?'

'Correct.'

'Why not?'

'You want a list of reasons?'

'Well, no, but—'

'First of all, it's not my problem. Second of all, it's not yours. And third of all—'

'Yeah, all right,' said Israel. 'That's plenty of reasons, thanks.'

'—the girl'll turn up soon enough anyway. She'll be raking about with her mates somewhere.'

'Right. Well,' said Israel. 'I'll just go it alone, then.'

'With yer fancy woman.'

'She is not my fancy woman.'

'Well, if she's not, ye've a funny way of showin' it. Anyway,' said Ted, conclusively, 'if ye just tidy up my breakfast things there and I'll—'

'Actually, Ted,' said Israel, nodding coyly towards the breakfast things.

'What now?'

'I wonder if I might perhaps prevail upon you for a slice of bread?'

'What?'

'A slice of bread?'

'My bread?'

'Erm. Yes.'

'From my table?' said Ted.

'Yes.'

'Why?'

'Well, it's just—'

'Have ye not had any breakfast?'

'No, actually.'

'Ye should always have breakfast.'

'My toaster's broken.'

'And you can't fix your own toaster?'

'No.'

'What sort of an idiot can't fix his own toaster?'

'Erm . . .'

'Aye, well, answered me own question there, didn't
I. All right, ye can help yerself to a slice.'

'Really?'

'Aye. But ye'll not be making a habit of this, mind.'

'What?'

'Eating your breakfast at another man's table.'

'No.'

'It's not natural. You'll have to give that plate a wee
rench in the sink there.'

'Sorry?'

'The plate, a wee rench in the sink?'

Israel gave the plate a wee rench in the sink, while
Ted ceremoniously removed his apron and put on his
black leather car coat and his cap, and sat down at the
kitchen table waiting for Israel to eat.

It was good bread.

'Mmm,' said Israel, mid-mouthful. 'Ted?'

'What?'

'Do you happen to know the man who owns the
Venice Fish Bar?'

'Ach, big Gerry Blair? Surely. You know him.'

'No,' said Israel. 'I don't think so.'

'Yes, you do. He'd the franchise on a load of fish and
chip places. Sold 'em up, so he did, and he just has
the Venice Fish Bar now. He's retired.'

'What sort of car does he drive?'

'What sort of car does he drive?'

'Yes.'

'I have no idea.'

'Mercedes?'

'I wouldn't be surprised.'

'And how old is he?'

'I don't know. Fifty?'

'What does he look like?'

'You'd know him if ye saw him. He's a couple of bay pacers he trains down at the beach sometimes. Has a tan. Looks a wee bit like yer man . . . what's he called?'

'I don't know.'

'Actor.'

'Who?'

'He's in all sorts.'

'Brad Pitt?'

'No!' said Ted. 'Dark hair.'

'Johnny Depp?'

'No! Does coffee adverts.'

'George Clooney?'

'That's him,' said Ted. 'With a wonky nose, but. Few pounds heavier. Big Gerry Blair. You know him.'

'No, I don't think so. What's he like?'

'He's all right. A bit full of the smell of himself.'

'How do you know him?'

'I've played golf with him a couple of times.'

'I didn't have you down as a golfing man,' said Israel, polishing off the slice of bread.

'Well,' said Ted. 'You know what they say. When in—'

'Rome?' said Israel.

'Portstewart,' said Ted.

Israel reached for another slice of Ted's wheaten bread. Ted scowled.

'May I?' said Israel.

'Ach, right,' said Ted. 'Don't ye stint yerself, eh? Ye want to be eating a proper breakfast, mind.'

'Yes,' said Israel. 'You said.' It was delicious bread. 'The Venice Fish Bar man, is he married?'

'Gerry? That he is.'

'I see.'

'Why? What are ye fishing around for?' said Ted.

'Nothing.'

'You're finagling around for something.'

'Just,' said Israel, 'the Morris girl works at the Venice Fish Bar at weekends, and one of the people she works with kind of implied that she and the boss were . . . close.'

'Right. And what did they mean by close?'

'Close,' said Israel.

'Aye, well, there's close and then there's close. What did they mean by close?'

'Intimate.'

'Intumate?' said Ted.

'Intimate,' corrected Israel.

'Exactly,' said Ted. 'And how old's the Morris girl?'

'Fourteen.'

'For goodness' sake! They're implicating that Gerry'd . . .'

'I don't know,' said Israel. 'It's not . . . impossible, is it?'

'Who was it telling you about this?'

'It was a Romanian girl who works in the Venice Fish Bar.'

'Ah, well, there you are, then.'

'What do you mean, there you are?'

'Romanians. They're like the Poles, aren't they?'

'What?'

'Shifty bunch. Trying to cause trouble.'

'I don't think they were trying to cause trouble.'

'What, accusing a well-respected member of the community, and a member of the golf club, of some kind of . . . relationship with this young girl? You want to ask yourself why they're telling you that.'

'I think they were just trying to be helpful.'

'Aye, right. Helpful! Ye need yer brains tested, boy! This is Tumdrum! It's not Sodom and blinkin' Gomorrah! I'll tell ye what'd be helpful: what'd be helpful would be if ye talked to her actual boyfriend, rather than listening to tittle-tattle about some imaginary intumacy—'

'Intimacy,' said Israel.

'Exactly, with some imaginary boyfriend.'

'Why? Who's her actual boyfriend?'

'Colin.'

'Colin who?'

'Colin Wilson? Sammy Wilson's boy.'

'No, sorry, I don't—'

'Ach, Israel. He's one of these computer nerds. Always at that place on High Street.'

'How do you know he's her boyfriend?'

'Well, if ye listened to the young ones on the library for a change, ye'd get to know quite a few things. They split up, though, I think.'

'Do you think the police will have talked to him?'

'Mebbe. If they've got the inside information.' Ted tapped the side of his nose.

'Why didn't you mention this before?'

'You didn't ask. I doubt he's anything to do with it, mind. He's a wee squirt. No hair on his balls.'

'And where was it you said he hangs around?'

'At the game place on High Street.'

'Game On!?'

'That's it.'

By which point Israel had got up and was by the kitchen door.

'Come on, then!' he said.

'Come on where?' said Ted.

'Let's go.'

'Ye've not finished your piece of wheaten,' said Ted. 'Ye're not going to waste it, are ye?'

'We haven't any time to lose,' said Israel.

'We?'

'Yes!'

'To do what?'

'To get to the bottom of this mystery—'

'The only thing ye could get to the bottom of is a packet of crisps, ye eejit. Leave it to the police.'

'But if I leave it to the police my name'll end up in all the papers and—'

'The reek'll go up the chimley just the same.'

'Which means?'

'It's just a sayin',' said Ted. 'She's blackmailing you, then, is she, your wee friend, the journalist, to help her out?'

'No, we've come to an arrangement.'

'Well, if that's what you call an arrangement you need your brains tested as well as your balls. I'm not getting involved.'

'You're not going to help me?'

'No.' Ted crossed his arms, implacably.

'Would you be able to drop me off on the way through town, and you can go on to the day's run?'

'By myself?'

'Yes.'

'Why?'

'So I could have a quick word with this boy Colin.'

'For why?'

'So I can start to get to the—'

'Don't make me laugh,' said Ted.

'Please!' said Israel.

'Ach. Only because it's a wee girl involved,' said Ted. 'I wouldn't be helping you otherwise.'

'Fine. No. Of course not.'

'So don't ask me again.'

'Never.'

'Promise?'

'Absolutely.'

They drove into town. Ted dropped Israel at Game On!

'Just remember,' said Ted, as he drove away. 'A bird in the hand can't see the wood for the trees.'

'Right,' said Israel. 'Thank you, Dalai Lama.'

18

Game On! was located above Crumbz! and not far from Cutz!, just off the main square, on Market Street, which was that street in every town which attracts the slightly off the wall and out of kilter. Market Street was Tumdrum's Bay Area: Market Street was out there. Crumbz!, for example, was a little bakery – half the size of the Trusty Crusty – that did just a few regular sodas and wheatens but mostly a range of its own gluten-free breads and cakes: in Ireland, where whcat intolerance and coeliac disease were becoming almost as commonplace as Guinness and potatoes, Crumbz! was on to a winner. Their lemon drizzle cake – using quinoa as a wheat substitute – literally had to be tasted to be believed. Cutz! was doing pretty well also: it was one of those hairdressers in which all the staff have multiple piercings and are wise beyond their years. Cutz! attracted mostly the younger crowd in Tumdrum, although Mrs Onions had booked herself in for a shampoo and set a few months ago and had unwisely agreed to try henna and straighteners; she'd worn a headscarf ever since. And Tatz!, next door to Cutz!, was Tumdrum's tattoo parlour with a difference: it was run by born-again Christian ex-Hells Angel Little Stevie, who specialised in full-body biblical scenes and themes. When he'd converted some years ago Little Stevie had taken as his inspiration Robert De Niro's character in the film *Cape Fear*, and he'd had the scales of Justice and Mercy done on his back, plus Moses with the Ten Commandments across his chest. Little Stevie was an arm-wrestling, chain-smoking, shotgun-toting (for the purposes of legal hunting) man-mountain who was yet somehow deeply in touch if not with his feminine then certainly with his spiritual and creative side, and he'd done a big wall-painting inside the shop of the vision of Christ in the Book of Revelation: the white horse, eyes flaming like fire, head crowned with many crowns, and the clothes dipped in blood, and the words 'And he hath on his vesture and on his thigh a name written, KING OF KINGS AND LORD OF LORDS' in Gothic lettering scrolling all around the top. It didn't seem to put people off. In fact, people came not just from all over the island of Ireland, but also from the UK and farther afield, to have Little Stevie do seraphim and cherubim on their forearms and ankles, and Celtic crosses on their shoulders: one man had been travelling over regularly from Germany for the past five years to have Stevie work on an illustrated Bible, in full colour, with (abridged) text; so far they'd reached the minor prophets and were heading fast down his waist.

At this rate they were going to reach the Acts of the Apostles at an unfortunate physical juncture.

Managing to resist the temptation to get his hair cut, have a biblical tattoo, or buy a gluten-free loaf of bread, Israel walked boldly – or as boldly as any vaguely bearded man wearing a duffel coat and brogues was able – up the stairs to Game On!

There was a brightly lit booth at the top of the stairs with a thick, scratched, stained plexiglas screen, which looked as if it had been used as a very large chopping board in a very dirty kitchen; in places you could barely see the scratches for the dreck. Crammed inside the booth, and just visible, was a portable TV, a kettle, mugs, boxes and boxes of Mars bars, and Red Bull, and packets of Tayto cheese-and-onion crisps, an old cash register, an armchair, and a middle-aged man, his greying hair cut short except for a ponytail sprouting from the back of his head, which gave him the appearance of an extra in the film of *The Lord of the Rings*. He sat, gaunt, the man, on the armchair, with a can of Red Bull in one hand, staring blankly into the distance. He looked like someone who might enjoy listening to a Kate Bush album. And then eat you. He certainly belonged on Market Street.

'Hello,' said Israel. 'I wonder if you could help me . . . I'm looking for a Colin Wilson, who I think is a member here?'

The ponytailed man snapped out of his middle-distance reverie and focused on Israel with narrowed eyes.

'Annual membership is forty pounds,' he said. 'OK?'

'Yes,' said Israel. 'I mean, no. I just want to—'

'One-day entry without membership is twenty pounds.'

'But I just want to talk to—'

The ponytailed man tapped a sign stuck up on the plexiglas which stated the terms and conditions he'd just explained.

'But I just want to—'

'The rules are the rules. OK? If you don't want to pay you can wait outside. There's a big free street out there.'

'Right. Could you not make an exception, on this one . . .'

The ponytailed man could not make an exception.

Israel reluctantly dug out his money. He went for the day membership. The annual membership was obviously the better deal, but he couldn't imagine he'd be coming back any time soon.

The money rung into the till, the ponytailed man pressed a buzzer and said 'Through the door' and Israel pushed against the door next to the booth and entered a dark room.

There were blinds drawn at the windows, and young men – all men, as far as Israel could tell, in the gloom – were ranged around all four walls, at computer monitors, frantically tapping away. Those who weren't wearing headphones or earpieces were able to enjoy the kind of splintering, yelling, thrashing music that might have been the theme tune to Dante's *Inferno*, being blasted out from vibrating speakers set high up on the walls. There was cracked lino on the floor, and a smell of damp and adolescent deodorant. Even though it was on the first floor, it felt like a dungeon. It was horrible. Gustave Doré might just have done it justice.

No one looked up as Israel entered. He wasn't quite sure how he was going to make an impact in the room: to be sure of getting anyone's attention he'd have had to switch off the mains power supply. Instead, he did the next best thing and went and tapped one of the young men on the shoulder. The young man's computer screen showed a chariot racing around the rim of a canyon filled with flames and, unfortunately, as Israel tapped him on the shoulder the chariot skidded and went hurtling over the edge into the fiery pits below. The young man turned round furiously and pulled an earpiece from one ear.

'What the fuck are ye doing?'

'Hi,' shouted Israel, as best he could above the sounds of death metal. 'Sorry. I'm looking for Colin? Colin Wilson?'

'You interrupted me!' said the young man.

'Sorry,' said Israel.

'I'm playing fucking *Chariots of War* here!'

'Right. Yes. It looks very—'

'It's a fucking beast! And you've fucking killed me!'

'I'm sure it is a beast,' said Israel. 'And I'm very sorry. But do you happen to know where I could find Colin Wilson?'

'Yeah!'

'Oh, good.'

'How about up your fucking arse! You fucking idiot!'

'Right. Well, thank you. Thank you very much,' said Israel.

'Fuck off!' said the young man, turning back to the screen.

'Charming!' said Israel, as he walked away.

It took two more taps on the equally unforgiving shoulders of equally charming individuals before Israel managed to track down the person he thought was possibly Colin. He was rocking slightly backwards and forwards in his seat, twirling a biro between the fingers of his left hand. He looked like a cross between a computer nerd and a bodybuilder. With dyed black hair. Israel took a deep breath and tapped again.

The young man swivelled his seat round, much as a computer-game-playing Bond villain might swivel round.

'Hello!' said Israel. 'Colin? Colin Wilson?'

'Yes?'

'I wonder if I might talk to you for a few moments?'

'Are you the police?'

'No. I'm a librarian.'

'Ha!' said Colin.

'What's funny?' said Israel.

'You're joking, are you?'

'No.'

'You're a librarian?'

'Yes. And I'm investigating the disappearance of Lyndsay Morris.'

'I thought you just said you were a librarian?'

'Well, I'm sort of doubling up as a—'

'Detective?'

'Sort of.'

'You're a librarian slash private detective?'

'Yes, I suppose you could—'

'Wicked! Is this some sort of set-up or what?'

'No.'

Colin punched the man sitting at the next terminal on the shoulder.

'Hey!' he said. 'Is this a prank?'

'What?' said the young man.

'Is this a prank?'

'Is what a prank? What are you talking about?'

'This bloke says he's a librarian slash detective.'

'Yeah?'

'Yeah.'

'I don't know anything about it,' said the young man, turning back to his screen.

Israel continued smiling, trying to look suitably like a librarian slash detective.

'So you're for real, are you?' said Colin.

'Yes,' said Israel. 'I am definitely for real. One hundred per cent.'

'I've already spoken to the police,' said Colin.

'Well. I just wondered if I could have a few minutes of your time, it would be a big help to me and might help find Lyndsay.'

Colin looked Israel up and down.

'All right,' he said. 'This is totally random, but.'

'Great. Thank you,' said Israel, as Colin got up. 'Is there somewhere quiet we can talk for a moment?'

'All right,' said Colin. 'But only because you're a

librarian slash detective. You guys are an endangered species.'

'Thanks,' said Israel.

They went out through the main door and then straight out a fire door on to a narrow fire escape.

'Nice,' said Israel.

'It's the smoking terrace,' said Colin. 'Do you smoke?'

'No,' said Israel.

'Me neither,' said Colin. 'I just come here for the views.'

The smoking terrace afforded unenviable views of the back of Tumdrum High Street's various takeaway establishments, and the main car park.

They stood leaning over the fire escape railing.

'So, librarian slash private detective, how can I help you?' said Colin.

'Well, I'm looking for Lyndsay.'

'Why?'

'Well . . .' Israel didn't feel he could say that if he didn't find her his name would be in the *Impartial Recorder*. 'I know you two were . . . close. I just wondered what you thought had happened to her.'

'Like I told the police, I think she's just having a benny.'

'A benny?'

'Yeah.'

'I'm sorry, I'm not sure I quite catch your drift.'

'Catch my drift?' said Colin, mimicking Israel's Estuary accent. 'Are you for real? Where are you from?'

'Not from round here,' said Israel.

'No. I can tell that. She'll be back soon—'

'Right,' said Israel. 'Can I ask – I know it's personal, and please don't feel you have to . . . if you aren't . . . – anyway, you and her, your relationship was . . .'

'It was just caj, you know,' said Colin.

'Casual?'

'Yeah. Like, we were going out, it was OK. It was jokes, ye know.'

'Jokes?'

'Yeah. She was all right, we were into the same music, you know.'

'Goth?'

'No, not just Goth. Grime, dubstep, gabber, crunk, nu-rave.'

'Uh-huh,' said Israel, painfully realising his youth was slipping away from him.

'But in the end, I was, like, CBA.'

'CBA?'

'Can't be arsed?'

'Right, I see.' Israel was feeling older by the minute. 'Can I ask how you got to know each other?'

'I don't know. I think I had a mate who Facebooked her and then, well, you know . . . We'd cotch around at hers.'

'I see.'

'But then she was getting into this whole church thing, man, which is just dry, ye know.'

'Which church thing?'

'The whole house church thing. The happy clappies.'

'The happy clappies?'

'Yeah. It's weird. I was brought up Presbyterian, but I'm much more do what you want, you know.'

'Yes, I think I know,' said Israel.

'Why don't you just Facebook her and ye can find out everything?'

'There's nothing like the personal touch,' said Israel.

'Right,' said Colin. 'When it comes to private investigating.'

'Yeah,' said Israel.

The fire door opened and they were joined by another man who was wearing a white hoodie. His hair had been shaved completely at the back and sides, and the tufty remainder bleached into blondness. It gave him the look of a ferret. He looked Israel up and down as he lit a cigarette.

'Who's this?'

'Librarian,' said Colin.

'Yeah, right.'

'No, he is,' said Colin.

'I am,' agreed Israel.

'Hufter,' said the man. 'What's he want?'

'He's looking for Lyndsay.'

'Is he all right?'

'Yeah. He's a librarian. But he's all right.'

'Thanks,' said Israel.

The man looked at him.

'I'm Rory,' he said.

'Hello, Rory,' said Israel.

'I didn't realise there were librarians any more,' said Rory.

'Well, yes there are.'

'I thought Google had it all sewn up.'

'We're struggling on,' said Israel.

'You want to think about retraining, mate.'

'Yes,' said Israel, wistfully. 'Probably I do.'

'Still no sign of Lynds, then?' said Rory to Colin.

'No.'

'You'd already split up, mate, though, hadn't you?'

'Yeah.'

'What happened?'

'You want the real answer or the answer I gave the police?' said Colin, who seemed momentarily to have forgotten that Israel was there.

'The real answer would be great,' said Israel, chipping in.

'She was fed up with the time I spent editing Wikipedia!' said Colin.

Rory laughed.

'Really?'

'Yeah.'

'You edit Wikipedia?' said Israel.

'Yeah, that's right,' said Colin.

'I've never met anyone who edits Wikipedia before.'

'Well, you've met one now.'

'Gosh. I didn't think . . . Can anyone do it?'

'Doh! That's the whole idea, isn't it?' said Rory.

'Yes, well, I suppose,' said Israel. 'Does it take long?'

'I do about fifty hours a week.'

'Fifty hours a week! Fifty? Or fifteen?'

'Fifty.'

'That's a full-time job.'

'Yeah. I suppose.'

'Do you get paid?'

'Of course you don't get paid.'

'Do you get paid?!' said Rory. 'Doh!'

'Would I be familiar with your work?' asked Israel.

'Would I be familiar with your work?' repeated Rory. 'Fuck's sake! Where d'ye get him, Colin!'

'Yeah,' said Colin, ignoring Rory's provocations. 'I've got a couple of Featured Articles: Saruman you might know.'

'Sorry?'

'From *The Lord of the Rings*?'

'Oh, right. Yes, of course.'

'And a piece about James Thurber.'

'I love James Thurber!' said Israel.

'I'd never heard of him, actually,' said Colin. 'I just like editing them.'

'I'll tell ye what,' said Rory, finishing his cigarette.

'What?' said Israel.

'Libraries are fucking finished, man.'

'Well, I don't know if I'd go that—'

'Who needs a fucking encyclopedia when you can get it all online?'

'Libraries are repositories,' said Israel.

'That's random,' said Colin.

'Yeah,' said Rory. 'Repositories! Doh!'

'Well, gents, anyway, thank you for your assistance.'

'Well, gents,' said Rory, 'thank you for your assistance. Are you some sort of perv, or what, mate? Looking for Lyndsay. You're old enough to be her dad, you know.'

'Well, I'm not, I think I . . .' Israel did the sum in his head. Actually, he was old enough to be her dad. *Technically* old enough to be her father. He thought it was probably time to beat a retreat. 'Thanks again, anyway, gents.'

'Check out that whole church thing,' said Colin, as Israel backed towards the door. 'They are total weirdos. It's like a cult, almost.'

'Right. Will do,' said Israel. 'Thanks.'

'Hufter!' said Rory.

19

That evening, Israel went up to the manse to visit the Reverend Roberts again. The Reverend was working on a sermon.

'Another bloody sermon,' he said, as he brought Israel through to the kitchen, where dozens of thick biblical commentaries were scattered on the table, like discarded bottles after an all-night party.

'Stuck?' said Israel.

'As always,' said the Reverend Roberts.

'Any ideas?'

'Alas, no. Any ideas yourself?'

'For a sermon? Something from the Bible perhaps?' said Israel.

'Ha!' boomed the Reverend, straightening up the books and putting them into a neat pile. 'Very good! You know, sometimes, Israel, I feel like the preacher in that Kierkegaard parable.'

'That Kierkegaard parable . . .' said Israel, attempting

to sound as though he knew what the Reverend Roberts was talking about.

'You know it?'

'Is that the Kierkegaard parable about the . . .'

'The ducks.'

'Ah, yes, the ducks,' said Israel.

'Who go into church every week, and the preacher duck says to them, "You can fly! You can fly!" and then every week the ducks waddle home, and waddle back to church again the following week.'

'Ah,' said Israel.

'Anyway,' said the Reverend Roberts. 'Coffee?'

'I wouldn't say no,' said Israel.

'Good man! Good man!' said the Reverend.

'You're sure I'm not disturbing you?'

'I need a break,' said the Reverend. 'There's only so much biblical Hebrew a man can take in one sitting.'

Having made the coffee the Reverend sat with Israel, the two of them taking up their traditional positions flanking the oven, as though they were sitting around an electric campfire, or a dual-fuel burning bush.

'So?' said the Reverend, leaning back on his chair. 'Social call?'

'Actually,' said Israel, 'I wondered if I could talk to you on a sort of . . . a religious matter.'

'Uh-oh,' said the Reverend Roberts. 'Doctrinal? Or more of a pastoral matter?'

'Erm . . . Not sure. I'm looking for Lyndsay Morris.'

'Ah, yes, the missing girl.'

'That's right.'

'Lovely girl,' said the Reverend Roberts, stroking his chin.

'You know her?'

'Oh, yes. Maurice Morris's daughter? She used to come to the church, actually.'

'Really?'

'Yes. She was a very valued member of the young people's group.'

'She was?'

'Yes, *was*. Past tense. I'm afraid she left.'

'When?' said Israel.

'It was about . . . six months ago. A lot of the young people left then, unfortunately.'

'Why?'

'Why!' The Reverend Roberts laughed. 'To ask the hard question is simple, Israel. It's a long story.' He spooned more sugar into his coffee.

'I've got plenty of time,' said Israel. 'And it might help, as part of the investigation.'

'Investigation?'

'Into Lyndsay's disappearance. I'm sort of . . . trying to find her.'

'Aren't the police trying to find her?'

'Yes, but I'm . . .'

'Helping them out?'

'That's it.'

'Is that wise?' said the Reverend Roberts, pinching his forehead and making a 'that sounds very unwise' sort of a face. 'Given your rather troubled history with Tumdrum's law enforcement officers?'

'Well, it's . . . slightly complicated. I need to . . . Anyway, tell me about Lyndsay.'

'What do you want to know?' said the Reverend Roberts. 'It's not as if I knew her well.'

'Well, erm . . .' Israel's interviewing technique required some work. 'I'm not sure. Anything you think might be relevant.'

'Everything is relevant, Israel, isn't it? It just depends on your perspective. *Sub specie aeternitatis* and all that.'

'Quite,' said Israel, having no idea what *sub specie aeternitatis* might mean, or how to spell it.

'Pen?' said the Reverend Roberts, offering Israel a biro from the table.

'Thanks, but . . .'

'For taking notes, as a part of your investigation?'

'Ah, yes,' said Israel. 'Absolutely. Good idea. You wouldn't have any—'

'Paper?' said the Reverend Roberts, tearing a couple of sheets of A4 from a jotter on the table.

'Super,' said Israel.

'Ready now, Detective?' said the Reverend Roberts.

'Absolutely.'

The Reverend Roberts drained his coffee cup and started to talk.

'About six months ago we suffered a schism in the church.'

'Sounds painful,' said Israel.

'It was,' said the Reverend Roberts, threading his fingers together, as though in prayer.

'S. C.—' began Israel.

'H,' said the Reverend Roberts. 'From the Greek. Meaning disunion. Or division.'

'Right,' said Israel.

'Now, as you doubtless know, Israel, the Protestant Church is of course prone to schism: it's where we're from.'

'Right,' said Israel, whose knowledge of church history rivalled only his knowledge of local, Irish, British, Jewish and in fact almost all other history in his premier league of virtual-know-nothingness. They'd done mostly the Nazis at school.

'It's probably to do with the priesthood of all believers,' said the Reverend Roberts.

'Uh-huh,' agreed Israel, sniffing, faux-knowledgeably.

'1 Peter 2:9.'

'I'll maybe look that up,' said Israel.

'Yes, you do that. Anyway,' said the Reverend Roberts, 'as is traditional with schisms, there was a . . . man in the congregation – and it's always a man, Israel, I'm afraid – I know of no great female schismatics—'

'Too sensible?' said Israel.

'Well, frankly, why would they bother?' said the Reverend Roberts. 'Anyway, this man decided that Tumdrum First Presbyterian was not going in the direction that God intended.'

'Right. And how did he know?'

'Good question,' said the Reverend Roberts. 'Some kind of hotline to Jesus? I don't know. They all have them.'

'Who?'

'Schismatics. Religious fanatics. Fundamentalists. The

274

Good Lord forgot to give me His direct line, alas. We seem to be disconnected.'

'"The number you have dialled has not been recognised",' said Israel.

'Ha!' boomed the Reverend Roberts. 'Exactly! But anyway, however he knew the Lord's intentions, our schismatic, he decided to split off from the church.'

'How do you mean, split off?' said Israel.

'He went and set up his own church.'

'Are you allowed to do that?'

'Of course,' said the Reverend Roberts.

'You don't need permission?'

'No more than you need permission to set up your own hairdressing salon, or a sandwich shop.'

'Right.'

'I mean, obviously he doesn't benefit from the support of the Presbyterian Church,' explained the Reverend Roberts, 'or have access to any of its resources, but if someone thinks they can survive as a minister, and they can draw a congregation, then they're perfectly entitled to set up whatever church they see fit.'

'Like Jesus?' said Israel.

'Yes,' said the Reverend, sounding unconvinced. 'Although you have to remember that Jesus had the obvious advantage of being the Son of God.'

'Arguably,' said Israel.

'Arguably indeed,' said the Reverend Roberts. 'Many people who set up their own churches do seem to fancy themselves rather as the Messiah.'

'Right,' said Israel. 'So . . . What was it the schismatic didn't like about your church?'

The Reverend Roberts looked uncomfortable. He fiddled with his coffee cup.

'Well, I should point out first of all, it's not *my* church as such, Israel: the church is of course the people, the body of believers—'

'Like a synagogue.'

'Well, no,' said the Reverend Roberts. 'Not exactly. A synagogue is a *beit tefilah*.'

'Yeah. Right. Which means?'

'House of prayer?' said the Reverend Roberts.

'You know Hebrew?' said Israel.

'A little,' he said.

'That's more than I know,' said Israel.

'I'm a Christian minister,' said the Reverend Roberts. 'I also know Greek.'

'Wow.'

'It's part of the job. Anyway, a synagogue is also a *beit knesset* – a gathering place. And a *beit midrash*. House of study. The church, on the other hand, is *ekklesia*—'

'Could you spell—'

'It's probably not relevant, actually, Israel, to your investigation. I'm just showing off here really.'

'Ah, right. Yes. So. The man who didn't agree with the rest of the body of believers?'

'Our schismatic, yes. He believed that there had been what's called a "charismatic awakening" in the church.'

'A what?' said Israel.

'A pouring out of the gifts of the Spirit?' said the Reverend Roberts.

'Right.'

'Never heard of it?'

'No.'

'The *charismata*? The nine gifts of the Spirit?'

'No. Sorry,' said Israel. 'No idea what you're talking about. You've got me there.'

'Words of wisdom?' said the Reverend Roberts, hopelessly. Israel shook his head. 'Words of knowledge? Faith? Healing? Miracles? Prophecy?' He was drawing a total blank. 'Anyway. Discernment of spirits. Speaking in tongues. Interpretation of tongues. It's First Corinthians, chapter twelve.'

'Uh-huh,' said Israel. 'That's another one I'll maybe need to—'

'Yes. Take a note. Look it up,' said the Reverend Roberts. 'Yes. It's basically . . . spiritual manifestations.'

'What, like in a Pentecostal church?' said Israel.

'Kind of.'

'Wow.' Israel was genuinely impressed. 'And what, all these things were happening in your church?'

'Not exactly,' said the Reverend Roberts. 'Mr Burns—'

'The schismatic?'

'Him. Yes. Mr Burns claimed that these so-called "gifts" were happening among himself and a few friends, and that I was stifling – I'm quoting here – *stifling* their expression.'

'Oh.'

'More coffee?'

'No, I'm fine,' said Israel. 'So he upped and left?'

'Upped and left,' agreed the Reverend Roberts. 'That about covers it.'

The two men stared outside for a moment at the

black nothingness of the Reverend Roberts's back garden.

'It was my own fault, in a sense,' said the Reverend Roberts, sighing deeply. 'I should have seen it coming.'

'The schism?'

'Yes. I made the mistake of letting the young people's group start to incorporate worship dance and flag-waving into some of the evening services.'

'Sorry?' said Israel. 'Did you say "flag-waving"?'

'Yes. It's often the first step.'

'What is?'

'Flag-waving,' said the Reverend Roberts. 'Sadly.'

'Flag-waving?'

'Flag-waving, yes. Yes. It's to do with David and the linen ephod.'

'The linen what-odd?'

'2 Samuel. Look it up.' The Reverend Roberts waved his hands dismissively. 'Anyway, it could be anything, to be honest, it's just a fashion thing, really. It just so happens that this time around it's flag-waving.'

'The waving of flags?'

'Precisely.'

'In the church?'

'Yes. Big banners, really, and sort of . . . bunting. People dancing with them. A bit like Jewish folk dance.'

'Right. Sounds . . . unusual.'

'Oh no. Not at all. It's become a standard part of the renewal movement within the church. I don't know exactly why. I suppose people want to express themselves creatively. Praise props, I call them, the flags.'

'I'm sure that goes down well.'

'Yes, you can imagine. Anyway, so Mr Burns and the charismatic group within the church exerted a big influence over the young people, and so they broke away and . . . set up on their own.'

'And Lyndsay Morris is one of them?'

'As far as I'm aware, yes.'

'She's part of this whole charismatic thing?'

'So I believe. She had been a regular attender, but she hasn't been for a long time now.'

'She's really into it, though, is she? I mean, she's a Christian and everything?'

'I couldn't possibly say, Israel. We all stand before our God naked and alone. As it were.'

'But I thought she was a Goth?' said Israel.

'The two things are not mutually exclusive.'

'Really? I sort of thought Goths were devil-worshipping sort of . . . people.'

The Reverend Roberts laughed. 'Ha! It's more a fashion thing, isn't it? And who are we to judge fashions? God created us in His likeness, not in your or my image. Genesis 1.'

'Right,' agreed Israel, with a faraway sound to his voice.

'Anyway,' said the Reverend Roberts. 'That's the story of our schism, for what it's worth.'

Israel slurped the remains of his coffee, and glanced at his unreadable scribbled notes.

'Well, that's very helpful, thank you.'

'Is it?' said the Reverend Roberts.

'Yes, absolutely.'

'Good. Well, glad to be of help.'

'Erm. Where do they meet, the charismatic people?'

'They have various meetings. The church is called Kerugma.'

'Kerugma?'

'Yes,' said the Reverend Roberts, disdainfully. 'From the Greek. Meaning proclamation, or proclaimer.'

'Right.'

'The young people attend a group called the Retreat at the community halls. That's tonight, actually.' The Reverend Roberts glanced at his watch. 'Starts in half an hour.'

'Ah. Right. Well, maybe I should . . .'

'Check it out?'

'Exactly.' Israel got up to leave. 'And anyway, I should let you get back to doing your sermon—'

'Bloody sermon,' said the Reverend Roberts, glancing at the accusatory commentaries on the table. 'But just hold on a minute.' He put a heavy hand on Israel's shoulder and pushed him back down into his seat.

'What?'

'You've been here sitting listening to me talk about my troubles—'

'Which was very helpful,' said Israel, brandishing his sheet of A4. 'For my investigation.'

'That may be,' said the Reverend Roberts. 'But tell me, how the devil are you?'

'I'm fine,' said Israel.

'I was worried about you the other evening,' said the Reverend Roberts, leaning back.

'Really, I'm fine.'

'You didn't seem fine, if you don't mind my saying so.'

'Well, it was the . . . shock, I suppose, of Pearce, and . . . Anyway, I'm fine now.'

'Are you sure? I know that grief can be a terrible shock.'

'Yes. Well. I went to see the doctor, actually.'

'You did?' said the Reverend Roberts.

'Yeah. He gave me a prescription for some SSRIs.'

'Really?'

'Yes. They're tablets. Like Prozac, apparently.'

'Yes. I know. Not personally. Pastorally, if you like. And you're going to give them a go?'

'Yeah, I think so,' said Israel. 'I haven't picked up the prescription yet, but I think it might make a difference . . .'

'With what?'

'Well. Just . . . everything, I suppose. You know, that sort of feeling . . .'

'I'm not sure I do know exactly which feeling you're talking about, actually,' said the Reverend Roberts.

'That sort of feeling of not . . . I don't know. Failure, I suppose.'

'Failure?'

'Yes.'

'I see.'

'I feel like I'm a failure.'

'Oh. But doesn't that rather depend on your definition of success, Israel?'

'I don't know. I suppose.'

'So what's success?'

'I don't know. Someone who succeeds at what they're doing. A businessman, or J. K. Rowling, or—'

'It's just money and fame, then, is it?'

'No,' said Israel.

'So you can have a successful social worker, or a window cleaner or a bus driver?'

'Yes. Of course.'

'And what would make them a success?'

'Doing their job well, I suppose. Enjoying it. Making a contribution.'

'And what is there to stop you doing that in your job?'

'I don't know. I just . . . It doesn't feel right. I just feel I don't fit in, I suppose.'

'Mmm.'

'I just feel . . . The milieu here, the—'

The Reverend Roberts laughed again. 'The *milieu*?'

'Yes.'

'You know, Israel, maybe you don't fit in here. Milieu!' He slapped his thighs with mirth.

'What's wrong with milieu?' said Israel.

'Israel! Nobody says *milieu*,' said the Reverend Roberts.

'Well, I do,' said Israel.

'Sorry, sorry,' said the Reverend Roberts, chuckling. 'Seriously. Where do you think you would find your milieu, Israel? Where would you thrive?'

'I don't know.' Israel thought for a moment. 'Vienna in the 1920s? Or Paris. Les Deux Magots?'

'Ah, yes, the old café cultures,' said the Reverend Roberts.

'Conversation and intellectual stimulation,' said Israel.

'There's always Zelda's,' said the Reverend Roberts.

'It's hardly the same.'

'No. But there are cafés down in Belfast now. They're everywhere. Starbucks.'

'Yes, but—'

'I know, I know. I'm joking.'

'It doesn't seem that funny, being stuck here,' said Israel.

'I know what you mean,' said the Reverend Roberts. 'We are rather on the edge of things, I suppose.'

'Exactly.'

'In a funny way that's what makes it attractive, though, isn't it?'

'I don't know about that.'

'Feeling isolated, removed, yearning to connect to the centre? Being here, it's a kind of metaphor, really, isn't it?'

'A metaphor for?'

'I'm not sure,' said the Reverend Roberts. 'Our need for redemption? That desire to resolve that sense of alienation from ourselves which I think we all have, and that derives from our recognition and knowledge of our own destructive impulses?'

'Erm . . .'

'I think living here excites in me that same feeling that religion, or art, or music, or literature raises and simultaneously answers in us, and yet not completely answers . . . Do you know what I mean?'

'I think I do,' said Israel. 'Although I never thought of Tumdrum as a metaphor, I must admit.'

'Well, maybe you should,' said the Reverend Roberts. 'It might help answer some of your sense of—'

'Having sort of lost the thread a bit,' said Israel.

'Yes,' said the Reverend Roberts. 'Yes. And do you think drugs are going to help you pick up the thread, and make you feel like a success?'

'I don't know. Maybe. I just . . . feel like . . . I'm not . . . at home. I don't seem to have found what I'm supposed to be doing with my life.'

'Well, I think we can all identify with that feeling!' said the Reverend Roberts, with a sigh. '*Ardens sed virens.*'

'Sorry?'

'Burning yet flourishing,' said the Reverend Roberts. 'It's the motto of the Presbyterian Church.'

'Right,' said Israel. 'It's different for you, though, isn't it? You have a calling, don't you?'

'It doesn't often feel like it,' said the Reverend Roberts.

'Really? But you're like the preacher to Kierkegaard's ducks, aren't you? The man up the front, telling people they can fly?'

'Mmm. You know, Israel, usually, to be absolutely honest, I feel like one of the duck congregation myself.'

'Oh.'

The two men gazed again outside at the blankness beyond the kitchen windows.

'I think we're all destined to live our lives in darkness, don't you, Israel?'

Israel coughed nervously.

'The Bible promises us that God will divide light from obscurity, yes. But not necessarily in our lifetimes, I think. It's amazing to me, actually, that more people don't . . .'

Israel huffed. The Reverend sighed.

'But! Enough of this sort of talk,' said the Reverend. 'Come on! Onwards! I've got a sermon to write, and you've got a young woman to try and find. Let's not indulge ourselves.'

'Right enough,' said Israel, standing up again.

'If you need any help, let me know,' said the Reverend Roberts, reaching for a commentary.

'Likewise,' said Israel, shaking the Reverend's hand.

'I appreciate that,' said the Reverend Roberts. 'Thank you.' And 'Now,' he continued, to himself, as Israel let himself out, 'Prevenient Grace: where to begin?'

20

The Retreat, as the Reverend Roberts suggested, was indeed held in Tumdrum's community halls, a bizarre, dilapidated warren of buildings just off the town's main square. The halls had metastasised over the years from their original, simple 1930s wooden incarnation into a horribly deformed red-brick and concrete monstrosity, which sprawled lazily and decrepitly across a large area surrounded by brown weeds and broken paving stones. But, of course, like a church, the community halls were more than a mere building; you couldn't really judge Tumdrum community halls on the basis of their looks alone. Which was fortunate, because they really were quite horrid.

A big bright luminescent sign had been erected outside the halls saying 'The Retreat', with another sign in luminescent orange saying 'FREE TRIP TO HEAVEN. DETAILS INSIDE!' alongside it, and there was a loud, forceful, jolly man with a clipboard at the door, the sort of man who in middle age was somehow both fully mature and yet still fully a child, his plump neck and receding hair the perfect complement to his hilarious Hawaiian shirt and character Buddy Holly-style glasses. He was directing young people to different rooms in the halls, with an air of grand and efficient theatricality, as though he were a stage manager and the halls were the backstage dressing rooms for a large and important show. Israel was surprised: at 8 p.m. on a Friday night there were crowds jostling to get in. The range of weekend and night-time recreational activities for young people in Tumdrum was neither alluring nor extensive: the bright lights of Rathkeltair tended to draw the over-eighteens for dancing and drinking, which left the town to the younger teens to do what they wished, and what they wished was what other teens wished on Friday nights in small towns all around the world, which was to hang around on street corners, smoking, drinking and shouting at one another, and at passers-by. But when they got bored, or cold, or they wanted someone new to annoy or to intimidate, or they just had the urge to play table tennis or pool on slightly broken-down pool and table-tennis tables, the Retreat was there for them.

'OK,' the clipboard man was saying to the crowds of people pushing through the doors, manically high-fiving whoever he could as they passed. 'Good to see you! Good to see you! Hi! Hi! Hi! High-five! OK, people,' he yelled, 'you know the score. It's table tennis through to the left, sock hockey in the main hall, refreshments in the dining room, prayer room next to the toilets.' He caught his breath and then yelled over the heads of the crowd to address a gang of even-more-disenfranchised-than-most Tumdrum young people standing across the other side of the street, who were shouting the traditional abuse at those going into the club. 'Hey! Hey! Come on over,' he said, waving them across. 'Come in. Come on. You might like it! Table tennis! Pool! Sock hockey. Come on! Check it out!'

'Loser,' shouted one young man across the road.

'Double loser,' added another.

The man with the clipboard smiled beatifically – like a saint. Or Ned Flanders, thought Israel.

'Hi! Hi! Hi! High-five!' came his repeated greeting as young people flocked through the doors.

Israel stood skulking until the rush and the high-fives had died down and then he wandered over.

'Hi!' he said.

'I'm sorry,' said the clipboard man. 'The Retreat's for under-eighteens only. But if you're in need of a bed for the night—'

'Ha!' said Israel. 'Very funny.' By the look on the man's face Israel realised he wasn't joking: he really thought he was homeless. 'No. No. I'm not . . . homeless or anything.'

'Oh, apologies,' said the man. 'I thought maybe you were . . .'

'No, no,' said Israel, tugging at his beard. Maybe he needed to shave.

'And you're not here for the youth club?'

'No.'

'Ah. OK. Well, hi anyway. I'm Adam. Adam Burns.'

'Hello,' said Israel, shaking his proffered hand. So this, he was thinking, is what a schismatic looks like: a Club 18–30 holiday rep.

'And you are?' said Adam.

'Sorry. Israel. Armstrong. I was wondering if I could have a word with you, actually?'

'Now?' said Adam Burns.

'If possible, that would be great.'

'Well. That might be difficult, actually. It's Retreat night, you see.'

'Yes, I understand. I just wanted to talk to you about Lyndsay Morris.'

'Ah. Terrible,' said Adam Burns, shaking his head. 'We're all so worried about her.' He looked Israel up and down. 'Look. Just give me a few minutes, and I'll see what I can do?'

'I'd appreciate that, thank you,' said Israel.

Israel hung around inside the entrance to the halls, where young people were milling around aimlessly, and where it was possible to hear loud music playing from one room, people singing along to a song that seemed to consist simply of the words 'Our God Reigns' repeated again and again, and again, and again.

Adam had disappeared and then came back a few minutes later, clipboardless, his smile intact.

'Do you want to come into the prayer room?' he asked, touching Israel on the arm.

'Yeah. That'd be great,' said Israel. He'd never really liked men who touched him on the arm.

The room was empty, and clearly used as a nursery or a creche the rest of the time: there were terrible finger paintings and laminated posters with the alphabet and numbers. Adam and Israel squatted down on a couple of miniature plastic chairs.

'So, Israel?' said Adam Burns. 'Unusual name.'

'I suppose,' said Israel.

'You're Jewish?'

'No. I'm a Hindu.'

'Really?'

'No. No. I'm joking.'

'Oh,' said Adam Burns, who despite his hilarious Hawaiian shirt was clearly not a man who was easily amused. 'How can I help you?'

'Well, I wanted to ask you about Lyndsay Morris.'

'Yes. We're all so terribly worried about her. Are you a friend or a family member?'

'No. I'm not actually. I'm a . . . librarian.'

'OK,' said Adam Burns, looking momentarily confused: the old 'l' word again.

'And we are . . . helping to coordinate the police search?' suggested Israel.

'Oh, really?'

'Yes.'

'Right.' Adam – perhaps because he was a good Christian – seemed to take Israel's claim at face value.

'Is it right that she would come here?' said Israel, seizing the advantage of Adam's obvious credulity.

'Yes. Yes. She did.'

'And she came here often?'

'Yes.'

'Did you know her well?'

'I think you could say that, Israel, yes. I'm privileged

to say that I was one of those present when she gave her life to Christ.' Adam smiled the kind of inward smile that expressed itself outwardly as a smirk. 'Sorry. I should have offered: can I get you a cup of tea?'

'No thanks. Erm. You say she gave her life to Christ?'

'Yes.'

'Erm. You mean she became a Christian?'

'Absolutely, Israel, that's right.'

'When was that?'

'That was maybe just a few months ago.'

'But she was a Goth as well?'

'Yes. I think that's right. But the Bible teaches us, Israel, that Jesus died for *all* our sins.'

'Right.'

'His work of atonement was for all, whoever we are.'

'Even Goths,' said Israel.

'Absolutely,' said Adam Burns. 'And Muslims, and Jews, and prostitutes, and sinners of every kind.'

Israel felt a little uncomfortable being lumped together with the world's outcasts.

'We believe in one body of Christ,' continued Adam Burns.

'Uh-huh,' said Israel. 'Really? What about the . . . I mean, I hope you don't mind if I ask about the . . . split with Tumdrum First Presbyterian?'

Adam Burns looked sharply at Israel, as though someone had mentioned Supralapsarianism.

'Why are you asking?'

'Just. I'm . . . interested. I must have read about it in the . . . *Impartial Recorder*?'

'Well, it was really a doctrinal matter,' said Adam Burns.

'Right,' said Israel. 'And what doctrine exactly was it that you disagreed about?'

'You're a theologian?'

'No, just . . . an interested layman.'

Adam sat up straight, put his shoulders back, and looked Israel in the eye, as though delivering a lecture, or a reprimand. 'Well, first of all, the Presbyterian Church in Ireland has become home to a number of unscriptural practices and traditions, and at Tumdrum's First Presbyterian Church in particular—'

'The Reverend Roberts's church?'

'That's right. And under the—' And here Adam Burns coughed, as though pausing nervously in confession. '—guidance of the Reverend Roberts, Tumdrum Presbyterian has been teaching a kind of liberal humanism in the guise of the Gospel, which I as a Christian would have to reject.'

'Right.'

'The Reverend Roberts, I'm afraid—' And he coughed again, and looked away from Israel. '—I would have to say is a false teacher.'

'A false teacher.'

'That's correct. The Reverend Roberts has replaced the true Gospel with something more commercially acceptable to—'

'*Commercially acceptable?*' said Israel, unable to work out what on earth was commercially acceptable about the Reverend Roberts.

'Yes. Something that sells more easily to people. Jesus said, "I am the Way, the Truth and the Life, there is no way to the Father except through me."'

'Right.'

'And I'm afraid I don't hear that simple, plain Gospel message being preached by the Reverend Roberts.'

'So you think he's too . . . lenient?'

'Well, that's certainly a layman's way of expressing it, yes.'

Israel laughed. 'I'm definitely a layman.'

'Can I ask if you've read the New Testament, Israel?'

'Not often,' said Israel. 'No.'

'And have you ever considered your future, Israel?'

'Well, again, no, alas, not often,' said Israel. He thought about that brownstone in New York, his true home and his future, which had maybe a little balustrade out front, and he thought about breakfast with Paul Auster, and lunch with Philip Roth, and cocktails with friends from the *New Yorker*, and returning home late at night to listen to the sound of John Coltrane playing 'A Love Supreme'. The utterly complete, beautiful, urban bourgeois solidity of his unfulfillable fantasy life . . .

'You are aware we are living in the End Times?' Adam was saying.

'Are we?' said Israel.

'Look around you,' said Adam.

Israel glanced around the room.

'Erm . . .'

'Not just in Tumdrum. Around the world. Economic catastrophes. Natural disasters. Tsunamis,' said Adam. 'Hurricane Katrina. Hurricane Wilma.'

'Ah, right, I see what you mean.'

'Disease,' continued Adam. 'Famine. Strife. War.'

'Yes,' agreed Israel. But Adam wasn't listening: he was preaching. He'd got into a rhythm. He was even rocking slightly on his seat.

'Just take the weather. Swollen rivers. Devastating floods. Southern China, northern India, Pakistan, Bangladesh. In Europe, Israel, last year, people died from the extreme heat – and this was in Europe, mind.'

'Right.'

'Drought and wildfires.'

'Well, you're certainly painting a picture of—'

'It's not my picture I'm painting, Israel. It's the Book of Revelation. The consequences of man's rebellion against God.'

'Erm . . .'

'Look at the Middle East, Israel. Israel, Israel. The war against terror. Bird flu. SARS. Soaring crime. I believe we are witnessing the beginning of the outpouring of the bowls of wrath, Israel.'

'Doesn't sound good, certainly,' said Israel.

'When you look in the papers, Israel, isn't all you see photos of people drinking and cavorting and in states of undress? Celebrities? Low-lifes?'

'Erm. I'm not sure about the paper thing, actually. Doesn't it depend rather which . . .'

'The angels are pouring out God's wrath.'

'Uh-huh,' said Israel, nervously.

And then Adam Burns broke off suddenly from his litany of wrath and woes, as though awakening from a trance.

'You say you're a librarian?'

'Yes.'

'Can I ask, does the library stock the *Left Behind* series?'

'I don't think so,' said Israel. 'I can always run a check for you.'

'My sense is,' said Adam, 'that the forces of the secular state don't want that kind of literature in the libraries.'

'Well, I'd hardly regard myself as an agent of the secular state. We have a very open policy on what's admitted,' said Israel.

'Really?'

'Yes.'

'Mmm,' said Adam, unconvinced.

Israel felt that the conversation had perhaps drifted away from where he wanted it to be going. He shifted in his tiny seat.

'Sorry. Just to get back to Lyndsay Morris.'

'Ah, yes, of course.'

'When was the last time she was at the club here?'

'It would be about a month or so ago, I think.'

'OK. And can you think of any reason why she hasn't been back since?'

'I'm afraid I had to ask her to leave the Retreat.' Adam did his cough.

'Right. Why?'

'She was becoming rather . . . a problem.'

'Really?'

'It was a question of behaviour.'

'Oh dear. What sort of behaviour?'

'I'm afraid Lyndsay was self-harming,' said Adam Burns.

'What?'

'She was cutting her arms with a razor blade.'

'Oh dear.'

'It's not uncommon, actually, among the young people we work with, Israel. More girls than boys.'

'Why was she self-harming?'

'Personally, I think it was something to do with home.'

'Really?'

'Yes.'

'How do you know?'

'Well, I believe, Israel, that I have what the Bible calls the gift of knowledge.'

'The gift of knowledge?'

'Yes. One of the gifts of the Spirit.'

'1 Corinthians 12?' said Israel.

'Yes,' agreed Adam Burns, rather surprised. 'That's right. And I felt I had to ask her to leave.'

'Why? Shouldn't you be—'

'It's complicated, Israel. Lyndsay had become a part of our church group—'

'Kerugma?'

'That's right. So she wasn't just coming on Friday nights. She had become part of our fellowship. And when someone . . . breaks covenant with us within the fellowship we feel we have no choice but to defellowship them.'

'Defellowship?'

'That's correct.'

'Sorry, I still don't quite understand how a young girl who is self-harming would be breaking—'

'Let me put it this way, Israel. We believe that Jesus

shed His blood in our place, and that His was the perfect sacrifice. And so in self-harming we believe the young person is denying this once only act of atonement. Do you see?'

Israel nodded sceptically.

'So,' continued Adam Burns, 'persisting in this sort of behaviour, we believe, is behaving in many ways like the priests of the Old Testament, who continually offered sacrifices which could in no way atone for their sins.'

'Right,' said Israel, feeling increasingly uncomfortable with Adam Burns's logic.

'Which is wrong. It's a sin.'

'OK.'

'Jesus wants to transform us, Israel. He wants to make us into His likeness. And if we resist that, and continue to set our face against the Lord's will for our lives, then I'm afraid it's difficult for us to share fellowship with such a person.'

Israel smiled, falsely.

'The aim of Kerugma is not merely to proclaim the Gospel but also to offer to one another mutual encouragement and edification in Christ. 2 Thessalonians 2:15.'

'Uh-huh.'

'Where the churches are instructed to "stand firm and hold to the traditions which you were taught, whether by word of mouth or by letter from us".'

'Yeah.'

'So, if we believers are part of the body of Christ, shouldn't we be unified, as His one bride?'

'Erm . . .' said Israel, his voice strained and high. 'So, basically, when you found out she was self-harming—'

'Persisting in self-harming.'
'Right. You then asked her to leave?'
'Yes.'

After thanking Adam Burns for his time, Israel left the community halls as quickly as possible. As he hurried down the street he remembered something his mother would sometimes say to him. 'All Christians,' she would say, 'are crazy.' He'd never quite understood what she meant.

He'd never been so glad to see teenagers hanging around on street corners drinking, and smoking, and shouting abuse.

21

Israel rang Veronica.

'Hi.'

'Who's this?'

'It's Israel.'

'Oh, right. So, shoot.'

'What?'

'How are you getting on, Israel?'

'Fine.'

'What have you got?'

'I went to the Venice Fish Bar.'

'And?'

'I spoke to some people there.'

'Yes. And?'

'They thought Lyndsay was close to the owner.'

'Gerry Blair?'

'Yes.'

'No!'

'Yeah.'

'He's married.'

'I know.'

'So how close is she?'

'They didn't say.'

'God, well. That's brilliant. We're talking tabloid there.'

'Are we?'

'Absolutely! And what else?'

'I also spoke to her ex-boyfriend.'

'Who?'

'He's called Colin. He spends all his time editing Wikipedia and playing computer games.'

'Computer nerd?'

'He was quite nice, actually.'

'Boring. God, I hope it's Gerry Blair.'

'Anyway, he put me on to this guy who runs a sort of Christian youth group thing that Lyndsay used to attend.'

'Uh-huh.'

'And he thinks there were maybe problems at home.'

'What sort of problems?'

'He didn't say.'

'Your interviewing skills are not that great, Armstrong, d'ye know that? You have to ask the supplementary.'

'The what?'

'Never mind.'

'Anyway, how did you get on with Maurice?'

'Fine, yeah. He's quite dishy, actually.'

'*Dishy?*'

'Yeah.'

'Anything to go on?'

'Not yet, no.'

'So what do we do next?'

'I think I need to follow up some of the leads we've established.'

'We?'

'Yeah. I'll get on to the Gerry Blair angle, and the computer nerd boyfriend – what was he called?'

'Colin.'

'Him, yeah.'

'Can't I follow them up?'

'That's very sweet of you, but I don't think you have the necessary skills, Israel. You're more use to us out on the street.'

'Out on the street.'

'Yeah. I think you need to speak to Mrs Morris, without Maurice there. See what she has to say about it all.'

'Can't you talk to her?'

'D'ye want me to do all the work, Israel?'

'No.'

'Look, Maurice is going to be busy with last-minute door-to-doors and what have you. I'll keep an eye on him and I'll start on Gerry Blair as well. If you go and see Mrs Morris—'

'What should I say?'

'Just tell her . . . I don't know. Tell her you're a librarian. That usually works, doesn't it?'

'Yes. But—'

'OK, Israel, sorry, got to go, thanks. Bye.'

* * *

Which is how Israel ended up the next morning, ringing the doorbell at Maurice Morris's luxuriously appointed home, where there didn't seem to be anyone in, and then wandering around the back of the house, towards the sea – where waves lapped up against the shore – and peering in through the windows of one of the many restored outbuildings, the old grain store, where he saw a woman lying on a sunlounger, smoking, wearing sunglasses, and which is how he ended up tapping on the window, and putting his head round the door, allowing a little rush of wind into the room, and saying:

'Hello? Mrs Morris?'

'Hi,' said Mrs Morris, raising her sunglasses momentarily, as if she were expecting him. She squinted. The room – which was an enormous, exquisite jumble of paints and canvases, and sofas, and easels, and which seemed simultaneously both bare and plush – was filled with harsh natural light.

Mrs Morris remained one of Maurice's greatest assets, not least because she herself happened to be one of the best-looking women in Northern Ireland, or at least one of the best-looking women over fifty-five in Northern Ireland, and certainly the best-looking woman over fifty-five who was a politician's wife in Northern Ireland, where there was a surprising amount of competition, politician-wife-wise; in Northern Ireland ambitious men still preferred to marry women who would look good and keep home for them; the career woman was only just emerging.

This morning, Mrs Morris was wearing a white, paint-splattered shirt. Her dark, shoulder-length hair was tucked behind her ears and her fingernails were painted a purply red, like bruises at her fingertips. Israel noticed that she was probably wearing perfume – he'd almost forgotten what it smelt like, perfume – and in his excitement a terrible shiver ran through him, like ripples of shot silk, or fingers through water. She didn't bother getting up.

'Sorry, am I disturbing you?' said Israel.

Mrs Morris flipped her sunglasses back down.

'Not at all.'

'Are you . . . painting?' asked Israel, looking around at the empty canvases, and the shelves lined with paint.

'Preparing to paint,' said Mrs Morris, continuing to smoke.

'Right.'

'As I have been for almost twenty years.'

'Lovely music,' said Israel. The music seemed to be being piped in from recessed speakers around the room.

'Sigur Rós,' said Mrs Morris.

'I've not heard of him.'

'It's a *them*,' said Mrs Morris. 'A beat combo. From Iceland. With an accent.'

'It's very nice music.'

'The title is a parenthesis.'

'Sorry?'

'The title of this piece of music is a parenthesis. It has no title.'

'Right. Well, it's a very nice studio you have here,' said Israel.

'Isn't it,' agreed Mrs Morris.

'Wonderful views.'

'Yes. The full gamut,' agreed Mrs Morris. 'Summer, autumn, winter and spring.'

She drew contemplatively on her cigarette, as though trying to overcome some terrible deep discomfort.

'You're an artist, then?' said Israel.

'I was going to be an artist,' she said. 'But I wasn't allowed to go to college. I had to go to work.'

'Right.'

'Cheltenham, I would have gone to,' said Mrs Morris. 'If I'd had the chance.'

'You could still go to art college,' said Israel.

'Ha!' said Mrs Morris. 'Perhaps you don't quite understand what art college is all about.'

'Perhaps not.'

'Practical anatomy,' said Mrs Morris.

'Sorry?'

'Sex and drugs and rock and roll.'

'Right.'

'Although you're not supposed to talk about that, obviously. If you're a politician's wife.'

'No. I guess that would be—'

'I used to go to dances at the art college in Belfast.'

'Sounds like fun.'

'It was. Tea, we used to call it,' she said. 'Would you like to try some tea?'

'No, thanks,' said Israel.

'That's what we used to say, if there was any weed or hash.'

'Oh, right. Yes.'

'And then when I was eighteen I hitch-hiked down

to Cork with my boyfriend from the art college. And we took the ferry to France and my boyfriend, he imported forty kilos of kif from Morocco. Made a fortune. Went back a few months later to try and do a similar deal, was thrown in jail in Tunisia.'

'God.'

'Six months later I met Morris.'

'Right.'

'And the rest, as they say, is history.'

'Right.'

Mrs Morris sat up slightly on the sunlounger, as though awaking from a dream.

'Anyway, how can I help you, young man?'

'Sorry. I should have introduced myself. My name's Israel Armstrong.'

'And you are?'

'A librarian.'

'*The* librarian?'

'Well, in Tumdrum, yes.'

'The mobile librarian?'

'Yes.'

Israel expected the usual wary response.

'Well, well,' said Mrs Morris, raising her sunglasses again. Her blue eyes bored into him. 'I've heard a lot about you.'

'Really?'

'Oh yes. Maurice doesn't like you at all.'

'Right.'

'He thinks you're a corrupting influence.'

'I see.'

'Like Mellors.'

'Well . . .'

'In *Lady Chatterley's Lover*?'

'Yes, I know . . .'

'So, Mellors, how can I help you?'

Israel felt a little uncomfortable about the tone of the conversation. He could hear the incoming waves outside smashing up against the shore.

'I was just . . . I'm interested in helping find your daughter.'

'Are you now? And why is that, Mellors?'

'I'd rather you called me Israel, actually.'

'Would you, Israel?'

'Yes, please.'

'Well, I'm going to call you Mellors anyway.'

'Right.'

'Until you tell me what your interest in my daughter is.'

'The police seem to be under the impression that my lending her books from the Unshelved in the library may have influenced her decision to run away.'

'I see. Like *The Catcher in the Rye* and the man who shot John Lennon?'

'That sort of a thing, yes. So I'm rather interested in finding out where she is.'

'I see.'

'You seem remarkably relaxed, erm, Mrs Morris, for someone whose daughter has gone missing, if you don't mind me saying so.'

'I'm rather delighted she's gone, to be honest,' said Mrs Morris.

'Really?'

'It's an adventure, isn't it? What chance for escape and adventure does she have, living here?'

'Why would she want to get away from here?'

Mrs Morris laughed.

'You're not from round here, are you, Mr Armstrong?'

'No, I'm not. I'm from London.'

'Well, then, why do you think she'd want to get away from here?'

'Erm . . .'

'Or are you one of these people who thinks this is a great wee country and won't have a word said against it?'

'No, I . . .'

'I have a sister in Dubai. She's not been back here for twenty years, and I can't say I blame her.'

'So you think Lyndsay's just run off on an adventure?'

'Seems most likely, doesn't it? Why? Do you have a theory, Mellors?'

'No. I . . .'

'If I was her I'd run away.'

'Really?'

'Yes.'

'And where would you go?'

'Me? Marrakesh, of course!' Mrs Morris laughed a deep, throaty laugh that echoed the sound of the waves. 'Although we also have a little place down in the Mournes, Slievenaman. We used to go there sometimes when Lyndsay was little.'

'Slievenaman?'

'That's right. Wonderful quality of light. She's probably

in London, though, isn't she? I hope so. Experiencing the world. That's what life's about, isn't it, Mellors?'

'Yes.'

'Seizing an opportunity when it presents itself to you?'

'Yes, I'm sure.'

'Perhaps you'd like to join me for some coffee – or some tea? – before you go?'

'Actually, no . . . I . . . should be getting on.'

'Of course,' said Mrs Morris, sinking back into her sunlounger. 'You run along there.'

'Well, thanks.'

Mrs Morris did not reply. She seemed lost again to the light, and the sound of the waves.

And Israel, if he wasn't mistaken, had a lead.

22

Ted agreed to drive down to the Mournes with Israel as long as they could listen to an audiobook in the van.

'An accompaniment to another wild-goose chase,' he said.

Israel had been an audiobook virgin before arriving in Tumdrum, a Gentile; by now he was thoroughly deflowered, his ears circumcised. In the past few weeks alone they'd worked their way, exhaustingly, through Lance Armstrong's *It's Not about the Bike* (a book that rather contradicted its title, in Israel's opinion), plus an unidentifiable Ian Rankin (Nazi war criminal, Chechen people smuggler, Japanese gangster; or was it Japanese war criminal, Nazi people smuggler, Chechen gangster; or . . .), Sebastian Faulks's *Birdsong* (again), and one of the ones about the African lady detective who was so smart, so wise, so gentle and so patient that she made Nelson Mandela look bad. Today, they were spending the journey down to the

Mournes in the company of the ever-fruity Stephen Fry reading from *Harry Potter and the Philosopher's Stone* – an audiobook classic, according to Ted. Ted had worked his way through all the Harry Potter audiobooks; they were his absolute favourites. Sometimes, if young people were causing trouble on the van, he would point at them and shout 'Expelliarmus!' and the young people would quake and Ted would bellow with laughter. Israel had tried the technique himself, but it didn't seem to work for him in quite the same way. Ted somehow had the necessary . . . oomph to carry it off, while Israel rather lacked oomph: when he said 'Expelliarmus' to the gathered Goths, casuals, emos and wannabe rap artistes who plagued him on the van, *they* laughed at *him*, which was the opposite of what was supposed to happen. He did not therefore share Ted's enthusiasm for Stephen Fry's celebrated readings of J. K. Rowling's celebrated tales of public school wizardry and japes, but since no publisher had yet seen fit to produce an audiobook of *Infinite Jest*, or of any Donald Barthelme, he seemed to be stuck with it. Then again, at least Harry Potter wasn't Allen Carr, whose *Easy Way to Stop Smoking* Ted had inflicted upon Israel several times since his arrival in Tumdrum, despite its obvious flaw: Ted had not given up smoking as a result of listening to Mr Carr's billion-selling audiobook, and Israel had seriously considered taking it up, out of sheer spite.

Today, though, by the time they had reached the Sandyknowes roundabout, just outside Belfast, Stephen Fry had got to one of those long boring Potter passages in which inexplicable parts of the plot had to be explained in excruciating detail by characters with no other apparent role or function, and Israel had cracked and had lunged for the tape in frustration, but Ted had swatted him away, so there he was, condemned to another interminable journey listening to a story about a scarred, bespectacled orphan trying to find his way in the world, and what was the use or appeal of that?

It was the last day of his twenties. And this was not what was supposed to happen.

Israel wound down the window of the van, to try to drown out the sound of some guff about dragon's eggs, and to savour the crisp air of an Irish autumn. Floral tributes to car crash victims flashed by them, and blue plastic bags lined the roadside, like ornamental flags in the whin bushes. They had long since left behind the Glens of Antrim, with its home-made signs promising 'Dulse and Potatoe's, 100 Yards' and were now deep into the long soul-destroying stretches of the A24 where all that was on offer were intermittent bar snacks and novelty ornamental concrete products.

Just outside Ballynahinch, Ted abruptly pulled the van over into a pub car park.

'I'm hefted,' he said, unbuckling his seat belt and clambering out.

'What?'

'I'm away for the toilet here.'

'Right,' said Israel, stretching, uncomfortably; the library wasn't really built for distance.

'Might be a while,' said Ted.

'Fine, take your time,' said Israel. 'No hurry.'

'Been holding on since Carryduff.'

'Right.'

Ted patted the van affectionately.

'Gives ye a quiver in the liver, doesn't she?'

'Yep. Too much information, thanks, Ted. You go ahead and treat yourself. Bye. Bye!'

The pub they'd stopped at was called the International, and looked anything but. It was an old cottage which had long since been pebble-dashed and had its old wooden windows replaced by uPVC, and its garden turned into the car park. A sign boasted of 'Live Big Screen Sport', and the inevitable alcopop 'Happy Hours', and a range of bar snacks that called themselves, unpromisingly, 'Belt-Busters' and 'Monster-Bites'. Along its road-facing gable wall a crude mural had been painted, depicting an Ulster fry: bacon, potato farls, soda bread, and a very large-yolked fried egg. The detailing on the bacon was reminiscent of a Lucian Freud: quease-making man-size marbled fat. But the place did have one saving grace – a good old-fashioned red telephone box by its front door. Israel hadn't seen an old red phone box in years: it was like seeing an old friend. When he was young back home in north London he would often slip out of the house in the evenings to make calls from a filthy old red phone box to his first girlfriend, who was called Leah. He'd spend hours on the phone to Leah, breathing in the smell of rusting metal, and urine, and other people's stale cigarette smoke, and kicking restlessly at the takeaway cartons at his feet, hardly saying anything, gazing up at the moon, and space, and the innumerable prostitutes' cards, and his own fantasies, while angry dog-walkers and fellow students, and immigrants, and men in overcoats would tap impatiently on the window, willing him to finish. He had happy, happy memories of the old red telephone box.

He wandered over, pulled open the heavy door and picked up the phone. He'd forgotten how heavy the handsets were, and how cold, and grey. But, miraculously, to his surprise, there was a dial tone: the phone was working.

He jangled the change in his pocket, just as he would when he was fifteen, and desperate to talk to Leah, and he wondered for a moment who he might possibly ring. Just for old times' sake.

He could ring Leah, of course, but he'd no idea what had become of her. She'd gone to university and that was that. Had disappeared, in the way that people do. She was probably married by now. Career. Children. All the things that Israel had somehow failed to achieve. He feared it might be a rather one-sided conversation. A near-thirty-year-old man couldn't really go around ringing up ex-girlfriends: it was weird. Leah existed now only in his mind. For a moment he thought he could smell her revolting, come-hitherish pineapple lip-gloss.

There was always Gloria, of course. He could ring Gloria.

No need.

He found these days he only thought about Gloria once or twice a day.

Or, actually, maybe six or seven times.

Or a dozen.

In fact, he thought about Gloria all the time, even though they hadn't actually spoken since he'd left London with Ted, months ago. When he'd arrived safely back in Ireland she'd sent him a single, solitary text which read 'Sorry. Plse do not get in touch. Hope you understand'. He didn't, and he'd tried ringing hundreds of times, but she was obviously screening his calls and never picked up. He'd tried writing letters. 'Dear Gloria,' he would begin. 'I am writing to you to . . .' but that was no good. It sounded as if he was writing to a solicitor asking about a point of probate. And 'Dear Gloria, So?' Or 'Dear Gloria, Why?' He just couldn't find the words. She had struck him dumb.

He definitely wasn't going to ring Gloria.

He rang the number.

And before he knew what was happening someone had picked up, and Israel was frantically pushing money into the slot and saying, breathlessly, 'Hello, Gloria?'

'No,' said a man's voice.

'Oh.' He couldn't quite place the voice. 'Who's that?'

'Can I help you?'

'Yes. Can I speak to Gloria, please?'

The voice said, witheringly, 'Who's calling?'

'My name's Israel. I'm a . . . friend of Gloria's.'

Israel detected a slight pause, and the voice said, 'I'll just check if she's here.'

He could hear voices in the background.

He stared deeply into the plexiglas of the phone

box, and thought about Gloria in the flat – *their* flat
– and the mystery of this man's voice. He had no
idea . . . And then suddenly he did have an idea. He
recognised the voice. It wasn't anything he'd said;
they'd only spoken for a moment. It was the
intonation, the smart-arse, sing-songing, pleading,
wheedling intonation of a Bill Clinton, or a Tony
Blair, or Bing bloody Crosby crooning his way carefully up and down and between the scales. It was
Danny, his old friend from school. Danny! Danny
the lecturer. Danny the author of the book *Postmodern
Allegories*. Danny, a complete fraud, and a show-off,
and an arrogant, selfish shit who thought Foucault
was a major twentieth-century thinker . . . Danny,
who was . . . what? Visiting?

Israel slammed the phone down and walked back to
the van, leaned up against the front of it, took a deep
breath, hung his head and gave out a long low moan
of 'No!'

At which point, Ted sauntered back from the toilet.

'Need the toilet?' said Ted.

'No,' said Israel, breathing deeply.

'Ye sure?'

'Yes, thank you.'

'All right, then, ye set?'

Israel was staring down at his broken-down brogues,
his head resting against the cool flank of the mobile
library.

'Hello?' said Ted. 'Wakey wakey! Time to go?'

'Sorry,' said Israel. 'What did you say?'

'Have you taken the strunt, or what?'

315

'Taken the—'

'Strunt, for goodness' sake. Somebody said something that's upset ye?'

'No. I'm fine. I just feel a bit . . . queasy, that's all.'

'Aye, well, whatever it is, ye'll get over it.'

'I don't know if I will, actually.'

'Aye, right. Heard it all before. Let's get on. I want to be back home for my tea tonight, and I've choir practice later.'

'Right.'

Ted walked round to the passenger side of the van.

'What are you doing?' said Israel. 'Where are you going?'

'You're driving, remember?' said Ted.

'What?'

'Half and half is what we agreed.'

'Yes, but—'

'And I've already done more than my share.'

'Actually, Ted, I'm feeling a little bit . . .'

'Aye, right,' said Ted, walking back beside Israel, shaking his head. 'I might have known. Always the blinkin' same with you, isn't it, eh?'

'No.'

'Aye. Ye shirker.'

'I am not a shirker.'

'Could have fooled me,' said Ted.

'I don't mind driving,' said Israel, becoming agitated.

'Aye, right.'

'No, really, it's fine, I'll—'

'I'll drive,' said Ted, walking round the other side of the van, towards the driver's side.

'No, I'll drive,' said Israel, catching up with him.

'I said, I'll drive!' said Ted.

'I don't—'

'Shut up and go and sit down,' said Ted. 'And stop mucking me about. Ye give me the jandies, so you do.'

'The whatties?'

'Ach!'

Israel went and sat miserably in the passenger seat while Ted got back into the driver's seat.

'Sorry,' said Israel, 'I just—'

'I don't want your apologies,' said Ted, starting up the engine, and slamming the van into reverse. 'I don't know . . . What's the point of having a dog and barking yerself? Eh?'

'What?'

'Nothing. It's a saying, just.'

'Right, well, I—'

'One of yer headaches, is it?' said Ted, without sounding in any way sympathetic.

'No, it's . . .'

'Ye'd only be deedlin' along at ten miles an hour, anyway.'

'Deedling?' said Israel.

'That's right,' said Ted, flooring the accelerator as he pulled back out on to the main road.

'Is that a word?'

'Of course it's a word. I just said it, didn't I?'

'Is it a proper word, though?' said Israel.

'What do you think?'

'Well, I don't know. I've just never heard it before. It's like "jandies", and —'

'What, ye've heard every word in the English language, have ye, Professor?'

'No, not—'

'All fifty billion of them?'

'I don't think there's fifty billion words in the English language—' began Israel, as they began to pick up speed past the outlying areas of Ballynahinch.

'Aye, well,' said Ted. 'However many, deedlin's one of them.'

'Right,' agreed Israel.

'And jandies.'

'Sure. And what would be the opposite of deedling?'

'The opposite of deedlin'?' said Ted, as if no one had ever asked a more stupid question. 'Going a dinger.'

'You're making all these words up, aren't you?' said Israel.

Ted's response was to press play on the cassette recorder.

'Expelliarmus!' he bellowed, and then Stephen Fry resumed reading.

They drove in silence the rest of the way down and into the Mournes, Israel spending most of the journey with his eyes half closed, hoping it might somehow lessen the impact of his discovery of Gloria's betrayal, as you might try and lessen the impact of a horror film by watching it through your fingers. It didn't work. Scenes played before his mind, in appalling Technicolor: Gloria and Danny in flagrante, the whole thing in close-up, in detail, and in its entirety, as if he were in the clutch of some perverse mania or delirium, or in that film by Michael Winterbottom that he and Gloria had

gone to see in the Coronet in Notting Hill. How had
he not realised? Was he stupid? Had he missed something? Some intimation of this . . . outrage, this . . .
betrayal, this . . . inevitability.

As they drove farther into the mountains the roads
became narrower, and the bends sharper, and Israel's
anxieties rose as Ted's driving style became correspondingly more relaxed. As they lurched round one corner,
the van leaning dangerously to the left, Israel broke
off from the explicit screenings in his mind and sat up
with a start.

Ted, as usual, was driving with his knees.

'Can you stop driving with your knees?!'

'I am not driving with my knees,' said Ted, casually.

'Yes, you are.'

'I am driving with my thighs,' said Ted.

'Well, can you stop!'

'What, the van?'

'No, driving with your knees. You need both hands
on the wheel here!'

'I was not driving with my knees. I was driving with
my—'

'Yeah. Right. Whatever. It's dangerous.'

'Ach,' Ted grunted, putting his hands firmly and
deliberately on the wheel. 'That all right?'

'Yes. Thank you,' said Israel.

Ted instantly lifted his hands off the wheel.

'Aaghh!' screamed Israel.

'Relax!' said Ted, laughing. 'Ye're wound up tight,
boy, let me tell ye.'

'Right. Are we nearly there yet?'

'I don't know,' said Ted. 'You've got the map.'

'I thought you said you wouldn't need the map?' said Israel.

'Aye, well,' said Ted.

'Oh, so we do need the map?' said Israel, pulling an old, damp, dog-eared Ordnance Survey map from the glove compartment.

'Well, for the last bit of the journey, mebbe,' said Ted.

'"I won't need a map, sure" were your exact words, I think,' said Israel. 'As we were leaving Tumdrum.'

'Well,' said Ted. 'Where is it we're headed again?'

'We need the map,' said Israel, spreading the map out over his knees.

'All right,' said Ted. 'Yes. We do.'

'You were wrong,' said Israel, his finger poised on the sheet.

'Aye, all right,' said Ted. 'I was wrong.'

'Sorry?' said Israel, leaning over and cupping a hand to his ear. 'What did you say? I didn't quite catch it.'

'I was wrong,' repeated Ted.

'Say it again,' said Israel.

'No,' said Ted.

'I like hearing you say it,' said Israel.

'Aye, right. Wise up,' said Ted. 'And tell us where we are.'

Israel squinted at the map.

'Where are we?' he asked.

'That's your job,' said Ted. 'I'm driving.'

'That's not my fault,' said Israel. 'You wanted to drive.'

'No, you *didn't* want to drive,' said Ted. 'So, *you're* reading the map.'

'Well, I don't know where we are,' said Israel.

'What did the last sign say?' said Ted.

'I don't know. Have you seen a sign recently?'

'Not recently,' said Ted. 'No.'

'I thought you said you'd been down here before.'

'I've been down to Newcastle,' said Ted. 'The Slieve Donard. Old friend of mine had his wedding reception there. Beautiful meal, so it was. We had braised lamb, so we did, with—'

'Yeah, maybe another time. At this moment I think we should—'

'Where is it we want again?' said Ted.

'Slievenaman,' said Israel. 'I can't see it here. Is that how you say it?'

'No idea,' said Ted.

'Anyway, some little cottage on Slievenaman, is what I think she said.'

'We'll need to ask someone,' said Ted.

Israel stared out at the bleak mountain landscape all around them.

'What, a leprechaun? Or one of the little people? Or—'

'We'll find someone,' said Ted.

'Yeah, right,' said Israel.

They drove for another mile until they did find someone – an old man out walking, wearing a yellow fluorescent jacket and carrying a long stick. He didn't look like a walker. He looked, worryingly, like a local.

Israel wound down his window.

'Hello!' he said, as brightly as possible.

'Ye sellin' fish?' said the old man.

'No, no,' said Israel. 'We're not selling fish. We're a mobile library.'

'Potatoes?' said the old man.

'No. Sorry. No potatoes either. We were just wondering—'

'Thon's a brave yin the day,' said the man.

'Erm . . .' said Israel.

'Quare and warm.'

'Indeed,' said Israel. 'I wonder if you could—'

'But she's comin' on plump,' said the man, pointing into the sky with his walking stick.

'Sorry? Coming on plump?'

'Aye,' said the man. 'I used to cut turf up here.'

'Right, lovely,' said Israel.

'Until the peelers and all put a stop to it. The world's a miserable, crabbit sort of a place, isn't it?'

'Actually,' said Israel, who knew when he was beaten, 'you know what? I'm just going to hand you over to my colleague here.' He leant back, to let Ted do the talking.

'Hi. How are ye?' said Ted.

'All right,' said the man.

'We're after—' He spoke to Israel. 'Where is it we're after?'

'Slievenaman,' said Israel.

'Slievenaman?' said the old man. 'Ye'll not get to Slievenaman from here.'

'Oh,' said Israel.

'Ye'd need to be back down the road.'

'Right.'

'And ye know the Fofanny Dam?'

'Er, no.'

'Turn yerself around,' said the old man.

'Hold on,' said Israel. 'Let me find a pen here, and I'll just make a quick note.' But 'Where are ye from?' the old man had asked, and before the pen could be successfully retrieved for a quick note and a speedy getaway, the old man and Ted had started swapping stories about dance halls and places and people from long ago. After five minutes of hit-and-miss reminiscence, Israel managed to wrestle the conversation back to the question of how to get to Slievenaman, and they were finally away again, Ted executing a tricky three-point turn, the old man conducting them with his stick.

'He's right about the weather,' said Ted, as they drove away.

'How do you mean?'

'She is coming on plump,' said Ted, pointing up towards grey clouds in the distance. 'Let's swoop in, grab her and get home again. Like the SAS in the Iranian embassy siege.'

'Right,' said Israel.

Eventually they found the narrow lane that led towards a cottage, and parked up on the gravel by the stone boundary wall. The cottage sloped away before them, built on the incline of the mountain, as though it were not so much a building as a glacial deposit. The roof was thatched. There were small outbuildings, a little courtyard.

'Would have been a nice little farm once, I suppose,' said Ted.

'It's not bad now, is it?' said Israel, looking at the rough open moorland spread as far as the eye could see. 'Rural idyll, isn't it?'

'If you say so,' said Ted.

They pushed open the wooden gate and went and knocked at the door. There was no answer. The knock seemed to echo across the fields and mountains.

'Now what?' said Ted.

Israel was bending over, peering inside the windows of the cottage: it had clearly been expensively reno-vated inside, in a traditional style, with a prominent pine dresser, and stone floors, and what looked like milking stools for seats.

'Wow,' he said, to Ted, 'come and look at this.'

'It's a cottage,' said Ted. 'I've seen plenty of cottages before.'

'It's really cool, though,' said Israel.

'Aye, right,' said Ted.

There were colourful cushions on thick-string-seated chairs, a plain rug, oil lamps, and a huge wall-mounted plasma-screen TV over the open fire.

'It's lovely,' said Israel.

'Looks dark and damp to me,' said Ted. 'So, now what?'

'Well, she's clearly here,' said Israel, straightening up.

'The Morris girl?'

'Yes.'

'Aye, how can you tell, Sherlock Holmes?'

'There's a pink iPod Nano sitting on the table in there.'

'And what's that when it's at home, then?'

'An iPod?'

'I'm joking,' said Ted.

'So she can't have gone far.'

'Why not?'

'They don't go anywhere without their iPods, do they?'

'Does she not have a car?' said Ted.

'She's only fourteen,' said Israel.

'Hmm,' said Ted.

Israel gazed around.

'If you were fourteen, Ted, and you were hiding in this cottage, what would you do?'

'Get the bus to Newcastle and go home?'

'No. If you were here, hiding. I think she's gone for a walk,' said Israel.

'In the mountains?'

'Yes.'

'Ach, don't be soft.'

'Why?'

'If you live in the mountains, you don't go walking in them,' said Ted. 'Sure, I've lived in the Glens most of my life, and I've never been walking out. It's only tourists go walking.'

'But she is a tourist, isn't she? This is her parents' second home.'

'Aye,' said Ted, dismissively. 'Second home. One not good enough for them.'

'Walk,' Israel confirmed to himself. 'That's definitely what she'd do.'

'Aye,' said Ted.

'That's what I'd do.'

'Aye, you would,' said Ted. 'Go all naturalistic, wouldn't you?'

'Yes, well, sort of,' said Israel, who was walking away past the stone boundary wall. 'Like Thoreau. I think if we follow this path . . .'

'Aye, right,' said Ted, dismissively. 'You follow away there. I'm going to sit in the van for a wee smoke.'

'You sure you don't want to come?'

'Do I look like I want to go walking in the mountains?'

'No.'

'There you are, then. You work away there.'

So Israel went walking alone. He'd not walked in mountains for years: the last time was probably when he'd gone on holiday with his mum and dad to Wales when he was eight or nine years old. He'd never really understood the whole nature and sublimity thing: he found his sublimity in a nice cup of coffee on a bustling city street, a crisp copy of the *Guardian* before him, and the prospect of a day's *flâneur*ing ahead.

He followed the worn path up and up.

And after just ten minutes he sat down on a rock, exhausted, and shut his eyes. Even though he'd lost the weight, he was maybe not as fit as he could have been. Not that there was any previous, perfect state of fitness he'd fallen away from: he'd never been as fit as he could have been. He was sweating. And his knees hurt. But at least he hadn't been thinking about Gloria

and Danny. The walking had somehow allowed him
to stop thinking. Just for a moment he had escaped his
imagination, and he was living in the here and now.
He allowed his breathing to become regular and deep,
and he felt the warm autumn sun on his eyelids.

'Hi.'

Israel leapt up off the rock, like a chamois leaping
from a mountain peak.

'Oh God!' he yelled.

'Sorry, sorry.'

'You gave me the fright of my life!'

'Are you OK?'

'Yes. I'm fine, thank you. Yes,' gasped Israel.

'You're the librarian, aren't you? From Tumdrum.'

'Yes.'

'I thought so.'

'And you're Lyndsay,' said Israel, for Lyndsay indeed
it was.

'What are you doing here?' said Lyndsay. 'Out
walking?'

'Yes. I mean, no. Actually, no, I've come to find you,'
said Israel.

'Oh,' said Lyndsay. 'You know, then?'

'I know that people back home are worried sick about
you.'

'Yeah, right.'

'They are. Your parents are beside themselves.'

'They don't care at all about me,' said Lyndsay, who
looked remarkably well for someone who'd been hiding
away in a remote cottage halfway up a mountain.

'Of course they care,' said Israel.

'My father is a scummy politician.'

'No,' said Israel, finding it difficult to disagree. 'He's
. . . a man doing a very difficult job.'

'He's a total scumbag,' said Lyndsay.

'No . . . ' said Israel. 'I wouldn't say that. I think he's
a man who . . .'

'You don't know him,' said Lyndsay.

'No. But I know of him,' said Israel.

Lyndsay sat down beside him on the rock. They both
stared in silence at the vista – the admittedly sublime
vista – before them.

'What did you think of the Philip Roth then?' said
Israel.

'*American Pastoral*?'

'Yes.'

'I haven't started it yet,' said Lyndsay. 'I'm reading
the Stephenie Meyers at the moment.'

'The vampire books?'

'Yeah.'

'Oh,' said Israel. 'Really? I thought maybe you'd . . .
Anyway.'

'I hate living there,' said Lyndsay.

'Where?' said Israel.

'Tumdrum.'

'You're not the only one,' said Israel.

'Really?'

'Of course.'

'Where are you from?' said Lyndsay. 'Originally?'

'London,' said Israel.

'I'd love to live in London.'

'Well, you can, when you're older,' said Israel. 'It's open to all.'

'What's it like living in Tumdrum, if you're from London?' said Lyndsay. In all his time in Tumdrum no one had ever asked him that simple question. He didn't quite know how to answer.

'Well,' he said. 'I suppose it's a bit like . . . It's a bit like *Groundhog Day*.'

'I love that film!' said Lyndsay.

'Yeah,' said Israel. 'Punxsutawney Phil.'

'Bill Murray,' said Lyndsay. 'I love Bill Murray in that film.'

'Yeah. He's good, isn't he?'

'And in *Lost in Translation*.'

'Yeah,' agreed Israel. 'And what was that other one? *About Schmidt*.'

'I think that was Jack Nicholson,' said Lyndsay.

'Was it?'

'Yeah, but he was . . . a bit like Bill Murray in that, I suppose.'

'Yes, he was,' agreed Israel.

He glanced up at the gathering clouds above them.

'She's coming on plump,' said Israel. 'And you really shouldn't be out in the mountains in this weather. In clothes like . . .' Lyndsay was wearing a sort of black miniskirt, with black leggings, and black pixie boots, and a black T-shirt. 'Sorry, I sound like my mother.'

'You sound like my father,' said Lyndsay.

'Shall we go back to the cottage, then?' said Israel.

They began walking back down the mountain, side by side.

'How did you find me, though?' said Lyndsay. 'I didn't think anyone would find me here.'

'I spoke to your mother,' said Israel.

'Is she all right?' said Lyndsay.

'She's very upset,' said Israel.

'I'm sorry,' said Lyndsay. 'I didn't mean to cause any trouble.'

'I'm sure she'll be delighted that you're safe and sound.'

'Did she tell you where I was?'

'No,' said Israel. 'I just sort of pieced it together. I spoke to your boyfriend—'

'Who?'

'Colin.'

'He's my ex, actually.'

'Well, he seemed very . . . nice.'

'God, no. He's an idiot. He spends all his time gaming, it's so boring.'

'It could be worse,' said Israel.

'Really?'

'He could be a librarian.'

Lyndsay laughed.

'What made you become a librarian?'

'You make it sound like a conscious decision.'

'Why? Was it not?'

'Well. As you get older,' Israel started saying – what was he saying? – 'you realise that all your decisions are not necessarily made consciously by you, if you see what I mean. I mean, it would be like me asking you why you're a Goth.'

'I don't know,' said Lyndsay.

'There you are,' said Israel.

'I just . . . am. It's just like . . . a state of mind.'

'Well, that's me being a librarian,' said Israel.

'It's a state of mind?'

'Something like that.'

'People think being a Goth is just, you know, Morticia Addams fashion,' said Lyndsay.

'But it's not?'

'Not at all. It's about experiencing the world in a more intense way.'

'Right. I spoke to Adam Burns, as well.'

'From Kerugma? Did you?'

'Yes.'

'You've been stalking me, then, basically?'

'No,' said Israel. 'I've been trying to find you.'

'Why?'

Israel thought this probably not the moment to explain about Veronica and the police.

'Just . . . doing a good turn, I suppose.'

'I do love it here,' said Lyndsay. There was a clap of thunder as they approached the cottage, and the first fat rain drops began falling. Israel could see Ted in the distance.

'It is beautiful,' agreed Israel.

'I used to come here with my mother when I was young, when my dad was too busy working.'

'What's that over there?' asked Israel, pointing to something shimmering in the distance.

'That's the Trassey river,' said Lyndsay.

'Right.'

'And that,' she said. 'You see there, between the two peaks?'

'Yes.'

'That's the Hare's Gap.'

'Right.'

'And there's a path there called the Brandy Pad, where people used to smuggle stuff.'

'Wow.'

'And there's Clonachullion Hill there, and the Spellack cliffs.'

'You really know your stuff,' said Israel.

'I guess.'

'You're very lucky.'

'Yes,' agreed Lyndsay. 'I suppose I am.'

They reached the cottage.

'Well, well,' said Ted, as they approached. 'By the seven secrets of the Ballymena coachbuilders! If it's not our missing young lady.'

'Hi, Ted,' said Lyndsay.

'How are ye?' said Ted.

'Fine,' said Lyndsay.

'We takin' ye home, then?'

'Yeah.'

'We should ring her parents and let them know,' said Israel. 'They're worried sick.'

'No,' said Ted. 'Let's ring later.'

'Why?'

'There's no reception here, you'll not get through.'

'But weren't you just on your—' began Israel.

'No reception,' said Ted. 'Quicker we get back in this weather the better.'

After Lyndsay had gathered her things from the cottage, they climbed into the van and began the long, rain-soaked drive back to Tumdrum, Ted and Israel up front, Lyndsay perched on the children's book trough behind them.

'What are we going to do about this little lady, then?' said Ted, as they accelerated through the torrential rain up the A24 towards the north coast.

'Get her back to where she belongs,' said Israel. 'Reunite her.'

'Hmmm,' said Ted.

'What?' said Israel.

'I think you owe us an explanation first, young lady, don't ye?' said Ted.

'I just had to get away,' said Lyndsay.

'Aye,' said Ted. 'Why was that, then?'

'The place was doing my head in.'

'Ye'd be better off telling us the truth, ye know.'

'That is the truth,' said Lyndsay.

'The actual truth,' said Ted.

'That is the truth, Ted,' said Israel, turning around and looking at Lyndsay. 'Isn't it?'

'The actual truth?' said Ted.

'Yes,' said Lyndsay.

'Ye pitched up down at the cottage all by yerself, did ye?' said Ted.

'Yes.'

'Get a lift?'

'No,' said Lyndsay. 'I got the bus to Newcastle, and then just walked up to the cottage—'

'And no one knew you were there?'

'No.'

'You haven't seen a soul?'

'No.'

'Funny, that,' said Ted. 'Because there were fresh tyre marks on the gravel up at the cottage there.'

'Were there?'

'Mercedes-type tyre marks, if I'm not mistaken.'

'How can you tell—' began Israel.

'I don't know who that could have been . . .' said Lyndsay.

'No?' said Ted. 'Who do we know who drives a Mercedes?'

'Lots of people,' said Lyndsay.

'Including your da?'

'Well . . .'

'Hold on,' said Israel. 'Do you mean Maurice Morris has already been down here looking for her?'

'No,' said Ted.

'No!' agreed Lyndsay.

'I don't think he's been down here looking for her,' said Ted.

'Right,' said Israel, confused.

'Because he wouldn't need to look for her, would he? He knew full well that she was here all along. Didn't he, Lyndsay?'

Israel looked into the rear-view mirror, and could see that Lyndsay was looking shamefaced.

'No?' said Israel.

Lyndsay wiped away a tear.

'Steady on,' said Israel. 'What do you mean?'

'I mean that our little Miss Runaway here was in caboots—'

'Cahoots?'

'Exactly. With her father.'

'No!' said Israel. 'That's ridiculous. That can't be right. That's not right, is it?'

'Yes,' said Lyndsay, from the children's book trough. 'It's true. I'm sorry . . .'

'But you told me you'd run away!' Israel protested.

'Do you believe everything everyone tells you?' said Ted.

'No,' said Israel. 'But . . . if he knew she was here, why didn't he bring her back?'

'I think we'd best ask Lyndsay that one, hadn't we?'

'Lyndsay?' said Israel, turning round to face her.

'Sorry,' she said, between sobs.

'Best to tell the truth,' said Ted.

'Yes!' said Israel, rather more forcefully than was necessary. 'Tell us the truth!'

Ted slapped him round the head.

'We're not the KGT.'

'KGB,' said Israel.

'Or them,' agreed Ted. 'In your own time, my dear.'

Lyndsay wiped her eyes.

'My dad asked me to come down here,' she said.

'Why?' said Israel.

'He wanted the publicity.'

'What?'

'He thought it would get him the sympathy vote. In the election. After the way he'd treated Mum, everyone hated him. And he'd gone from being Mr Popular to being . . .'

'A total scumbag,' said Ted.

'Yes.'

'Did your mum know about it as well?'

'No, no,' said Lyndsay. 'She didn't know. They don't really get on any more. They just argue at home. But I thought if Dad got elected again, things might—' And she started sobbing again.

'That's all right, darling,' said Ted.

All three of them sat in silence as they drove through Ballynahinch.

'Well, now what?' said Israel.

'Please,' said Lyndsay. 'You mustn't tell anyone. If people find out—'

'If people find out yer da put you up to it, he'll not be able to show his face in Tumdrum again,' said Ted. 'And he'd lose the election, for sure.'

'Which wouldn't be such a bad—' began Israel. 'Sorry, Lyndsay.'

'It's all right. I wouldn't vote for him anyway,' said Lyndsay.

'But you were prepared to do all . . . this for him.'

'He's my dad,' said Lyndsay.

'Well,' said Israel. 'That's . . .'

'Let's listen to some Harry Potter, shall we?' said Ted.

'Which one is it?' said Lyndsay.

'*Harry Potter and the Philosopher's Stone*,' said Ted.

'Oh, great.'

'Oh, no,' said Israel.

'And we'll have a little think for a bit,' said Ted.

Lyndsay eventually dozed off to Stephen Fry's susurrations. And they were finally back on the coast road up to Tumdrum.

'She's asleep,' said Ted.

'Seems to be,' said Israel. 'And we're nearly back.'

'We've a decision to make, then,' said Ted.

'Yes.'

'What about your journalist friend?'

'What about her?'

'If you tell her, it'd be fate accomplished.'

'Fait accompli,' said Israel.

'Be in all the papers. The big fella'll be finished. Divorce of the wife, I wouldn't wonder.'

'God. So what if we don't tell anyone?'

'Yon Lyndsay's just a runaway, then, who's happily reunited with her parents.'

'And Maurice Morris gets the sympathy vote.'

'He thinks,' said Ted.

'A moral dilemma, isn't it?' said Israel.

'That it is,' said Ted.

'Between public and private,' said Isracl.

'Probably,' said Ted.

'E. M. Forster again,' said Israel.

'Who?' said Ted.

'E. M. Forster.'

'He play for Chelsea?'

'No! He's a famous writer.'

'Well, I wouldn't know him if he offered me a sausage sandwich,' said Ted.

'He's dead,' said Israel. 'So it's not likely.'

'Aye.'

'Anyway, he famously said that if offered the choice between betraying a friend and betraying his country he hoped he'd have the courage to betray his country.'

'Hmm,' said Ted.

'What?'

'I don't know about that.'

The sign up ahead said 'Welcome to Tumdrum'.

'Decision time,' said Ted.

23

Maurice Morris was not a bad man as such. He'd gone into politics for the same reason that everyone else goes into politics – to make a difference, and to do good. And he believed that he had done good. He had nothing whatsoever to reproach himself with.

Which is why, on the morning of the election, he was able to look himself fair and square in the eye in the bathroom mirror, and to find nothing amiss. If he said so himself – and he did say so, Maurice believed in articulating his own self-worth – he was looking pretty good. 'Looking pretty good,' he said. He had a radiance about him. He wasn't only blessed with good looks, and with good luck, he was pretty damn smart too. He knew he must be smart because he didn't know anyone else who'd grown up on the Shankill Road in Belfast, and gone to Campbell College, even though his father was only a postman, and then gone on to found Northern Ireland's most successful independent financial advisers, and then gone on to become an MLA in the local assembly, and who had lost their seat, but who was now about to be gloriously re-elected. He had achieved far and away above what might have been expected of him. His life had a trajectory, a story.

And he had pulled off quite a coup. His daughter had been reunited with him the night before the election – graciously returned by the librarians – and in enough time for the six o'clock news to cover it. And for the papers to have it for their headline. If that didn't win him votes, then nothing would.

He looked good in his plain black suit. He should wear black suits more often: he was usually inclined towards pinstripes, with statement linings. Frank Sinatra wore plain black suits, of course, and Frank was one of his great heroes, the epitome of fifties cool. He was lucky enough to have seen Sinatra sing with Tony Bennett, in Vegas, late 1980s. The voice was gone, but Frank was still soldiering on. Still in the tux. 'My Way'. 'Luck Be A Lady'. 'Come Fly With Me'. When people said Sinatra was a crook, what they didn't understand was where he was coming from – born the son of immigrants, worked as a young man as a riveter in the shipyard. This was someone who had made himself what he was. And that took courage, and bravado, and commitment. That's just what it took.

His wife called from downstairs.

'It's time to go!'

He winked at himself in the mirror, and intoned

his current favourite motivational slogan: 'Winners Do Things Differently'.

At the Devines' farm, meanwhile, Israel Armstrong splashed some cold water on his face, dried himself off, and forced himself to eat a spoonful of peanut butter. He already had his migraine, which had started, as usual, with a sort of headache just over his left eye, a piercing pain, and then he'd started feeling nauseous, as though on the verge of vomiting. He still had the prescription in his pocket for the SSRIs, from Dr Withers. He hadn't yet decided: drugs; counselling? Maybe he just needed to get away from here.

He took deep breaths.

Maybe all English Jewish vegetarian mobile librarians were condemned to a life of headaches, weariness and existential despair.

He glanced at himself in the mirror. He'd decided to keep the beard, at least for the time being; it made him look suitably sombre, but it was a shame he didn't have a black suit. He was wearing a black jacket that he'd borrowed from Brownie, and an old pair of black corduroys. His only shoes were his brown brogues, which didn't look right with the jacket and trousers, so he'd found a dark brown shoe polish in the Devines', and had dabbed some on and made them look darker. He'd bought a pair of black laces, from the Spar. They were too long.

He rang Gloria, pointlessly.

The pain in his temples was awful. He was thinking

about Gloria, and about Maurice Morris, and Pearce Pyper, and none of it was good, and he felt inside himself a deep inclination to cry.

He decided not to.

He stepped out instead into the yard and made his way over to the farmhouse, passing the chickens in the yard, waving to the goats.

George was in the kitchen, by the Rayburn, and there was a familiar smell – not just the usual smell. This was a smell that reminded Israel of something. A homely smell. The smell of home. It smelt of parents. And Saturday traffic outside. It smelt of north London.

'What are you making?' he asked.

'Chicken livers,' said George, wiping her hands on her apron. She was wearing a black dress. Her hair was scraped back. She looked kind of Italian.

'Chicken livers,' said Israel. 'I didn't know you did chicken livers.'

'We live on a farm with chickens, Armstrong. What do you think we do with the chickens?'

'I love chicken livers.'

'I thought you were a vegetarian,' said George.

'Yes, but . . . Chicken livers.'

He thought for a moment of all the chickens he must have eaten in his time – all the white flesh, and the brown flesh, and the crispy skin, and those claws and entrails boiled up into soups. He wondered sometimes whether he'd become a vegetarian through sheer chicken fatigue, his mind and body sated with meat; fowl cravings completed.

'Do you want some?' said George.

'Well, I'll . . .'

'There's plenty: it's for the wake.'

'No,' said Israel. 'I shouldn't, no . . . How do you do your chicken livers?'

'You want me to explain?'

'Yes.'

'Why?' said George. 'You're going to make it yourself?'

'I might.'

George sighed, but she explained nonetheless.

'So, you need a boiling fowl, and then you stuff the neck with dumpling ingredients, stitched at both ends, and you boil that up alongside it.'

'Right.'

'And you save the fat.'

'Schmaltz?' said Israel.

'Bless you,' said George. 'And then you chop the onion, cook it in the fat.'

'OK,' said Israel.

'Then you take the livers.'

'Right.'

'And you add them.'

'OK.'

'Cook them. And then I add some hard-boiled eggs.'

She raised her hands in a gesture that suggested completion.

'And that's it?' said Israel.

'Pretty much.'

'That's delicious,' said Israel.

'Chickens are not what they were,' piped up old Mr Devine from his seat. 'The auld Sussex cockerel. Breastbone ye could shave with.'

'Right.'

'It's all the thigh now. Breast and thigh. Breasts like towers. Sin and greed and wickedness.'

'Uh-huh,' said Israel.

He turned his back to old Mr Devine, and helped George to wrap kitchen foil around platters of sandwiches.

'So. Are you OK, Armstrong?' she asked, tucking up the final platter.

'Yes, I'm fine,' said Israel. 'Totally fine. How are you?'

'Fine.'

'It's going to be a difficult day,' said Israel.

'Yes,' agreed George.

'We're all going to miss Pearce.'

'Yes we are,' said George, giving a little cough.

'Dear friends,' said old Mr Devine, 'do not be surprised at the painful trial that ye are suffering as though something strange were happening to you. But rejoice that you participate in the sufferings of Christ.'

'Father!' said George.

'1 Peter 4:12,' said old Mr Devine, with a distinctly self-satisfied air.

'Right. And that's meant to be some sort of comfort, is it?'

'It doesn't do a Christian good to grieve,' said old Mr Devine.

'All right,' said George. 'That's enough. I don't want to hear any more from you today. Do you understand?'

Mr Devine narrowed his eyes.

'Let's go,' said George. 'Or we'll be late.'

So, Israel drove to Pearce Pyper's funeral with George and old Mr Devine, sitting on the back seat, in total silence, surrounded by sandwiches, and bread, and chicken liver pâté.

Outside Tumdrum Presbyterian there were crowds of mourners. Men with white hair. Women in hats. Grey stone buildings all around, the sky an eggshell blue; it was as though Pearce himself had painted the scene. Israel saw Linda; said hello to Seamus Fitzgibbons, Green Party candidate; embraced Minnie; nodded to Zelda; shook hands with Mrs Onions; avoided Maurice Morris and Lyndsay, and Mrs Morris; and greeted at least half of the mobile library's regular clientele, who had turned out in force to say goodbye to Pearce. Veronica cut him dead. The talk was of the day's election, and the return of Lyndsay Morris: Israel and Ted were congratulated on having helped find her.

At two thirty the organ music began, and Pearce's coffin was taken into the church, Israel one of the pall-bearers, along with Brownie – who'd made it back from university – and a group of Pearce's friends, artists and aristocrats mostly, and some of them both, not the kind of people you saw every day around Tumdrum, people who wore hand-benched shoes, and inherited clothes, and novelty headgear. One man had a handlebar moustache; another sported a long grey ponytail, and wore battered brown cowboy boots; another wore a tam o'shanter and a kilt. The rich, it seems, wear fancy dress to a funeral. Tumdrum's Presbyterians wore black.

Israel had never carried a coffin before. He'd been too young when his father died, and at subsequent funerals there had always been others to take the burden. The coffin weighed more than he'd expected.

'On my count, gents,' said the undertaker, and on his count they made their slow, steady procession into the church, laying Pearce on a bier at the front, and the congregation filed in behind and sat down, and the Reverend Roberts stood up and led them in prayer, and then he began to speak.

'A Christian funeral,' he said, without any introduction or ado, 'is a service of worship in which God's people witness to their faith in the hope of the Gospel, the communion of saints, the resurrection of the body, and the life everlasting.'

People gulped and shifted in their seats as they began to adjust to the tone and the rhythm of what they were a part of. Israel took a deep breath.

'A funeral,' continued the Reverend Roberts, 'is God's way of bringing comfort to the hearts of those who mourn.' He paused. 'At a funeral we read the Scriptures, and prayer is offered, and praises are sung.' Another pause. 'And remembrance is cherished.' You could hear the sound of the cars outside the church, in the main square, with people going about their business, as if nothing had happened, as if life was going on as normal. 'A funeral is an occasion when we, by the grace of God, bless the name of the One who gives and who takes away. Though today we mourn our loss and remember our loved one, our eyes remain fixed on Jesus, the author and finisher of the faith.' Israel felt a tightness in his chest and his throat. He tried to concentrate on the Reverend Roberts's oratorical swing – the alliteration, the contrasts, his little triads of phrases.

Then they sang a hymn, 'The day thou gavest, Lord, is ended,/the darkness falls at thy behest' and Israel felt a prickling around his eyes, the early signs of tears. And then they prayed. And then there was a reading. An old friend of Pearce's – an old, old man with a shaky voice. 'A reading,' he wobbled, 'from the Gospel of John, chapter fourteen.' It wasn't the words. It was the pathos of the words being spoken, the ceremony. Israel felt himself on the brink.

And then the Reverend Roberts stood up again to speak.

'Pearce Aloysius Pyper –' began the Reverend Roberts, in sonorous tones, pausing respectfully between each word – and Israel was crying now, without shame, ' – our dear friend Pearce – was born on the twenty-sixth of June 1918, in the last months of the First World War. He was the third child of the Reverend Julian and Margaret Pyper. They were a privileged family – Pearce's mother, Margaret, being a descendant of the Earls of Tyrone – who had a long history of serving the poor through good works.

Margaret was a suffragette, and Pearce would often recall in later years his memories of the destitute and the homeless coming to his father for assistance at the Rectory in Ballycastle. Pearce was sent to Sherborne preparatory school, in England, and then to Marlborough, and from there on to Brasenose College, Oxford, where, as he was always glad to report, he graduated with what he called the poet's degree: a Third.' There was wry laughter among the university-educated in the congregation. 'On coming down from university Pearce found work as a teacher before becoming a commissioned officer in the Second Battalion of the Royal Ulster Rifles. He was most proud in his life, he said, of having gained the Distinguished Conduct Medal – during the Second World War, for his bravery during some of the fiercest fighting following the retreat from Dunkirk.'

The congregation was able to relax now into the flow of the Reverend Roberts's narrative. Israel found himself breathing more easily.

'After the war Pearce married Lillian Jabotinsky, the celebrated soprano, and they had two sons, both of whom alas predeceased their father. Pearce and Lillian's elder son, Jacob, who some of you will doubtless remember, became a surgeon and died aged only thirty-three, in a car crash, in 1983. Their younger son, Leon, was a conservator at the Courtauld Institute of Art, and he alas died of a brain haemorrhage in 1999. Pearce was enormously proud of his children, and their early and tragic deaths brought him a great sadness. We should perhaps remember today that this was a man' – and here the Reverend Roberts nodded towards Pearce's coffin – 'who was not himself unacquainted with grief.'

Some among the congregation could be heard sniffing.

'The young Pearce and his wife lived in London, where Pearce, who taught at Westminster School, turned increasingly towards art as a means of self-expression. He held a number of exhibitions of his work, and was a friend of many of the great artistic figures of the day. He returned increasingly to his work as an artist after the death of his sons, and seemed to find great consolation in it.'

Israel thought of the telegraph totem poles, and the giant concrete heads, and the bright, childlike sculptures that adorned Pearce's gardens, and for the first time they made sense.

'After the death of his wife in 1966 Pearce remarried and returned to live in Ireland with his second wife, Vivian Farrell, the actress. After Vivian's death, Pearce was to marry and divorce twice more; the triumph, one might say, of hope over experience.' The congregation smiled.

'It is perhaps worth recalling on a day such as today that Pearce stood for Parliament – unsuccessfully – on a number of occasions, and as well as being an artist and philanthropist, he was a keen yachtsman, a cyclist, and as many of you will know, a great letter writer. His was, by any means, a life well lived.'

There was now a steady dabbing of eyes around the church.

'You will all, of course, have your own memories of Pearce – a man distinguished not merely by his worldly achievements, but more importantly by his very self, by his magnanimity, his good humour, and, of course, his wisdom and generosity. Personally, I got to know Pearce only recently, and was lucky enough to witness how he bore the burden of years, and his final illness, with a resolve and with a verve and a style characteristically his own. He was of course not always an easy man to get on with – none of us are saints – and we are here today to give thanks for the life of Pearce as he was, not as we might imagine him to have been. He was a man of great passions – and those of us who occasionally felt the lash of his tongue will know that those passions extended to a great dislike of those who he felt were foolish, ignorant, or pretentious, "stupid bloody bastards", as he called them.

'In short, Pearce Pyper was a man who was fully human, who knew who he was, and who was prepared to share himself and his life with others. Gathered here today, in our grief, we should be mindful of what the Bible teaches us: that to every thing there is a season, and a time to every purpose under heaven; a time to be born, and a time to die; a time to laugh, and a time to mourn. As Christians, we believe in the life eternal, and the world to come. But we also believe in the good of *this* life, and that the lives of the good show us what it means to be truly human. And so today we should not only mourn, but we should celebrate the life of our brother, Pearce

Pyper, born twenty-sixth of June 1918. Died twenty-ninth of September 2008.'

More hymns followed – 'Praise to the holiest in the height', 'Ye holy angels bright'. Hopeless sobbing. Prayers. The blessing. And finally the escape outside.

'Well,' said Ted, who stood smoking outside the church, waiting for Israel and the other pall-bearers to load the coffin back into the hearse. 'There we are, then. Another man down.'

'Yep,' said Israel.

'Can't be all bad, if it's got you in a shirt and tie, mind.'

'Yeah.' Israel wiped at his eyes. Ted had teamed his usual black leather car coat with a black tie and shiny black slip-on shoes.

'Ach, ye're all beblubbered there, look. Here.' Ted thrust a crumpled, unironed handkerchief into Israel's hands.

'Thanks.'

'Good elegy,' said Ted.

'Eulogy,' said Israel. 'Yes. It was good, wasn't it?'

'I tell you what he didn't say about Pearce, though,' said Ted, crushing his cigarette butt under his heel, and bending over to pick it up and pocket it. 'Ouch.'

'You all right?'

'Yeah. My back, just. You know what he didn't say?'

'What?'

'He didn't mention that the old fella was completely buck mad,' said Ted.

Israel gave a little laugh.

'Mind, takes all sorts, I suppose.'

'Yes,' agreed Israel. 'I suppose it does.'

It was a private interment, so Israel drove with Ted back to Pearce's for the wake. Cars were parked all along the driveway up to the house, and inside there was an atmosphere of unforced joviality, quite different to anything Israel had experienced at any funeral in England. Women were busy serving tea and coffee, and men stood around chatting, in their overcoats. Everyone who was anyone in Tumdrum – which is to say, just about everyone – was there. Sandwiches were piled into pyramids, and bottles of whiskey were being passed casually from hand to hand. Minnie was doing the rounds with a platter of sandwiches.

'Och, Israel,' she said. 'Sandwich?'

'What are they?'

'Ham. Ham and cheese. Ham and pickle.'

'Erm. No thanks. I'm vegetarian.'

'Oh, are you? I always forget. There's crab paste somewhere.'

'Right. Thanks.'

'Lovely service, wasn't it? I might get him to do mine.'

'Yes,' agreed Israel. 'Very good.'

Israel wandered among the crowds, from room to room. Linda Wei waylaid him in the library. She was wearing a man's dinner jacket and trousers, with a corsage, a pillbox hat and bright red glasses.

'You've heard about the books, have you?' she said.

'Pearce has bequeathed them to the library service?'

'You knew?'

'He mentioned it to me, yeah.'

Linda raised her eyebrows in dissatisfaction.

'I don't know what we're going to do with all these,' she said, glancing around despairingly at the tens of thousands of leather volumes. 'Sell them, probably.'

'Right.'

'Pay for some new computers.'

'Uh-huh.' Israel couldn't be bothered to take the bait.

'You're unusually quiet, Armstrong.'

'Yeah, well, you know. Just thinking about Pearce.' He was staring at the space on one wall where bookshelves had been removed: the shelves that had done for Pearce.

'Have you voted yet?' said Linda.

'No,' said Israel. 'I don't think I'm going to bother.'

'If you don't vote you've no right to complain about whoever gets in.'

'That's true,' said Israel. 'That is very true.'

He made his way out of the library, out on to the terrace, where he found George sitting on a bench, smoking, staring out across Pearce's garden towards the farm in the distance.

'I didn't know you smoked,' said Israel.

'I don't,' said George, stubbing out her cigarette. 'I've something for you, actually.'

'For me?'

'For your birthday.'

'Really?'

'It is your birthday, isn't it?'

353

'Yeah, it is.'

She took a small package from her handbag.

'It's a book, I'm afraid,' she said, handing it over.

'I don't know what to say,' said Israel.

'Thank you?'

'Thanks. Shall I open it?'

'Maybe save it for later,' said George.

'OK.'

They sat in silence together, shivering. Israel sighed.

'Big sigh,' said George.

'Was it?'

'Yeah.'

'I don't belong here,' said Israel.

George laughed.

'What's funny?'

'Nothing.'

'No, what? What's funny about that?'

George took a deep breath.

'Let me tell you a secret, Israel. No one belongs anywhere.'

'But you're from here. You were born here. You grew up. You're going to—'

'And you think I don't ever wish I wasn't?'

'Well. I don't know. I just . . .'

'Everyone's the same, Israel. We want what we can't have. That's the meaning of life, isn't it?'

'I don't know. Is it?'

She turned and looked at him. He looked at her.

His phone rang.

'Sorry,' he said.

'I'll maybe see you back inside,' said George.

'Yeah. Sure. Fine.'
It was Gloria.
He thought. For a moment.
He let it ring.

Acknowledgements

For previous acknowledgements see *The Truth about Babies* (Granta Books, 2002), *Ring Road* (4th Estate, 2004), *The Mobile Library: The Case of the Missing Books* (Harper Perennial, 2006), *The Mobile Library: Mr Dixon Disappears* (Harper Perennial, 2006), *The Mobile Library: The Delegates' Choice* (Harper Perennial, 2008). These stand, with exceptions. In addition I would like to thank the following. (The previous terms and conditions apply: some of them are dead; most of them are strangers; the famous are not friends; none of them bears any responsibility.)

Amy Adams, Thomas Adès, Ingeborg Bachmann, Korrena Bailie, Georges Bataille, H. E. Bates, Hector Berlioz, Ingrid Betancourt, Dirk Bogarde, W. E. Bowman, Susan Boyle, Max Bruch, Carla Bruni, John Burnside, Vince Cable, June Caldwell, Lucy Caldwell, Eric Cantona, Helen Carr, Nina Cassian, Steve Chamberlain, Stavroula Constantinou, Alan Coren, Simon Cowell, Curious Candy, Boris Cyrulnik, Charles D'Ambrosio, Edwidge Danticat,

Jacobus De Voragine, Denis Diderot, William Donaldson, Ed Dorn, Scott Douglas, Gwyneth Dunwoody, Francine Du Plessix Gray, Geoff Dyer, Mircea Eliade, George Ewart Evans, Harold Evans, Maureen Evans, J. G. Farrell, Penelope Fitzgerald, F. S. Flint, Kinky Friedman, Elaine Gaston, Elizabeth Gilbert, Ben Goldacre, William Golding, Martin Green, Hannah Hagan, Patrick Hamilton, Salma Hayek, Geoff Hill, Tom Hodgkinson, Holywood Cricket Club, Steven Isserlis, Philippe Jaccottet, Stephen Kelly, Natalie Kirk, Janusz Korczak, Shane Leslie, Doris Lessing, Joshua Levine, Colm Liddy, Derek Lundy, Humphrey Lyttleton, James MacMillan, Marcel Marceau, Annie Martz, Simon Mawer, James McAvoy, David Mitchell, Haruki Murakami, Rafael Nadal, Nuala Ní Dhomhnaill, Barack Obama, Gina Ochsner, Jay Parini, William Parkhurst, Andrew Pepper, Grayson Perry, Richard Price, Elizabeth Reapy, Alasdair Reid, Derek A. Roberts, Robin Robertson, Eoghan Ryan, Julian Schnabel, 6th Bangor Scouts, Varlam Shalamov, Michael Shannon, Ammon Shea, Barrie Sherwood, Gary Shteyngart, Rory Stewart, Parminder Summon, Joyce Sutphen, Tilda Swinton, Margaret Twohy, Fred Voss, Sheena Wilkinson, Peter Wild, Qian Zhongshu.